The
BOOKSHOP
MURDER

The
BOOKSHOP
MURDER

Merryn Allingham

Bookouture

Published by Bookouture in 2021

An imprint of Storyfire Ltd.
Carmelite House
50 Victoria Embankment
London EC4Y 0DZ

www.bookouture.com

ISBN: 978-1-80019-682-7
eBook ISBN: 978-1-80019-681-0

ABBEYMEAD

Sussex, 1955

CHAPTER ONE

Locking the shop door carefully behind her, Flora heaved the last parcel of books into the basket. Betty wasn't the most beautiful of bikes but she was functional, her wide wicker tray already filled to overflowing. Time for the Friday evening chore they both hated. It was Aunt Violet who had begun a regular delivery slot from the All's Well bookshop several years ago. *A community service*, she'd told her niece. *Some of the old dears find it difficult to carry even one book home from the village.* The problem was that the number of old dears had increased rapidly and there was barely a week now that Flora wasn't packing the bike to its maximum and labouring her way through Abbeymead and its surrounding lanes.

Today shouldn't be too onerous, though – three village addresses and only one a mile or so beyond. Just as well, she thought, looking up at the autumn sky. In the last hour or so, puffs of white cotton had given way to a darkening bank of cloud. She would need to be swift.

Cycling to her first call, she found the village green deserted. It was that time of day when, school and work finished, people had only just arrived home and the evening had not yet begun. She stopped at one of the cottages lining the green. Thatched-roofed and rose-covered, it was everyone's rural dream, though the reality was less idyllic as Flora knew from her own experience of draughty windows and leaking pipes.

Leaning Betty against the low stone wall, she looked up to see Elsie waving to her from the window. The pensioner was among

All's Well's best customers, having an unquenchable thirst for the most gruesome crime stories Flora could find. A brief chat and Flora was back on her bicycle and posting the vicar's latest improving tome through the vicarage letter box, then on to the postmistress to deliver a large parcel of children's books – Dilys regularly entertained a swarm of nieces and nephews – only to be kept talking on the doorstep for far too long. One more call, Flora thought, disentangling herself from her garrulous customer.

Miss Lancaster lived at the top of a very steep hill, but even so, Flora reckoned she should be home for supper by seven. And what a supper! Alice Jenner, the cook at the Priory Hotel, had called this morning on her way to work and left Flora one of her famous pies. Steak and kidney – a sheer delight! Meat had come off ration only last year and still felt a wicked indulgence. Flora could almost smell that pie as she puffed her way up the last few yards to Miss Lancaster's neo-Gothic pile.

It was then that it happened. One minute she was straining every calf muscle to make it to the driveway and the next a blast of wind, or so it seemed, had knocked her off the bike and deposited her at the side of the road. The autumn leaves made a comfortable enough bed, but Betty was spreadeagled across her chest and she was finding it difficult to breathe. Pulling herself from under the bike's dead weight, she glimpsed the rear of a red sports car disappearing past Miss Lancaster's wrought-iron gates and on around the bend towards the Priory, the driver's cloud of fair hair blowing wildly in the wind.

Flora struggled to her feet, heaving the cycle upright and fixing the basket back in place, then wearily pushing Betty through the gates and up to the gloomy front door. That sports car, she thought, had to be from the hotel. Alice Jenner had been telling her only this morning how many new ideas the owner, Vernon Elliot, had introduced, in the hope of enticing more customers to book. According to Alice, a complimentary drive in a brand-new Aston Martin was on offer, but only for guests who reserved the most expensive suites. They might have money, Flora fumed, but they certainly didn't have manners. As Miss Lancaster's wintry face appeared in the doorway, she pasted on a bright smile.

It was all very different when Lord Edward Templeton was alive, she reflected, freewheeling down the hill, her long hair streaming behind, a banner of resistance. In the viscount's day, villagers had been free to walk in his fields and woods and welcome to call at the Priory. Every year, even during the war, his rolling parkland had been used for the summer fayre with special teas laid on in the rose garden and, at the very beginning of the conflict, the house had thrown open its doors to welcome dozens of evacuees, children from those parts of London considered most in danger – Silvertown, Stepney, Bethnal Green. As a child herself at the time, she had welcomed new playmates. Now, though, there were fences everywhere and notices that barked at people not to park here, not to enter there. These days the village, unless it chose to eat a very expensive meal in the Priory restaurant, never went near the place.

But Lord Templeton was gone and so was dear Aunt Violet. And so, Flora thought sadly, was her chance of escape. Her chance to leave the narrow life of Abbeymead and walk out into the world beyond.

The memorial clock opposite the All's Well was already striking nine when Flora pedalled furiously along the village high street the next morning, feeling for her shop keys as she rode. She was going to be late opening up. Aunt Violet had always insisted they were in the shop and ready to serve by ten minutes to nine every day, no matter that their first customer invariably walked through the door at least an hour later.

Her aunt's rules might sometimes irk, but Flora tried to keep them still. Violet Steele had been everything to her – mother, father, friend and confidante. But for Violet's intervention, an orphanage would have been Flora's childhood home, her parents dying together in an horrific road accident. Her aunt had nurtured the small child, loved and encouraged her, watching with pride as Flora grew to adulthood and became her closest companion. Six months ago, when Violet had been forced to bow out of her niece's life for good, she had placed all she possessed – a small cottage on the outskirts of Abbeymead and her beloved bookshop – into Flora's hands.

Flora had worked in the shop for as long as she could remember: first as a little girl making more mess than helping, then later in school days earning money as a Saturday job and, later still, home in the holidays from library school, working happily alongside her aunt. She had always meant to do something else, use her qualifications to travel, settle in a larger town perhaps, but then Violet had become sick and needed constant care. In the end, her aunt's decline had been swift and it had to be Flora who had stepped up. Was still stepping up.

She propped Betty against the wall's weathered red brick and took a deep breath. Opening the white-painted shop door, she allowed the familiar smell of books to wash over her – the sweet, musky warmth that she loved. Her first chores were always to check the till and dust at least two of the bookshelves. Then she could make a cup of tea. She would have plenty of time – the village had appeared half asleep as she'd pedalled through.

But in that Flora was wrong. She had barely hung up the pink swing jacket for which she'd saved so hard, and opened the cash register, when the shop bell rang and an unknown man walked through the door. Flora's eyes widened. Unknown men were rare in Abbeymead. This one was tall, lanky she'd say, his clothes hanging loose, seeming to have grown alongside him. He was wearing a strange hat, too. She'd seen something similar in her neighbour's magazine. A fedora, that's what it was called. She'd loved the name, it had such a ring about it, conjuring up colour and sun and everything exotic.

There wasn't much exotic about this man, though, and she felt slightly cheated.

'Miss Steele?' He raised his hat as he approached the counter. 'I'm here for books.'

'As you see.' Flora waved a hand at the book-lined walls surrounding them.

'No, I meant books that I've ordered.' He fixed her with an enquiring look. His eyes, she noticed, were an astonishing light grey.

'I think they should be here by now,' he prompted. 'There's a boy, Charlie – he usually collects my orders – but annoyingly he's caught the mumps and I need the books now. Urgently. Research,' he finished, as way of explanation.

Flora knew the boy he'd mentioned. Charlie Teague did all kinds of odd jobs around the village to earn money and she'd seen him in the bookshop several times, but it was Aunt Violet who had always dealt with him.

'I'll certainly look. If the books have arrived, they'll be downstairs. Could I have your name?'

'Carrington. Jack Carrington. They'll be marked for J.A. Carrington.' He said the words as though he were uncomfortable with them and she wondered why. It seemed a perfectly good name.

'I'll just pop down and get them, Mr Carrington, but do have a look around while you're here. You may find something else you'd like.'

Anything, she thought, to keep the shop going. For years, they had struggled to make a profit and constantly teetered on the verge of financial disaster. The war might have ended ten years before, but the make-do-and-mend culture of wartime continued, and few people had surplus money to spend. Books were a luxury, but Mr Carrington looked a good bet, a serial reader. The All's Well liked serial readers.

It took her some time to locate the right pile, packages of books being scattered haphazardly around the cellar. The building was old – parts of it from the fifteenth century, she'd been told – and its walls twisted and turned in dizzying fashion, often ending in a dead end. Storing goods in any kind of order was almost impossible. Above the cellar, the shop floor was similarly higgledy-piggledy and there had been a few times when Aunt Violet had had to ride to the rescue, discovering a customer in one of its hidden nooks, unable to find their way back to the front door.

J.A. Carrington, Flora read. A small pile of books had come but not the full order, it seemed. Every customer was given a label, and the books they'd ordered placed beneath as they arrived. Once the order was complete, Flora would telephone the customer and ask them to call, praying hard it wouldn't prove to be a Betty trip. Mr Carrington was different, though. It was Charlie Teague who delivered the man's order to the shop and called a week later to see if the books had arrived. When she'd mentioned to Violet how odd the arrangement seemed, her aunt had smiled. *Each to his own*, she'd said. *He's probably a man who doesn't like to mix much.*

Flora collected Mr Carrington's three volumes, hoping he'd be satisfied with half of what he'd expected. One, she saw, was on rare poisons, another a history of state executions, and this one with the blood-red jacket was a catalogue of evil-looking Turkish scimitars. What was this man up to?

Flora looked over her shoulder, thinking for a moment she'd heard a footstep on the stairs, and then scolded herself for her silliness. Quite clearly, these were reference books. But for what? J.A. Carrington – of course. She should have known, she had an entire half shelf of his books displayed a few yards from the till. Jack

Carrington. Crime writer. Determined recluse – according to the village. Or for the less generous among them, the local oddball. It was Charlie's sickness and desperation for his books that had finally winkled the man out into the open. Flora supposed she should feel proud. She must be one of the few villagers who had ever seen him, despite the fact that he'd rented Overlay House at least five years ago.

Quickly, she found a small box in which to pack the books, taping the lid securely, and heaving the parcel back up the stairs. It was surprisingly heavy. When she emerged onto the shop floor, though, it was to find that Jack Carrington had disappeared. She toppled the box onto the counter and was wondering if she should go and look for him – mindful of the building's quirks – when, suddenly, he was at her shoulder. She hadn't heard a thing. He might be lanky and wear a battered fedora, but he moved like a cat.

'Miss Steele, I think you should come.'

'Come where?'

His expression was grave and she saw the grey of his eyes had become dark. Like a winter sea.

'I ventured to the rear of the shop, where the wall turns sharply inwards,' he said over his shoulder, already walking back the way he'd come. 'There's a kind of small alcove there, diamond-shaped.'

'I know it,' she murmured, trying to keep up with his long strides as they threaded a winding path through the shop.

'I was surprised, I must say.'

'But why…?' she began.

They had almost reached the end of the shop and her voice faded away. There was a body sprawled across the wooden floor, a young man by the look of his unlined face. His head had toppled the line of books on one of the lower shelves and, at the other end, his suede boots had toppled another. But it was his hair that fixated Flora, spread like an arc of sunshine across the polished floorboards.

A familiar cloud of bright, fair hair.

CHAPTER TWO

Flora gave the crumpled figure another swift glance. 'Is he dead?' she asked faintly.

Kneeling beside the body, Jack held two fingers against the man's neck. 'Quite dead, I'm afraid.'

She pushed her long hair back from her face, as though this might help her think more clearly. 'But how on earth did he die here?'

'He was looking for a book?'

Jack Carrington was poker-faced and she was unsure whether or not he was joking. If he was, it was in poor taste.

'I doubt it,' she said coldly. 'You were the first person to walk through the door this morning, apart from me, and he certainly wasn't here last night when I left, alive or dead.'

'How extraordinary.' Jack got to his feet again. 'So what do you think?' He was looking at her as though she had the answer to some magic riddle.

'What do I think?' she demanded. 'That he shouldn't be here, whoever he is. That's what I think.'

Flora's nerves were beginning to fray. She felt sorry for the young man, naturally she did, even though he'd behaved so boorishly last night, but a dead body was the last thing the All's Well needed.

'You don't know him then?'

'I don't, though I have seen him before,' she admitted. 'Yesterday evening. I'm certain it's him – I recognise his hair. He nearly ran me down. I think he must be a guest at the Priory.'

'The Priory?' He sounded puzzled.

'It's a hotel.' Dear God, she thought, this man must never leave his house.

'You're talking of Lord Templeton's family home? It's the only priory I know of around here.'

This was an interesting development, a reclusive man who spoke to nobody, but knew the local aristocrat. Though it did nothing to solve her current problem, Flora couldn't resist asking, 'So you were acquainted with Lord Templeton?'

'Acquainted is the right word.' Jack gave her an enigmatic smile. 'But as for this poor chap… there's a wallet poking out of his trouser pocket. That might tell us his name.' He pointed to a square of brown leather, the tip of which was just visible.

'We should phone the police but not touch anything,' Flora said firmly. 'I thought you were a crime writer. Even I know that.'

She wondered if she should be more suspicious. Aunt Violet had been happy to have Jack Carrington as a customer, despite his interesting choice of books, but Flora had never met him before this morning. And *he'd* been the one to find the body. Yet, somehow she trusted him.

'The police can eliminate my fingerprints easily enough, and wouldn't you like to know who ran you down? It might give us a clue why he's turned up here.' Jack bent over and deftly slid the wallet out onto the floor. Opening it, he said. 'Kevin Anderson, that's his name. Mean anything?'

'Should it? If he was a guest at the Priory, I wouldn't know him.'

'Apparently, he's an Australian. Unusual. But I guess the tan rather gives that away. What was he doing here, do you think? Abbeymead is a delightful village, but would you come ten thousand miles to visit?'

Flora thought quickly. 'You might if you'd once owned the Priory or knew someone who had.'

For the first time since she'd met him, Jack looked interested. 'How come?'

'Lord Templeton had no immediate heir. His brother died when they were young, his son was killed in the war and within a year his wife had faded away. But you must know that from your "acquaintance". The solicitors searched but couldn't find anyone who was related, except for a second cousin in Australia. A farmer living miles out in the bush.'

'And he was the chap who inherited the house and the estate?' When Flora nodded, Jack let out a puff of air. 'That's quite an inheritance. Do you think this is our farmer?' He nudged the body with his toe.

'Far too young. I believe the man who inherited was well into middle age, if not older. He wanted nothing to do with the Priory. I suppose you couldn't blame him. It was thousands of miles away and the house was starting to fall to bits. Death duties over the years saw to that. I doubt there was much money in the bank to put it right either. Lord Templeton was a dear man but he wasn't very astute financially.'

'So the Australian sold it?'

'I guess he was keen to have the money. He employed an English firm to find a buyer, the same firm who'd told him the house was falling to bits. They dug up Vernon Elliot, who was keen to open a hotel.'

'Has it been a success?'

Flora put her head on one side to consider the question. 'I don't think anyone really knows. Mr Elliot seems to have a great many plans to put the hotel on the map. To be fair, he's employed local people, and that's gone down well in the village. Overall, though, his ideas haven't been popular.'

'Too modern for an old place. It happens.'

'Too out of step with local feeling. This is a big village and we're lucky to have a good many facilities. Shops and a post office, a pub, a doctor. But it's still a rural community, and still recovering from years of hardship during the war. Incomers aren't greatly welcome, especially if they turn out to be flashy.'

He grinned. 'Your description, I take it?'

Flora grinned back. 'Not mine, it's the village's word. But this man' – they really should get back to the poor dead person lying on her bookshop floor – 'even if Kevin Anderson knows the man who inherited the Priory, it's still a strange place for him to choose to stay.'

'It's possible he was doing a tour of England and stopped off for a few nights in Abbeymead so he could tell the tale back home.'

'I suppose…' She gave a small sigh. 'He won't be doing much tale-telling now. How do you think he died? There doesn't seem an obvious cause.'

'It will be for the police pathologist to decide, though by the look of it…' Jack bent down again, 'he has a nasty cut on his forehead. That could be where he hit the bookshelf on his way down. As an amateur, I'd say it looks very much like a heart attack.'

'But he's a young man,' she protested.

'As I said, extraordinary. And extraordinary how he got in here in the first place. Is there another door to the shop?'

She shook her head. 'There's a yard at the rear of the building, but no door. The powers that be have never allowed us one. Ruining a historic building, et cetera, et cetera. It's a complete bind. When I've rubbish for the dustbin, I have to carry it out of the front door and around the outside of the building. I wonder—'

Abruptly, she spun around, darting into the narrow passageway on her left, and almost running to its end. As soon she turned the last corner, she saw it.

'Look, look here!' she called out.

A surprised Jack followed in her footsteps and was soon standing beside her, staring down at the pile of shattered glass. The window above sported a gaping hole, the chill of an October morning frosting the air.

'That's one question answered at least,' he said.

A question that only created others. Flora wore a bewildered frown. 'So he broke in. But why?'

'To steal?'

'Not money, for sure. The till is untouched. And books – would anyone break in to steal books?'

'It's been known, but it is pretty—'

'Extraordinary, I know. And if this man is staying at the Priory Hotel, he could probably buy the Bodleian.'

'You exaggerate, I think.'

'Of course I'm exaggerating. My nerves are on end and now I have this mess to clear before I can let any customers in – and what do I do with the body?' Flora's fists tightened, fingernails biting into her palm.

'I don't think you'll have too many customers today,' Jack said gently. 'Leave the mess until the police get here. They'll want to see it in any case. Now, shall I telephone them or will you?'

'I will, though I can't think Constable Tring will know what to do.'

'He'll get Kevin collected, at least. There'll be a post-mortem and if the pathologist doesn't like the results, you'll have Brighton CID descend on you.'

'Wonderful, that's all I need.'

Rummaging through the big black diary Violet always insisted they kept, she found the number for the police house. Constable Tring took some time to answer and when he'd listened to everything Flora had to say, he wasn't a happy man.

'If he's young, he shouldn't be dead. And if he's a guest at the Priory, he's got money and money means trouble. I don't like it. I'll need to phone my superiors.'

'Meanwhile…?'

'You must shut the bookshop, Miss Steele. Yes, that's what you must do. Shut the shop and call the undertaker. No, I best call them. Just be ready to let them in.'

When she replaced the receiver, it was to see Jack Carrington doing an odd kind of hop around the cash register.

'I wonder,' he began, 'if I might pay and—'

'The police will want to speak to you, too,' she interrupted, seething with the injustice of it. He had found the body, yet he was planning to disappear. He'd get on with his life, while hers had been stopped dead. It was grossly unfair.

'They know where they can find me,' he said complacently. 'Now, Miss Steele, if I could just settle up.'

Feeling mutinous, she took his money, then watched him walk through the door and in seconds disappear from view. She turned the key in the lock, as Constable Tring had instructed, changing the shop sign to Closed. It was then that Flora realised she'd locked herself in with a dead body. She hoped the undertakers wouldn't be long…

It was a full five hours before she walked through her cottage gate. At the request of the police, the undertakers rather than an ambulance had taken Kevin Anderson's body to the pathology lab where he would undergo a post-mortem to establish cause of death. Meanwhile, the shop had to remain closed, Constable Tring told her, and the inspector from Brighton would probably call tomorrow, although being a Sunday, that wasn't certain. At least, Michael, the local odd-job man, had nailed sheets of wood across the broken window in order to secure the building. It was a comfort to know that she was unlikely to find another body when she returned on Monday.

But Flora was worried and that evening, as she sat by a fire she'd coaxed into being, she couldn't help but fret. It wasn't that cold for October, but she'd felt the need for warmth, and for the first time in months had fetched logs from the wood store. More than ever, she wished Violet was sitting beside her. Someone she knew and loved and with whom she could talk frankly about today's events.

There was a lot to talk about. What had Kevin been doing in her shop? Why had he broken in, if indeed he'd been the one to smash the window? Had there perhaps been two of them, accomplices in theft, and a quarrel between them had ended in death for Kevin? But there was nothing missing from the till. She'd checked again after Jack Carrington left, so if the break-in had been about money, the thieves or thief had gone away empty-handed, but left behind something they shouldn't have.

That was what bothered her most. Looking deep into the flames, listening to the spit and hiss of apple wood, she felt safe. Not at the All's Well, though. Not any longer. The bookshop had been a haven since she was so high, but now it felt violated and she worried that she might never feel comfortable there again.

If the police came up with a rational explanation for what had happened, it might be different, though what explanation there could be eluded her. Jack Carrington had offered none and he was a crime writer. A crime writer who had been next to useless, his interest waning swiftly. Once the demands of work reasserted themselves, he couldn't wash his hands of the affair quickly enough. He was a popular novelist – Flora knew that from the orders she received – and he must, she supposed, have deadlines to meet. Even so, he could have been more supportive. A girl in distress, that kind of thing.

Except that she was no longer a girl. Twenty-five did not count as girlhood. She was a grown woman and unused to feeling this feeble. She and her aunt had managed everything between them, two independent spirits. Not for a moment had Violet allowed the loss of her fiancé in the First War to determine her life, though Flora knew it had left a deep scar. And, she decided, she must be similarly resolute. She was on her own in the world and whatever tomorrow brought, she must deal with it.

CHAPTER THREE

Flora was forced to keep the bookshop closed for the next three days while the police waited for the pathology report. A detective sergeant from Brighton had visited on Monday, inspected the damage, made various notes, and went away. Flora never learned what he thought, if he thought anything. It was a relief when Constable Tring rang with the news that she could once more open her doors.

'So what's the verdict?' she asked him.

'Verdict?' The constable sounded fazed.

'How did the man die?'

'Ah, I see. The pathologist concluded it was death by natural causes,' Tring replied primly. 'A heart attack.'

'How old was Mr Anderson?' she asked.

There was a ruffling of papers while Constable Tring checked his notes. 'It says here twenty-one, Miss Steele, though only just.'

'He must have had some kind of health problem.'

'Not as far as I know,' the constable said cautiously. 'The inspector actually telephoned Australia.' He announced this in a solemn tone, pausing to let Flora absorb the immensity of calling a country so far distant, before he continued. 'Mr Anderson's doctor confirmed that he was a fit young man who took no medicine and had never sought medical help.'

'You're telling me that a man of twenty-one, who was otherwise fit and healthy, died of a heart attack?'

'It can happen, Miss Steele, even to young people. A freak occurrence. I've read about it.'

'And had the young people you read about just broken into a shop?' There was silence at the other end of the line. 'Isn't anyone interested that I suffered a break-in?' she demanded.

She could almost hear Constable Tring chewing his pencil. 'Was anything taken?' he said at last.

'No, but—'

'Well, then, least said, soonest mended, wouldn't you say? Whatever this chap wanted in your shop, he didn't succeed, and now he's dead there are no leads for the police to follow. We must consider the poor man's relatives, too. Suggesting he might be a burglar would cast a shadow and be very hurtful. Best to leave things as they are.'

'And my broken window? Who will mend that?' It was an irrelevance, Flora knew, but she was enraged that clearly the whole affair was to be swept beneath the carpet.

'I'm sure the insurance will pay, Miss Steele.'

'Damn the insurance,' she said loudly, and slammed the phone down.

She stomped into the small kitchenette and put the kettle on to boil. By the time she was stirring a cup of tea, she had calmed down enough to think sensibly. It was stupid that this break-in bothered her so much. The constable was right. The man was now beyond reach – you couldn't haul a dead body into court. And what real harm had been done, other than the shock of finding a defunct Kevin Anderson at the back of her shop?

But a week later, she had changed her mind. Trouble was in the offing. Harm *had* been done. It was what she'd sensed, brooding by the fire that first evening after finding the body. Now, her foreboding was turning out to be right. She glanced across at the photograph of Violet, her favourite photograph, taken the summer before her aunt fell ill. Wearing a faded pair of dungarees, a battered sunhat and a broad smile, Violet stood clutching a lettuce in one hand and a beetroot in the other. What would you do, Auntie? she wondered.

The problems had started the moment she'd re-opened after Constable Tring's phone call. A number of villagers, who had never before put a foot inside the bookshop, had 'popped in' that afternoon – *just to make sure you're all right, Miss Steele*. It was a voyeurism she should have expected and it went on for several days. But then, a sudden lull, and as more days passed, she could go for hours without serving a single customer. The shop was never hugely busy and there were times that were definitely more laggard than others, but the complete lack of custom was bewildering. For days, Flora was the only person in the bookshop.

The new sense of isolation was pervasive, spilling into her life beyond the shop. On her few forays along the high street – they were infrequent since Aunt Violet had grown every kind of fruit and vegetable in the long, narrow garden behind the cottage – Flora had felt people withdraw as she passed, seen looks of sympathy on their faces and heard the murmur of voices as she walked away. She had become a figure to view, a figure to discuss rather than talk to.

It was rumour to blame. It most often was in village communities. Rumours that there was something wrong with the All's Well's building. Something deadly. How could a fit young man die without explanation? Abbeymead clearly didn't believe in freak occurrences. Stories were exhumed from the past. There was the widow who had lived in the building as a private home. She'd sworn that the place was haunted. She had actually seen the ghost. Not only seen, but been terrorised by this violent apparition, she and her cat made sick and the water in her taps turned bitter. The older residents recalled how one of the soldiers, billeted in the building during the First War, had collapsed and died, seemingly without cause. It was whispered, though never proved, that a poison had seeped from the walls.

In the last day or so, Alice had overheard Dilys, the postmistress, regaling her customers with the way she'd always sensed something odd in the bookshop, a smell she could never put a name to. It had to be the poison, the one that had slaughtered the soldier and made the old woman sick. It might have been in abeyance for years but now it was killing again. Flora could have screamed, but was powerless to stop the gossip as one rumour supplanted another, all of them pointing squarely to the dangers residing in the All's Well building.

And something just as damaging, if that were possible, had reared its head on Saturday. A party of sensation-seekers had arrived from out of the village. The news, confirmed by the police, that the dead man was the nephew of the very Australian who'd inherited from Lord Templeton, and that he was young and fit and should never have died, had caught the public imagination. People always enjoyed seeing the wealthy brought low: *They might have had a lucky inheritance*, they said, *but money was no security. Even the rich could die early.* An enterprising bus driver from Steyning had tapped into this universal sentiment and hired a coach to offer a guided tour of Abbeymead, with particular focus on the bookshop where this dastardly event had occurred. If this inaugural trip was a success, Flora learned, he intended to make it a regular Saturday feature. The village was not amused.

A coachload of the day trippers had pounded their way into the All's Well, aimlessly wandering its winding passageways, gawping at nothing in particular, bombarding Flora with a pelter of questions – and buying nothing. Where was the body found? How had the man got into the shop? Had she locked him in overnight by mistake and he'd died of starvation? The more outrageous the comments, the tighter Flora's lips became.

The trippers' descent on the All's Well was not the worst of it. The village was up in arms over the coach trip, infuriated by the prospect of being overwhelmed every Saturday by visitors who bought nothing but prevented everyone else from going about their lawful business. Somehow this onslaught had become Flora's fault, and her pleas that she had been similarly inconvenienced fell on deaf ears.

Sales had fallen dramatically and the cellar was now almost empty of books, with few orders in the ledger to replace them. With trade so bad, she was forced to pillage her savings. It broke her heart to do so – not for the money itself, but for what it represented. The loss of a dream. Since she'd returned to Abbeymead to help her aunt run the shop, she had been saving hard. Through all the months and years of caring for Violet, she'd continued, saving for the time when she hoped her aunt would have recovered sufficiently for Flora to take a year out and set off on her travels.

Paris would be her first stop. She would find a small hotel in the Marais, enjoy coffee beneath the linden trees before she plundered the second-hand bookstalls along the Seine. A few months in France and then on to Italy. She knew she would love Italy – not just the cities, Rome, Florence, Venice, though they would be wonderful – but the countryside, too. Tuscany, Umbria, Le Marche. She had read about them all. Careful planning, she had reckoned, would allow her to pay for an assistant, a woman that both she and her aunt trusted, who would help in the shop and keep a careful eye on Violet. It had been a dream that after her aunt's death had faded. Now, forced to use her savings simply to keep the shop going, it had disappeared altogether.

If she could only see an end to it, but she couldn't. Anderson's death remained a dangerous mystery, at least as far as the village was concerned and, apart from some desultory questioning at the hotel, the police had shown little interest. Now, it seemed, they had walked away from the case entirely. Reggie Anderson, the young man's uncle and Lord Templeton's heir, had been contacted to arrange for the body to be shipped back to Australia. Reggie, apparently, was unhappy at being asked to pay for the repatriation of his dead nephew.

He can join me in the misery stakes, Flora thought. The only one who remained completely undisturbed by the whole wretched business was Jack Carrington. The final two books he'd ordered had arrived in the last few days and were in the cellar awaiting collection. Charlie Teague was still in quarantine and not able to mix, so unless Jack chose to break cover again, he would have to wait for his books. Meanwhile, Flora was faced with lonely hour after lonely hour, her savings account slowly dwindling, and an ache in her heart that her aunt's beloved shop was so badly despised.

Until one morning, she woke and made a decision. It was up to her to find a solution. If she could discover why Kevin Anderson had died – she didn't believe in freak occurrences any more than the rest of the village – if she could show there had been skulduggery at work and the bookshop was blameless – trade would return.

Where to begin, though? Investigating skulduggery was not exactly her forte. But didn't she know someone for whom it was? Sudden clarity, a spark of illumination: she would go to Jack Carrington. He could help her. He had to help her. He'd been the one to find the body and he lived crime constantly. So who better? Today, when she closed the shop at five – there was no point in staying open longer – she would wheel Betty round from her shelter in the yard and deliver Carrington's books to Overlay House.

CHAPTER FOUR

Jack Carrington had been more disturbed by his visit to the bookshop than he'd realised, for several nights finding it difficult to sleep. It was one thing to write about dead bodies, quite another to trip over a corpse when looking for books. The dead man, though, had appeared peaceful enough. There had been no visible injury except for the cut to his head and that was more than likely the result of his fall. Yet Jack was uneasy. He was unsure why and felt stupid that he couldn't pin the feeling down. He decided, though, that when he came to be interviewed by the police, it would be best to say nothing of the doubts hovering in his mind, but simply give a brief account of his movements on the day he'd found Anderson.

He was contacted a day later by a policeman whom he already knew. Jack had spoken to Inspector Ridley several times in the past when he'd consulted Brighton police, wanting to ensure he had the details of a current novel completely right. This time they met over a pint of beer at the Cross Keys, Abbeymead's historic pub. Jack had been reluctant when Alan Ridley had suggested it. He'd been hoping for a brief conversation at his door, the local constable ticking a few boxes. Now it was turning into the kind of social occasion he hated, and in a pub of all places. But Ridley had helped him in the past and he felt obligated to agree.

The smell of beer met him at the doorway, and inside a fug of cigarette smoke floated just below the dark timbers of the ceiling, making Jack's eyes water. A football table had been pushed up against one of the latticed windows, restricting the light even more severely, but through the gloom he caught sight of the inspector already waiting at the shabby bar. On one side of him a group of men were talking loudly together.

'Find a table,' Ridley called out, spotting him in the doorway. 'I'll bring the drinks over.'

The pub was crowded at this time of day, but Jack managed to find a table free that was as far as possible from the noisy laughter at the bar.

'This talk is off the record, Jack,' Alan Ridley said, bringing two foaming glasses to their table, 'but it's good to see you again.'

Jack was instantly cautious. 'Off the record? Why is that?'

'The old man' – he must mean his superintendent, Jack thought – 'wants this business wrapped up as soon as possible. He doesn't like the unusual and, you must admit, it's a bit of an oddity. A visitor to Abbeymead breaking into the local bookshop and dropping dead. We're pretty convinced, though, that it was a heart attack. Just waiting for the pathologist to confirm it.'

Jack felt confused. If it was such an open-and-shut case, why was he here with a beer glass in front of him and talking off the record?

'The papers have got hold of the story,' Ridley went on, 'and it looks like they're out to make a meal of it. You know the kind of thing, lost heir's nephew travels thousands of miles to Sussex and promptly dies. The sooner we can close it down, the better, but I need a line to spin them.'

'You think a cosy chat with me will give you one?'

'Everything helps. You were there – and you're a man steeped in crime. You must have some idea what happened.'

'I didn't know Kevin Anderson. I'd never seen him before. For that matter, I'd never seen Flora Steele before. I found the body while I was waiting for Miss Steele to fetch my books from the cellar.'

He felt the inspector's penetrating eyes on him. 'You don't know Miss Steele then? That's a pity.'

'I'd never been to the bookshop before. I pay a boy, Charlie Teague, who delivers and collects my orders. I'm not going to be much help, I'm afraid.'

Alan Ridley took a long draught of his beer. 'We're working on the assumption that Mr Anderson was in the bookshop for a reason. We thought he might have been meeting Miss Steele.'

'He would hardly have broken into the premises if that was the case.'

'The window was broken, true, but not necessarily by Kevin Anderson. He may have discovered someone breaking in, tackled him and paid for it with his life.'

'Flora, Miss Steele, told me she'd never met Anderson, except when he almost ran her off the road the previous evening.'

'That's what she told my sergeant, too, but she's a young woman. A pretty young woman. She might be bending the truth.'

'Why on earth would she do that?'

'Secret liaison? Villages talk and she didn't want people knowing?'

The suggestion made Jack's eyes widen. A relationship between Flora and the dead man? It was possible the girl had met Anderson elsewhere other than in a speeding sports car, but it seemed unlikely. She had been genuinely bewildered at finding Kevin's body in her bookshop. This was to be the old story, it seemed. The inspector was looking for a line and, in doubt, had fallen back on romance.

'You're sure she never dropped a hint?' Ridley pursued.

'As sure as I can be. In any case, Anderson is Australian and he's only been in England a few weeks.'

'These modern girls are fast workers, you know! And it could have been a long-distance romance. I've heard all this guff about his uncle inheriting the Priory, but it could just as well have been Flora Steele that had him make the journey.'

Jack frowned into his beer. 'Sorry,' he said, after a long pause, 'I can't really help.'

'Ah, well, it was a possibility. A titbit to feed the press.' The inspector gave a long sigh. 'They'll be disappointed when they discover they've been running a story that's going nowhere. Once they learn it's death by natural causes.'

'If it is.'

'Bound to be.' Ridley drained his glass. 'I best be off. Shouldn't be drinking on duty! But thanks for meeting me.'

'Before you go, I should mention that my fingerprints will be on the chap's wallet. I tried to find out who he was before Flora called the police.'

'I'll pass that on, for what it's worth. It's a rum do, that's for sure. The place was broken into but nothing stolen. If the dead man didn't know Miss Steele, what reason could he have for being there?'

It was what Jack would have dearly liked to know himself. 'Why he died seems just as important a question,' he said quietly. 'Anderson was a young, fit-looking man.'

'Like I said, we're waiting for the post-mortem to be sure.'

'Is it possible you could let me know the results?'

The inspector looked surprised.

'I was the one who found him,' Jack said quickly. 'I'd like to know, just to close the affair.'

'It's not really protocol, but… as a special favour, I'll drop you a note. Don't suppose you're on the telephone yet?'

Jack shook his head, and drank down the last of his pint. 'If you would, Alan. I'd best be off, too. I've a deadline to meet.'

The laughter at the bar had become raucous and he was glad to have an excuse to leave.

It wasn't the last he was to see of the inspector, however. A day or so later, he was returning from a walk he often took in the woods nearby, when he was surprised to see a car drawn up outside his house. Very few vehicles ever bumped along the muddy lane, but as he drew nearer, Alan Ridley jumped out and waved at him.

'Thought I'd call in person,' the inspector said. 'Better than trying to write it all down.'

'You'd best come in.'

Jack hardly sounded welcoming, but he couldn't help himself. If Ridley was here to tell him the results of the post-mortem, wouldn't they be simple enough to be written on the back of a postcard?

'I'll not stop, old chap, but I promised to let you know what the pathologist said. It's what we thought. A rogue heart attack.'

'That must be good news. It should take the case off the front page. Not much mileage in a heart attack.'

'They'll play the poignancy card, young man away from home, et cetera, but yes, we're hoping it will be an end to any furore the press were wanting to kick up.' Ridley paused, sucking in his teeth, then, moving closer, he said into Jack's ear, 'Between you and me, though, it isn't that certain.'

Was that the reason Ridley hadn't committed his words to paper? The uneasiness that had been lurking in the back of Jack's mind stirred into action.

'How is that?'

'The pathologist couldn't find any problem with the chap's heart, apart from the fact that it had stopped. No sign of disease or even wear or tear, and the bloke's doc Down Under confirmed as much. Anderson was fit enough to go surfing on a regular basis and rarely walked through his surgery door.'

'What do you make of it?' Jack asked cautiously.

'Me? Nothing. I'm not a medic and I'm happy enough to wrap the case up as natural causes. Unusual but natural. There was some speculation about poison, but—'

'Poison?'

'The pathologist wondered. It looked like the bloke's airways had narrowed and he'd suffered some respiratory distress, which isn't always the case in a simple heart attack.'

'Was there a trace of any poison?'

'Not a drop. That's the problem. If there was a poison, it was one that's not easily detected. Invisible once ingested. I don't suppose you've come across any oddities in the research you've done?'

Jack shook his head, then recalled the book on poisons that he'd recently bought. He would definitely check.

'Keep it under your hat, though, won't you?' the inspector said. 'The pathologist was flying a kite, I think. He only mentioned it to me because the chap's general health was so good that it was bothering him. Without definite evidence, we've decided it's best to go with the heart attack. The bloke's dead and we haven't anything to prove differently.'

Jack opened the car door for the inspector to climb back in and found himself nodding, though he wasn't sure why. Ridley's suggestion had done nothing to ease his mind and, letting himself into the house, he felt troubled.

For the next few nights, he slept badly, and during the day slumped gloomily at his desk, finding it difficult to write. Some sixth sense had been telling him that all wasn't what it seemed, and though he'd been at pains to stress to Flora Steele that a heart attack in a young man was perfectly possible, he hadn't really believed what he was saying. Not entirely. And she certainly hadn't. He'd rather liked her for that. Liked that she was a little fiery, a little too candid. Jack wondered how she was getting on.

He found out sooner than he'd expected. Having struggled unsuccessfully with the same paragraph for most of that day, he'd been about to give up and go down to the kitchen for yet another ham sandwich – he couldn't be bothered to cook – when there was a knock on the front door. He ignored it. He didn't welcome visitors. The only people he ever talked to were his publishers, his agent, and an occasional policeman, anything to do with what earned him a living. Everything else was out of contention.

The knocking began again, this time louder. He gritted his teeth. Some do-gooder from the village wanting him to donate to charity, or find Jesus, or join the Mother's Union. He thought he'd seen them all off by now. The third knock was more of a thump and caused him to spring out of his chair and slam the window wide open. He had been ready with a barrage of cutting remarks, until he saw the pair of hazel eyes looking up at him. Flora Steele.

He would have to go down, he supposed. He couldn't leave her standing there; even a hermit couldn't do that. Her eyes had held an angry glint, he'd noticed, though at the same time she looked quite fragile. Different from when he'd seen her last. He ran down the stairs, comforting himself with the thought that at least he'd get the books he'd ordered. She must have brought the new arrivals with her, and perhaps, just perhaps, they would push him towards writing fluently again.

At the front door, Flora made no attempt to hand over the books that Jack could see resting in her bicycle tray. In the bookshop, he'd thought her face lovely, paintable even if he'd been an artist, but now her hair was scraped back into some kind of bobble and her eyes held a warning spark.

'Good evening, Miss Steele.' He tried to sound welcoming. 'It's kind of you to bring my order. Can I take them for you?' He went to lift the books out of the bike tray, only to have his hand pushed aside.

'You can have them, certainly, but it's you I've come to see, Mr Carrington.'

'Really?'

'Yes, really. Can I come in? I need to speak to you.'

'The house is in a bit of a mess right now,' he began to bluster.

'I don't mind mess,' she said, collecting the books from the bicycle tray and walking across the threshold before he could stop her. 'Where to?' She turned to him with a bright smile.

'You'd better come in here,' he said, unable to keep the glum note from his voice.

She followed him into one of the two large reception rooms that covered most of the ground floor of Overlay House. He never used the room himself, or the other one for that matter. The kitchen provided everything he needed.

'This is a nice room,' she said, looking around her, 'or it could be.' She walked towards the tall glass doors that led on to the terrace. 'Pity about the garden, though.'

'I'm not aiming to win Gardener of the Year.'

'Evidently not. When Charlie Teague emerges from his quarantine, you could ask him to do the weeding for you. I believe he tidies quite a few gardens. So… your books,' she said, clearing a space for them on what the landlord had called an occasional table.

Jack leant forward, eager to scan the material he'd been waiting for.

'Have you noticed?' she asked suddenly, pointing to the invoice she'd laid beside the books. 'I suppose you must have. Your initials spell out your first name. Well, almost. JAC.'

He knew he was looking guilty but couldn't help himself.

Flora glanced sharply up at him. 'What's wrong with your name? Don't you like it?'

'Not much,' he admitted. 'But neither would you.' The question in her eyes had him blurt out, 'Not if your name was Jolyon Adolphus Carrington.' He didn't know why he'd confessed to a secret he always hugged to himself as tightly as possible.

'Jolyon? Really?' The broadest grin imaginable spread across her face.

'Yes, really. Now can we get on?'

Flora must have taken the hint because she said in a businesslike fashion, 'Shall we sit down and I can tell you why I'm here?'

Her briskness at least meant she wouldn't be staying long. Jack had been about to offer a cup of tea, it was the done thing and he should try to conform, but then decided that he would send her on her way as soon as possible. He was no longer comfortable around people and Flora Steele ruffled him more than most.

She plumped herself down on the stiff sofa he'd inherited with the house. 'Gosh,' she said, 'this is uncomfortable. How do you cope with it?'

'What is it you wanted, Miss Steele?'

'Flora,' she said. 'I really think you should call me Flora – if we're to be working together.'

He blinked. 'We're working together? In what way?'

'I have to discover why that man died in my shop and you can help me. You're a crime writer, you'll have ideas,' she finished vaguely.

'I doubt that crime fiction qualifies me to do better than the police, and they've made it clear that Kevin Anderson died of heart failure.'

'His heart failed, certainly, but why? I don't believe it was some kind of amazingly bad luck for him. I think it was a suspicious death.'

'You're alone in that… Flora. The police believe differently. It is possible for an otherwise fit young man to die suddenly. Don't forget, Anderson collapsed after breaking into your shop. The effort of doing so could have triggered a hidden problem.'

'That may be what the police prefer to believe. They simply want to tidy up loose ends, send Kevin back to his uncle, and forget it ever happened. That makes life easy for them, but it doesn't for me.'

Jack frowned. 'I don't understand. Why is this so important to you?'

'Because my business is being ruined by rumours that I need to scotch. Whispers that in some way the All's Well is a dangerous place and best avoided. The only way to put paid to those rumours is to find out what actually happened.'

Feeling uncertain, Jack got up and walked over to the glass doors. For a while, he stood looking out onto the wilderness of tall grass and straggling hydrangea, before turning back to her. 'Do you honestly think that if you discover there's been foul play, there'll be no more talk in the village?'

'There'll be talk, there always is. The incident will probably pass into village folklore. But the talk will be good. The bookshop will be seen as interesting, notorious, if you like, but notorious for the right reasons – a murder that's been solved.'

He was startled by the idea. 'If you say so. But I don't understand what you think I can do.'

'At the moment, I've no real idea, but you're the one who found the body. Will you help me?'

Jack didn't reply. Her suspicions chimed too well with his own feeling that something wasn't quite right, though his immediate response had been to refuse to be involved in anything so crazy. To be involved in anything, full stop. Particularly if there was a young woman in the mix. Not after Helen. Not ever. And not just after Helen, but his best friend, his colleagues, the whole world of work. He was happier now than he'd ever been, he told himself. Content to live alone, seeing no one he didn't absolutely have to. So why spoil it?

But then he looked across at Flora and saw the anxious expression on her face, the hands that weren't quite still, and some pernicious strand of chivalry caught hold of him. He could help her for a day or two, couldn't he? Though how he was to do that was a mystery. A day or two to keep her happy, and then he could fade from view. He had to face the truth, his new novel was dire. He was writing three words a day if he was lucky, and the books she'd brought – they were just a prop. Why not use a real crime case, if indeed there had been a crime, as distraction, possibly future material?

'Where do you want to start?' he asked.

He saw her expression clear and the hazel eyes sparkle with pleasure. This might not be such a great idea after all. She was a little too pretty, hair bobble and all, but if he were ever tempted, he had only to remember.

'How about the Priory Hotel?' she said eagerly. 'Kevin was a guest there. It was his last resting place, before my bookshop, that is.'

'So we just bowl up and start firing questions at his fellow guests?'

'Is that what your heroes do? Of course not. We need to be subtle. I know the cook at the Priory. Alice Jenner. We could start with her.'

'Insider knowledge!' He tapped his nose with a finger and gave a faint smile.

Flora smiled back at him. 'Let's hope.'

Jack was hoping, too, but for something different – that questioning Alice would be the beginning and end of the investigation.

CHAPTER FIVE

Just after ten the following morning, Flora met Jack Carrington at the gates of the Priory Hotel. Alice Jenner started her day early and by now, Flora reckoned, she would be taking a well-earned rest.

The weather was crisp but bright and, walking beside Jack up the gravelled drive, she felt warmed by a hazy sun. Gradually, the mist that had hung like a curtain over the smooth contours of the Downs was dissolving, their outline etched dark against the pale blue sky. The hills were sentinels, Flora thought, guarding the white stone mansion that she had known all her life, and in far happier times.

At least Vernon Elliot was keeping the parkland spruce. In Lord Templeton's last years it had run wild, only the home lawn ever seeing a mowing machine. Cyril Knight, Edward Templeton's gardener for most of his life, had struggled single-handedly to keep the long grass down, the rose garden blooming, and the trees and bushes in the remaining estate under some kind of control.

It had been an unequal struggle, but since Vernon Elliot had taken over with funds to employ a raft of new staff, and Cyril having retired disgruntled, the grounds had been transformed. In the distance, the smoke of a bonfire hazed the air. Fallen leaves, no doubt – the park was full of them. Flora shielded her eyes, trying to make out the figure wielding a rake. She frowned. Bernard Mitchell, it looked like. Was he working at the Priory now? Kate, her friend who ran the village café, had made no mention of her husband taking a job here.

'It's best we go through the servants' entrance,' she said. 'The kitchen is close by, just along the corridor. I don't want too many people to see us.'

'Cloak and dagger stuff, eh?'

She stopped walking, her figure tense. 'I need you to take this seriously,' she said crossly, looking directly into a pair of light grey eyes. 'The bookshop will go under if I don't turn things round, and finding out what really happened is the only thing that's likely to save it. I owe it to Violet to do what I can.'

'Sorry, I wasn't thinking. Charlie told me about your aunt.' He sounded genuine and she almost forgave him. 'It must be tough running the business on your own, especially after losing Violet. She told me once, when I telephoned an order, that together you were the best team in the world.'

It was more than tough. Violet hadn't just been her sole relative and her partner in business, but much, much more. She'd meant just about everything to Flora. The nearly three years she had cared for her aunt, while taking responsibility for the bookshop, had meant that most of the friends she'd once had had disappeared. There simply hadn't been time to include them in her life. Violet had tried to help, battling on until the last few weeks, taking orders and despatching them. Despatching Jack Carrington's books, in fact.

By the time they'd crunched their way to the servants' entrance, the sun was streaming down and Flora was feeling hot. She wished she hadn't worn her bright pink jacket – a light jumper would have been a far more sensible choice – but the swing coat was smart and she'd wanted to make a good impression. On whom? she wondered.

At the side door, they paused, neither of them quite sure of the propriety of bursting in on people during their working day. Jack took off his fedora and used it to fan his face. At close quarters, the hat looked to her more worn than ever.

'We can't stand here all day,' she said decidedly. 'Come on. Let's find Alice.'

Alice Jenner was easy enough to find and so was her kitchen. The most beautiful smell of baking laid a trail for them along the rough-flagged corridor to an open door at its end. The cook was taking a batch of scones out of the oven and nearly dropped the baking tray when she turned and saw the two figures hovering in the doorway.

'My, you gave me a scare! Flora, how are you, my love? Come for a scone, perhaps?' An unexpected dimple accompanied her smile.

'I could certainly do with one. They smell divine, but I don't want to hold you up.'

'Nonsense. It's time I had a rest. I've been bakin' since six this mornin'.' Alice adjusted her cook's hat, trapping several rogue strands of wiry grey hair, then waved a hand at the wooden counter that lined the large square kitchen. Several loaves of bread, two cakes, a scattering of small pies, and two more trays of scones bore testimony to her hard work.

'Put the kettle on, Ivy,' she said to the small dab of a girl washing dishes at the sink. 'Then have a break yourself.'

China mugs were laid out on the scrubbed wood table and an enormous brown teapot fetched down from a shelf above the counter. 'A cup of tea will go down nicely,' Alice said comfortably. 'Now, who's your friend? I don't think we've met.'

'I'm so sorry. How rude of me. This is Jack Carrington. He's a writer and he doesn't get out very much – which is why you don't know him.'

'A writer – my, that's a fancy occupation.' Her faded blue eyes surveyed him with interest.

'Not half as fancy as baking.' Jack looked along the counter with a smile.

'You'll take a scone, Mr Carrington?'

'Jack, please. I'd love one,' he said easily.

When they were all three settled at the table with butter and scones and large mugs of tea in front of them, Flora said tentatively, 'You know what happened at the bookshop, Alice?'

'It's been all around the Priory and back again. Poor young man.'

'It's very sad,' Flora agreed. 'Did you know that Jack was the person who found him?'

'No, really!' Alice's eyes were wide. 'How dreadful for you – and for you, too, my love. It's not somethin' you want to happen every day.'

'I was wondering, did you ever speak to Mr Anderson while he was staying at the hotel?'

Alice nodded vigorously. 'You couldn't escape him,' she said.

'How do you mean?'

'He was always askin' questions. About the house and the village. And the Templeton family.'

'I suppose that's understandable, with his uncle having inherited the place.'

'Mmm.' Alice took a bite of her scone. 'Mebbe. But he seemed too nosy for my likin', though perhaps I shouldn't say so, him not bein' with us any more.'

'You don't have to like every one of your guests,' Jack put in.

'Just as well.' Alice gave a broad smile. 'Some of them are plain nasty. That wasn't Kevin, though. He said for us to call him Kevin though if Mr Elliot had heard, he'd have had our guts for garters.'

'You liked him then?' Flora pursued.

'Not exactly liked. He was too pushy to like. Cyril found that, too. He was always questionin' us and we both got a bit fed up with it. But I didn't truly dislike him either. He was pushy but not unpleasant, if you know what I mean. Miss Horrocks, though, definitely didn't like him.'

'Who is Miss Horrocks? She wasn't here in Lord Templeton's day.'

'She's the new housekeeper.' Alice lowered her voice. 'West End trained.' She winked. 'And don't we know it.'

Flora slowly spread her scone with butter. 'Why did she dislike Mr Anderson so much?'

'He was always wanderin' around the house. Some of it's off limits to guests. Mr Elliot has his private quarters in the East Wing. It's where Lord Templeton used to live – you'll know it, Flora – and he don't like guests bargin' in. No need for them to do so. There's plenty of space they can wander in. Have another scone, Mr… Jack.'

'Better not, but it was delicious. Thank you, Mrs Jenner. You say this chap was in Mr Elliot's private rooms?'

'The library, he was in the library. It's right next door to where Mr Elliot has his private office and he's made sure to rope the area off. It's quite clear it's not part of the hotel. Kevin took down the rope, bold as brass, and let himself into the library.'

Flora exchanged a look with her companion. Books seemed to be important to Kevin Anderson. First the Priory library, then her bookshop.

'Anyways, Miss Horrocks told him to leave and he got quite abusive. We heard the row from down here. Still, he did offer to throw a party, staff included, I will say that.'

'Why a party?'

'It was his birthday. He was twenty-one, he said, and that was a great age to be, and since he was a long way from home, we had to help him celebrate. I thought it was a nice gesture. I was going to do the sandwiches and the cake, but he said no, I should have a rest for once and he'd get the village café to do it. Kate's a fine cook and she could do with the business, so it worked out well. She did this beautiful chocolate cake in the shape of a boomerang! It was quite a talkin' point.'

'Who is Kate?' Jack asked.

Alice looked surprised. 'You don't get out very much, do you? Kate Mitchell – she runs Katie's Nook, the tearoom on the north side of the high street. Lovely girl. Shame about the husband, but then you can't have everythin'.'

Flora ignored this, hit by a sudden thought. 'Did the cake taste as good as it looked?'

'I dunno. We never got to eat it. It was up in Kevin's room and he was goin' to bring it down to the kitchen later. After he'd had a drive. That was his treat, he said. Like I told you, Mr Elliot bought this sports car—'

'I know,' Flora said quickly, 'but are you saying that Kevin never appeared in the kitchen?'

'No, and neither did his cake. Miss Horrocks found it in his room the next day.'

'Had he eaten any of it?'

'One slice, I think she said. She was tuttin' about the waste. I thought it was a blessin' that he'd actually had some. At least he'd enjoyed a drive in that posh car and then a piece of his birthday cake – before it was too late.'

Flora felt Jack stiffen beside her and wondered if he was thinking the same thing as she, that the cake might have made Kevin ill. 'What happened to the cake?' she asked casually. 'After Miss Horrocks found it?'

'Mr Elliot told her to throw it out. That was after we knew about the poor man, of course. And the cards he'd been sent and the flowers in his room. Everythin' had to go. Like I say, all very sad.'

Flora dusted the scone crumbs from her hands and drained her mug. 'That was absolutely lovely, Alice, but you'll be wanting to get on, I know.'

'Well, I wouldn't mind,' the cook admitted. 'We've fifteen guests checked in for lunch and Ivy hasn't even started the vegetables. But come again, won't you? And you Mr... Jack.'

'You could tempt me.' He smiled down at the plump figure of the cook. He had a kind face, Flora thought, and a sharp intelligence. Nothing much escaped him, she could see.

When they were once more walking down the drive towards the tall, wrought-iron gates, she said, 'Katie's Nook?'

'Absolutely, but tell me more about Kate.'

CHAPTER SIX

'Kate Mitchell has lived in Abbeymead all her life. I was at school with her, in fact, though I didn't know her very well then. Different classes, different friends. She's Cyril Knight's daughter – the gardener who was here in Lord Templeton's time.'

'And Kate is another cook?'

'A very good one, too. I went on to do A levels – they were still relatively new at the time and a lot of the girls didn't want to do them, Kate included. She went off to catering college instead. I never saw her again until we both came back to the village.'

'Coming back seems to have worked for her.'

'She tried Worthing first, I remember Aunt Violet telling me. She was working in a hotel there for a while, but she wanted her own business and came back here to set up Katie's Nook. Her father helped her. The café is quite small, no more than ten tables, but it's been very popular. The food is excellent and Kate herself is well-liked in the village. She does a lot of business, too, at the weekly market. People coming in from the farms and smallholdings to sell their produce. Then there are the holidaymakers, they spend quite a bit. She's just started a new thing, taking orders for food to eat at home. Sandwiches and soup – she cooks fresh soup every day – and of course there are trays of luscious cakes! You should try her cooking some time.'

He could feel Flora looking quizzically at him, assessing him, no doubt passing judgement on the way he lived. That was the trouble with getting involved.

'What's wrong with the husband, by the way?' he asked, hoping it would prove a distraction. 'Alice seemed pretty dismissive of him.'

'Well, he's been in prison.'

'Really? How exciting this village is.'

'Not that exciting. It was petty theft, I think. Kate was going out with Bernard Mitchell before he got caught, then stood by him when he was sentenced to two years. She married him in jail. Her father was dead against the marriage but she went ahead anyway.'

'A two-year sentence doesn't sound much like petty theft. There's likely to have been some violence involved.'

Flora pursed her lips. 'Bernie Mitchell isn't an attractive character, and there have been rumours in the village that he doesn't treat his wife well. According to Cyril Knight, his daughter is bullied and abused, but I don't know how true that is. Mind you, her father has never accepted the marriage. He used to talk a lot to my aunt, and she said he was a very unhappy man, even reckoning his son-in-law had his hand in the till.'

'Does the man have a job other than stealing from the till?'

'He's supposed to help Kate – order in goods, do deliveries, keep the books up to date.'

'Cook the books?'

'Quite possibly. It's what Cyril believes.' She paused for a moment. 'Is there any way, do you think, that Bernard Mitchell could have been involved with Kevin? I think he must be working at the Priory now. I saw him in the distance on our way in.'

'I've no idea, but if he's an ex con…'

'Give a dog a bad name?'

'Yeah, I shouldn't do it, but it was his wife making Anderson's cake that lodged in my mind. I wondered if—'

'Me, too.' She gripped hold of his sleeve. 'Jack, if we could get hold of that cake or what's left of it…'

He tussled with himself as to whether or not he should tell her what Ridley had passed on. He was supposed to keep it under his hat, but if he were to be of any real help to Flora, she needed to know.

'I heard from the police – on the quiet – that the pathologist wasn't entirely happy with the diagnosis he'd made. Anderson's heart failed, but there was no sign of previous organ damage, no reason other than a freak accident to account for his death.'

Flora came to a halt. 'So?'

'The chap speculated that maybe poison could have caused the heart to fail, though he found no trace.'

'A poison,' she said excitedly. 'That's it. The one slice of cake.'

'Steady on. I've just said there was no trace of poison in Anderson's body,' Jack warned.

'Maybe it's one that's not widely known.'

'Any pathologist worth his salt would know his poisons.'

'Yet, in this case, he didn't,' she said stubbornly. 'We need to go back.'

Jack was alarmed. 'Back where? Not to the hotel?'

Flora nodded. 'To speak to the fearsome Miss Horrocks. Find out whether it's true there was only one slice missing, and what she actually did with the rest of the cake. If it's still around, we could rescue the remains and take them to the pathologist. He'd find the poison then.'

'The cake was dumped nearly two weeks ago,' he protested. 'It will have found its way to the rubbish tip by now.'

Flora wasn't listening. She had spun around and was marching back up the drive, forcing him to scramble after her. 'We'll go through the front entrance this time,' she said over her shoulder.

Jack sighed inwardly. How had he allowed himself to be cajoled into this? It would be a fiasco. If they started grilling the hotel staff, they would likely be thrown out.

Flora was still ahead of him, skipping up the front steps of the Priory and through the great oak doors that stood open. She walked across to the receptionist, Jack following. Like a pet lamb, he thought wryly. The receptionist's name badge told him she was Polly Dakers. She flashed him a brilliant smile, looking past Flora as though the girl wasn't there.

'We'd like to speak to Miss Horrocks,' Flora said, tapping the desk for attention. 'Is she around, do you know?'

Lazily, the girl looped her long blonde hair behind her ears, her mouth tightening into a small moue. 'She'll be around, but she'll be too busy to speak to anyone.'

'I think we can be the judge of that,' Flora said robustly. 'Where is she?'

Polly gave a casual glance across the foyer to the grandfather clock that stood opposite against the wood-panelled wall. 'At this time of day, supervising the chambermaids,' she said in a bored voice.

'The bedrooms then? Good.'

Jack's gaze was drawn unwillingly to the receptionist. Polly was giving him another of her blinding smiles. 'I don't think we've met,' she said. 'Are you new in the village?' Flora, already halfway to the oak staircase, looked back at them. He suspected she wanted to laugh.

'No, I'm not new,' Jack said quickly, 'and I don't believe we've met.' He hurried towards the staircase to join his partner in crime.

'Nothing like being blatant, is there?' Flora was taking two stairs at a time. 'I wonder if she tried that on with Kevin Anderson?'

'Don't tell me you're discounting my unique charms?'

'I'm sorry to disappoint you, Jack, but anyone wearing trousers…'

They had barely reached the top stair when a woman, dressed in grey from head to toe, materialised in front of them.

'Miss Horrocks?' Flora said brightly, wriggling her way past the housekeeper and onto the landing. She wasn't going to be intimidated, Jack could see, but this woman would be a tough nut to crack. He hoped Flora realised that.

'I am Miss Horrocks,' she said, brushing an imaginary speck from the lapel of her fitted jacket. 'And you are?'

'Flora Steele. I run the village bookshop and this is Jack Carrington. He's a…' She stumbled. He could see she'd bitten back the word 'crime'. 'He's a writer.'

Miss Horrocks's perfectly arched eyebrows travelled skywards. 'Really? And is there anything I can assist either of you with?'

'Yes, there is,' Flora said gratefully. 'We've come about one of your guests. One of your former guests, I should say. I'm not sure if you know, but Mr Anderson died in my bookshop.'

Miss Horrocks stiffened, but Flora went on. 'His death has upset me greatly. I know it happened nearly two weeks ago, but I can't get it out of my mind. I was hoping to talk to you about him.'

The housekeeper looked down her nose. Literally, Jack thought, fascinated by the sight.

'I can't think why you would wish to talk to me,' Miss Horrocks said. 'I'm unable to tell you anything more than you already know. Mr Anderson was a young man, an Australian, I'm told, who had an unfortunate heart attack and died thousands of miles from home.'

'It's such a sad story,' Flora said mournfully. Miss Horrocks did not look particularly sad. 'I expect he enjoyed his stay at the Priory, though. I hope you put him in the best room.'

'We have a number of best rooms, as you put it, and Mr Anderson was pleased with his premier suite.'

She made an impatient gesture with her hand to a bedroom nearly opposite to where they stood. It was front-facing and the door had been left open. Ready for cleaning, Jack imagined. He could see a small Juliet balcony at the far end, but little else.

'I understand it was Mr Anderson's birthday while he was here.'

Flora was like a small dog with a very large bone, Jack thought, and wondered if he, too, would end up gnawed.

When the housekeeper continued to stare at her, Flora prompted, 'Mr Anderson's birthday?'

'I believe it was,' the woman said finally. With an abrupt jerk of her hand, she marshalled a wisp of hair that had strayed from her chignon. 'Really, I cannot say any more, Miss Steele, and I do have a very busy morning.'

'I'm sure you do and I'm grateful for you taking the time to speak to me. There's just one small thing, though – was Mr Anderson able to celebrate before… you know?'

Frost had now settled firmly on the housekeeper's face. 'I understand he did,' she said tautly. 'A little.'

'A cake, maybe? Kate Mitchell does some wonderful novelty cakes.'

'Why are you asking me this? It is evident you are well aware of Mr Anderson's cake.'

'It's only that I wondered if Kevin got to eat any of it.'

The housekeeper had clearly lost all patience with the questions; Jack could see it was time for him to step in.

'How much did he eat?' he asked blandly.

Miss Horrocks looked mystified and angry at the same time.

'You must know,' Jack continued. 'You threw the cake away at Mr Elliot's instruction.'

'Precisely what is this about? Mr Anderson had one slice of cake, and the rest was deposited in the dustbin. Are you accusing me of eating the cake? Or my staff of eating it? How dare you come up here, trespassing, I might add, and throw accusations around?'

Her voice verged on a scream and she appeared to be working her way into a major fury when one of the maids glided up and said something in the housekeeper's ear.

Miss Horrocks turned a thunderous face towards them. 'I have work to do. I must go and I would advise you to do the same.' She disappeared down the corridor, whirling into a bedroom at the far end.

Jack looked down at his companion. 'Worth a try?' he asked.

She beamed up at him. 'Absolutely.'

Together they slid into the room Miss Horrocks had indicated. Jack closed the door softly behind them and looked around. The bed had been stripped ready for remaking and the wardrobe doors flung wide to reveal their emptiness.

'How disappointing,' Flora said, dejectedly.

'It was unlikely we'd find anything. The room will have had several occupants since the late-departed Kevin and been cleaned each time. It's just possible, though, that he left something behind the cleaners haven't found. It sometimes happens.'

'Let's make a quick search, then we can be sure. You take the bedside tables, I'll look in the chest of drawers.'

It took only seconds to ascertain that the chest was as empty as the wardrobe, although one of the bedside tables revealed a bright green electric clock hidden away in the top drawer and a Gideon bible in pride of place in the lower.

Jack shook the clock.

'Why are you doing that?'

He shrugged. 'You never know. I had a hero once who found a radioactive disc in a bedside clock just like this one.'

'We're not looking for a disc, we're looking for a cake,' she said sharply. 'Or even a few crumbs. They get everywhere and the cleaners could have missed some.'

'Unlikely. Anyway, the pathologist would need more than a few crumbs to come up with any kind of analysis.'

'Well since there aren't any, he won't be disappointed.'

Jack walked across the room to the long windows overlooking an expanse of rolling parkland. A table and chairs had been positioned to make the most of the view. 'Not crumbs,' he said, 'but there's a small crack in this table. And a few dots of pollen. Kevin was sent flowers, wasn't he? The vase must have sat here. I wonder who sent them?'

'I think we should stick to the cake. We need to keep asking questions about it.'

'If we must. Katie's Nook?' he repeated.

'Katie's Nook,' Flora agreed.

CHAPTER SEVEN

They were crossing the foyer, making their way towards the hotel's grand oak doors, when Flora found herself hailed from behind.

'Miss Steele, isn't it?'

She turned to see the tall, thin figure of Vernon Elliot emerging from the office behind the reception desk, his leanness exaggerated by a suit so smart that Flora thought he must be dressed for a wedding.

'Good morning, Mr Elliot,' she said guardedly.

She was uncertain how to tackle this encounter, how to explain their presence in his hotel when they were neither guests nor diners. Then she remembered Alice.

'We've been visiting Mrs Jenner,' she offered, inventing the reason as she spoke. 'I had to return some dishes – Alice has been spoiling me with her pies – and as it was such a lovely morning, I thought a walk would do me good. Mr Carrington felt like walking, too.'

Jack's expression was one of determined blankness. He evidently thought poorly of her excuse. Well, let him find a better one!

'It's always good to see you at the Priory,' Vernon said, his high thin voice sounding less than delighted. 'I don't think you've been here since our opening gala. You should come and eat with us some time. Mr Carrington, as well.'

She would never have the money to do so, but Flora replied to the invitation as enthusiastically as she could. 'I will, Mr Elliot. You have made the old house look beautiful.'

That wasn't true either. She much preferred the shabbiness of Lord Templeton's era to the fussy lampshades, elaborate drapes, figured wallpaper and acres of velvet that its new owner appeared to favour. It was an attempt at a country-house style, devised by a man who had never lived in one.

Elliot responded overwhelmingly to flattery – Flora had realised that from the first moment she'd met him – and his face cracked into something approaching a smile. 'Excellent, excellent. And your friend…?'

'He'll come and eat, too,' she promised.

At least Jack Carrington was more likely to. Judging by the number of his books she'd sold over the last few years, he could afford to eat for both of them. She gave him a nudge.

'I'll look forward to it,' Jack said. 'Right now, I'm afraid, I need to be elsewhere. Miss Steele, too.'

Vernon Elliot looked disappointed. And wary, Flora thought.

'Ah, well. Until next time, then. But make it soon!'

'That was awkward,' Jack commented, as they made their way back to the gates once more. 'I thought the fellow was going to demand an explanation of why we were in his hotel.'

'It felt like that,' she agreed, 'though there's no reason on earth why we shouldn't walk into the Priory. You could have been thinking of booking a room there and called in to give the place a look-over.'

'Highly unlikely.'

'But Elliot doesn't know that. He doesn't know you're a hermit.'

'I'm not,' Jack protested. 'I like a simple life, that's all.'

'That's what I said. A hermit. You've probably met more people today than you have in the last year.'

Jack was quiet, appearing to think about this surprising statistic, before he said wearily, 'And there's more to come, I expect.'

*

Kate Mitchell was clearing coffee cups and emptying plates when they walked through the door of Katie's Nook. She look tired, Flora thought, her face pale and her movements slow. The lank hair, scraped into a thin ponytail, suggested a woman who had given up caring.

She looked up when the café bell rang out. 'Flora, how nice! You're a bit late for coffee but I can make another pot.'

'No need. We're not here to drink coffee but to order a birthday cake.'

She hadn't cleared it with Jack, but all the way back from the hotel she'd been thinking of a good reason to call on Kate. She didn't want to be caught out again. A brilliant thought had dawned as they'd walked down the main street.

Kate's forehead wrinkled. 'It's not your birthday, is it? I thought that was April time.'

'It is. The cake is for Jack. This is Jack, by the way.'

He walked forward to shake Kate's hand. 'Jack Carrington,' he introduced himself.

Flora gave him brownie points. He had taken the birthday cake idea with equanimity.

'So what kind of cake?' Kate asked. 'Fruit, sponge? Traditional icing or maybe something more adventurous?'

'Jack is a writer,' Flora declared. 'I was thinking of a book-shaped cake. Would that be possible?'

Kate put her head on one side. 'I don't see why not.' She sounded cheerful, but Flora had the impression that every word was an effort.

'Wonderful! We've been to the Priory this morning to see Alice Jenner. She mentioned the boomerang cake you baked for the poor man who died. That was what gave me the idea.'

Kate looked down at her feet and said nothing. What did she know of Kevin's death? Flora wondered. Had she really been involved?

Uttering a silent prayer that Kate was completely innocent, she said casually, 'That was such a clever notion. I bet your customer loved it – I mean before he... you know...'

Kate nodded, walking back behind the counter. 'Bernie said he was delighted.'

'Your husband delivered the cake? It's a shame you didn't hear the praise for yourself.' When Kate said nothing, Flora continued, 'Anyway, we're lucky to have you in the village and Kevin was lucky to find you.'

'He didn't really,' Kate said suddenly. 'That was Bernie again. He suggested to Mr Anderson I make a cake for him. My husband is very good at drumming up business, especially now he works at the Priory.'

'We saw him this morning, sweeping leaves. How long has he been there?'

Kate thought for a moment, her soft brown eyes intent. 'Several months now. He helps out in the gardens – the contract firm only do so much – but mainly he's in the hotel, working in Mr Elliot's private office, preparing bills, paying invoices, dealing with confidential stuff. It's why he didn't want me to talk about it. Mr Elliot says he doesn't know what he'd do without Bernie. He's become the Priory's Man Friday. The money is good as well. It definitely helps out.'

With a wan smile, she reached across the counter for her notebook. As she did so, Flora saw a large bruise on the inside of her wrist.

'Now.' Kate tapped her pencil. 'What size cake would you like, Mr Carrington?'

'Jack, please. Medium, I think. Sponge – I'm not crazy about fruit cake. Will that be OK?'

'It should be. I'll enjoy the challenge. When is your birthday?'

He hesitated for a crucial second.

'It's next week.' Flora jumped in. 'Jack wasn't going to bother to mark the day, but when he came into the bookshop, I persuaded him to celebrate. Then when Alice told us about the boomerang, I thought a novelty cake was a great idea.'

'The boomerang cake *was* great fun,' Kate said. 'Dad found me a picture in one of his old encyclopaedias and I sketched on paper what I thought would be the right size. Measuring the ingredients was a bit hit and miss, but Dad gave it his seal of approval – I can never stop him scraping the bowl.'

'Did Mr Knight help you make it?' Flora asked disingenuously.

A rare smiled flashed across Kate's face. 'He doesn't usually, but this time he did. My electric mixer was having a bad day and Dad took a wooden spoon to the bowl. It was packed with fruit and needed a strong arm.'

'It's a shame the chap didn't get to eat it,' Jack said. 'I guess it arrived too late.'

'I hope he ate some. I asked Bernie to deliver it after lunch that day. There would have been time to snaffle a slice or two before he offered it to the staff. I think that's what he was going to do.' She chewed the end of her pencil. 'Now, the lettering? Happy Birthday, Jack?'

'What could be better? Shall I settle up now?'

Kate finished making a note in her order book. 'No need. You can pay me when you collect. Do you have a telephone number so I can let you know when it's ready?'

Jack shuffled uneasily and it was Flora again who bridged the awkward silence. 'You can telephone the bookshop, Kate. I'm only just up the street and I can drop by.'

They had walked the short distance to the door of the All's Well before either of them spoke.

'If poison was added to that cake,' Jack said, 'it could have been at any time – from Cyril Knight stirring it with his wooden spoon until the cake reached Anderson's bedroom. An awful lot of people could have handled it.' He held up his hands, counting the names on his fingers: 'Kate and her father, this man Bernie, the receptionist at the hotel, a chambermaid perhaps, Miss Horrocks herself.'

Flora gave him a shrewd glance. 'I wondered why you were interested in the time the cake was delivered.'

'If it was delivered after lunch, it was sitting around a long time before Anderson took his drive, then returned to his room and helped himself to a slice.'

'Before breaking into my bookshop,' she said, her hand on the large brass knob that opened the All's Well's door.

'That's likely to have been the order of events, but none of it explains why. Why on earth would any of these people want to kill Kevin Anderson?'

She stepped back from the door, her eyes searching his face, a genuine question on her lips. 'What do people in your novels kill for?'

'Love, revenge, money. Anderson was a stranger here so love seems a bit wide of the mark. Revenge? Possibly. Maybe something in his past history linked him to someone here. We can't discount that. After all, his uncle is part of the Templeton family, if only a distant relative. But it's money I'd place my bet on.'

'These days, everyone could do with more money. Only spivs benefited from the war – Aunt Violet loved that word, you know – and they're probably still benefitting. Still selling black market cigarettes, even if the fake ration books have gone. The rest of us have to do the best we can.'

'We need to narrow the field. At the moment, trying to nail the perpetrator is like looking for the proverbial needle. Bernard Mitchell seems a bit of a toerag, wouldn't you say? He was the one that introduced Kevin to his wife's café and persuaded him to order the cake.'

'But then Kate herself isn't beyond suspicion,' Flora said sadly. 'I know there's a whole cast of people who could have handled the cake, but she was the one who made it and would have had the best opportunity—'

'Not necessarily. Once the cake was finished, it would be possible to inject it with poison from a syringe.'

Flora looked startled. 'Is that what your villains do?'

'Not so far, though I could probably use the idea. I think it could be easily done. In any case, Kate wasn't alone in making the cake. Daddy was involved, too.'

'But why would either of them want money so much they were willing to kill?'

Jack was silent for some while, before he said, 'Did you see the bruise on Kate Mitchell's arm?'

'Yes,' she said slowly. 'I don't like to think what that means.'

'It could mean that she's desperate to escape an abusive marriage, and she'd need money for that. Her father, too – he mistrusts his son-in-law. He could have been willing to help dispatch Kevin, if it ensured his daughter escaped a man he despises.'

'But how does killing Kevin Anderson gain them money?'

'I'm supposing that Kevin had something valuable that they wanted.'

'His hotel room was quite bare. If there was ever anything worth taking, it's disappeared.'

'Except that it might not be a tangible object,' Jack said thoughtfully. 'Information can be just as valuable and knowledge can lead to blackmail.'

'You're saying that one of them could have been blackmailing Kevin? But then they wouldn't kill the golden egg, or whatever it is,' Flora protested.

'The goose, the goose that laid the golden egg. Kevin got fed up with paying and threatened to go to the police, so had to be silenced?

Or turn it around. He could have been the one blackmailing them. He'd come all the way from Australia to do just that.'

'Blackmail sounds far-fetched.'

'And poisoning a cake baked in a village café doesn't?'

Flora rested her back against the sun-warmed brick and flint of the shop wall. 'Kevin might have had something valuable that someone coveted – Kate, Bernie, Cyril Knight, the hotel staff – but he was looking for something, too. Miss Horrocks caught him in the library and we found him in my bookshop.'

'A coincidence?'

'I don't think so.'

Jack furrowed his hand through a head of dark hair. A 'short back and sides' was favoured by most of the men Flora knew, but Jack's hair was far more luxuriant, flopping forward over his forehead and tapering low on his neck. Flora liked it.

'What, though?' he asked. 'What could he have been after that any of these people wanted enough to murder for? Don't forget, whatever he was searching for – if he *was* searching – he never found.'

'I haven't forgotten. Not at all. But my theory makes a great deal more sense than yours. Blackmail? Nobody here had ever heard of Kevin Anderson until he died.'

'You can't know that.'

'But I do,' she said stubbornly. 'And if we only had a clue to what he was looking for, we could unlock the whole mystery.'

*

Flora Steele infuriated him. When she made up her mind, there was no budging her. Anderson may or may not have been searching for something – the fact that he'd broken into the shop suggested he had been, and that whatever he was after was important – but his search didn't necessarily connect to his death. The man or woman who'd rendered the cake deadly would not have known of Kevin's sudden impulse to break into the bookshop. They would have reckoned on him dying in his hotel room, and it being attributed to a dodgy heart and the excitement of cards, flowers and a celebration party to come. In which case, that person had another reason entirely for depriving the world of Mr Anderson's company. Blackmail seemed the most obvious motivation to Jack. It was what he'd used successfully in several of his novels. Why had Flora asked for his help if she wasn't prepared to listen to him?

He'd enjoyed today, he had to admit, and been surprised. Normally, too many people made his head ache, and his day had certainly been crowded. He'd enjoyed Flora's company, too: that was another admission. She was stubborn and annoying, but he liked watching her in action. Candid, he'd call her approach, candid and direct. It got results, though, and she'd thrown herself into this whole mad mission with enthusiasm.

That was understandable. When he'd left her at the bookshop this afternoon and watched her let herself in, it had seemed a sad place – the fact that she'd felt able to close the shop for most of the day testified to her lack of customers. He'd felt her loneliness acutely. She had friends in the village, but it was evident her aunt had been her emotional anchor. Was there a boyfriend somewhere? he wondered. At some point in their conversation, she'd mentioned that she had studied to be a librarian and had only been back in Abbeymead for three or four years. That would make her in her mid-twenties, though she looked younger. Most women of Flora's age were married by now with at least one child. Jack wondered what her story was. There was bound to be one. Everyone had a story.

He'd enjoyed Flora's company, true, but despite that he was tempted to call time on his involvement. The list of suspects was growing and they would be hard put to investigate all of them. The poison, if it existed, could have been administered by any number of people at any time over a period of hours. If Anderson had eaten cake before his joyride, the poison could have worked slowly, causing him to keel over in the shop several hours later. If he'd snatched a piece of birthday cake after the drive, but before slipping out of the hotel to break into the All's Well, then poisoning would have been more immediate. Either scenario was possible.

And so was the fact that the cake might be wholly innocent. All this talk of poison and blackmail could be laughable. Anderson might well have died from sudden, unexpected heart failure after all. The pathologist had plumped for it as being the most likely cause, and really there was nothing – except for the break-in – to suggest anything more sinister. But he wouldn't persuade Flora of that, he knew. She was adamant that Kevin's death was suspicious and convinced that until she got to the bottom of it, her shop was on a downward slope to failure. He gave a small groan. He couldn't let her down, not with her livelihood at stake.

Still, it would be a good idea to let the dust settle for a while. He'd hunker down at home, uncover his typewriter and try once more to get this benighted story moving. If he knew Flora, and he was beginning to, she'd be banging on his door at the slightest hint of progress.

CHAPTER EIGHT

Flora stared moodily through the bookshop window at the few pedestrians who had braved the rain, scurrying along wet pavements, heads bent and umbrellas at the tilt. The grocer opposite appeared to be the only shop in the high street doing any trade. She gave a small sigh. People had to eat, she supposed, but they didn't have to read. Still, this morning she'd had two customers, which was two more than for days past. They had travelled from Worthing, having heard of the All's Well's collection of second-hand books, and one of the ladies had actually bought an expensive volume of flower prints.

It had been Aunt Violet who had started the second-hand section, concentrating mainly on out-of-print books, though sometimes rare volumes: first editions, signed copies, those with special jackets. Her aunt had loved her afternoons at local auctions, or at the sales that occasionally took place when an old house in the district was sold and the new owners wished to create an entirely new library, or no library at all.

The last auction she'd attended had been at the Priory itself, a few months after Lord Edward's death, when the sale of the building had just been agreed. Despite her failing health – she was to follow Lord Edward a year later – Violet had returned from the sale triumphant. Items of furniture and a number of paintings had been up for sale, but she had acquired a lot that included a whole section of the Priory library – and beaten another dealer to it.

For the most part, the volumes she bid for stayed on the bookshop shelves, but they were still a draw to browsing customers and, most often, if they didn't buy an old book, they went on to buy something newly published. The year Violet had secured a large collection of original Agatha Christie books and Flora had arranged them in a tasteful window display, they'd had people pouring through the door. Not any more, though.

She pressed her face hard against the window pane. Had the rain stopped at last? If so, she might dash to Katie's Nook and treat herself to one of Kate's wonderful iced buns. A bun and a cup of tea should see her through to lunch. Grabbing her old raincoat, she locked the shop door and walked to the corner opposite the café. She had just begun to cross the road, the enticing smell of something warm and delicious reaching her through the damp air, when she was forced abruptly to jump back onto the pavement. A cyclist, covered from head to toe in bright yellow, had skidded on the water rushing along the gutters, and almost mowed her down. Flora stood still, her heart beating uncomfortably fast. It was the second time in as many weeks that she had risked injury on the roads. Was she invisible?

'Sorry,' the cyclist called out over a screech of brakes. Beneath the hood of the yellow waterproof, she saw it was Polly Dakers, the bored receptionist from the Priory.

'Sorry,' the girl said again. 'Are you OK?'

'Just about. A bit shaken,' Flora muttered.

'I had to borrow this riding cape and the hood keeps falling over my eyes,' Polly admitted.

'Perhaps not the best garment to be cycling in,' she said severely. Then a sudden thought had her mollify her tone. 'I was on my way over the road to Kate for a bun and a cup of tea. Would you like to join me?'

Polly looked surprised and seemed about to refuse. But then two large splashes of rain fell from her hood and trickled their way down her face and into her lap.

She grimaced. 'This rain!'

'Come and get warm,' Flora invited her.

'It's an idea. I'm supposed to be buying cigarettes for a guest, but he can wait. They won't miss me at the hotel for half an hour.'

Kate had a welcoming smile for them both as they pushed the door open, Polly dripping gently onto the rubber doormat. Flora felt guilty that she'd ever suspected her friend could have anything to do with Mr Anderson's death. But then took herself to task. An investigator must remain objective. Kate, sweet and kind as she was, was a suspect – until she was proved otherwise. If only, Flora thought, she could slip into the Nook's kitchen and search, she might find a clue as to what had gone on. Or maybe no clue, if there was nothing to find. One way or the other, it would be immensely helpful. But that wasn't possible.

The café was empty but the tables were set for lunch, sporting bright blue gingham tablecloths and cutlery that shone. The mouth-watering smell of onion soup drifted towards her on the air and, for a moment, made Flora reconsider the iced bun.

'Miss Dakers, isn't it?' Kate asked. 'You'd best take that cape off and I'll hang it in my office to dry.'

Polly shrugged off the clammy waterproof, immediately plumping herself down at one of the window tables. 'I like to look out,' she said, though what there was to see on a day like this, Flora couldn't fathom.

The girl seemed to be tense, possibly from the difficult ride she'd had, but once a pot of steaming tea and two sticky iced buns appeared on the table, her shoulders lost their stiffness.

'Why I have to go shopping for guests, I don't know,' she said between mouthfuls. 'I'm a receptionist, for goodness' sake. And most of the guests have their own cars. That chap could easily have driven down to the village and bought his own cigarettes.'

'Do you often get asked to shop for guests?'

'I get asked to do all sorts of things. Whenever there's something no one else wants to do, it's, Polly, could you just… Polly, could you take… Polly, could you ask…?'

'You don't sound too happy with the job,' Flora ventured.

'I could do a lot better,' the girl said decidedly. 'Elliot's a real misery to work for. The only time I've ever heard him laugh is when he's been drinking with the guests. Puts on a real show then. "You're not wanted here, young lady," he said to me when I went to meet Kevin at the bar one evening.'

The name had Flora's ears burning, but before she could say anything, Polly was once more launched on her complaints. 'And for all his airs and graces, Elliot works you to death and pays a rotten wage.'

Flora made a mental note. Kate had said that Elliot paid well, so perhaps Polly had got on the wrong side of her employer. Or perhaps Bernard Mitchell was a special case.

'Have you thought of looking elsewhere?' she asked.

Polly gave a cynical laugh. 'I've thought of it plenty, but there's precious little work around here. Not the kind of work I want to do anyway.'

'And what would that be?' Flora took a hefty bite of her bun.

'I've been told I could be a model.' Polly flicked her long blonde hair over her shoulders, her mouth adopting a small pout.

Flora looked across the table at the heart-shaped face, the wide blue eyes and the shapely figure. 'I can see that,' she said honestly.

Her companion glowed, her smile scintillating, the first genuine smile Flora had seen.

'My mum thinks I'd be a great success if I ever got the chance. Look at that Suzy Parker. I look quite like her, except for the hair colour. She must earn a fortune. Uncle Ted thinks so, too.'

Flora's knowledge of modelling was zero, but she scanned her memory for anything that might keep Polly talking.

'There are agencies, aren't there? Have you tried any of them?'

Polly leaned forward, her food forgotten. 'I wrote down a list that me and Mum got from the magazines, but all the model agencies are in London.'

'That's not far,' she said encouragingly. 'If you take a direct train from Brighton, you'll be in Victoria in an hour.'

'It's not the journey that's the problem.' The pout had changed from pensive to discontented. 'You have to have a portfolio.' The girl drew out the letters of the word, evidently enjoying the sound. 'It's a collection of photographs – of me,' she added, as though Flora might think they were of the Sussex landscape. 'Photos taken in different poses and costumes. The agencies won't look at you without a portfolio.'

Again there was that strangely drawn-out pronunciation.

'A portfolio sounds very businesslike. And very exciting.'

'It would be if it was ever going to happen.' Polly sank her teeth into the last piece of squishy icing. 'It costs a lot of money,' the girl said, her mouth full of bun. 'Uncle Ted gave me five pounds towards it, but the photographer in Steyning said it would cost double that. And he's not even a top bloke. In any case, his photographs probably wouldn't be right for the agencies. They're very particular.'

'What a shame.'

Flora tried to sound sympathetic, though why anyone, corseted and wearing the most uncomfortable clothes, would want to walk up and down a piece of carpet while being judged by other women, was beyond her.

'Is there no way you could raise the money? Take an additional job perhaps? Ask for a pay rise?'

From her limited knowledge of Vernon Elliot, she doubted any request would be successful. He was a man of surface show, Flora reckoned, not someone who would invest in the nuts and bolts of human relationships, but she wanted to get Polly to talk more of the hotel. That, after all, was where Kevin had spent most of his time.

'I'll be lucky,' Polly said gloomily, taking a glug of her tea. 'Kevin wanted to help me, but that's gone out of the window now.'

Flora's ears were again on the alert. She was getting somewhere at last. 'Kevin Anderson? The young man who died?'

Polly nodded. 'He said I was beautiful and that he really liked me.'

'Yes…' Flora prompted.

'We went out once, you know,' the girl confided. 'Nothing improper, but he was very keen.' She gave a small giggle. 'He said I was prettier than any girl he'd ever met Down Under and if he had anything to do with it, I'd be a model.'

'And did he have anything to do with it?'

'He died, didn't he? Before he could.' The full lips formed themselves into the biggest pout so far.

'That was so sad.' Flora looked suitably sorrowful. 'How do you think he would have helped if he was still here?'

'He was going to give me money for my photographs and then come up to London with me – to the agencies.'

'He didn't manage that, though?' Had Kevin been making for the shop's cash till after all, but collapsed before he could reach it? But then, he'd been found snooping in the Priory library and there was no cash till there.

Polly shook her head regretfully. 'He said he didn't have the money right now, but he was in a fair way of getting it.'

'That surprises me.'

'How come?' The girl cocked her head to one side.

'I wouldn't have thought money would be a problem. Mr Anderson was staying at the Priory. I imagine most of your guests are fairly wealthy.'

'You'd think so, but Kevin wasn't. He worked for his uncle back home, he told me, and Reggie Anderson didn't pay well. He reckoned his uncle got a fortune when he sold the Priory – he never told Kevin how much – but it made no difference anyway.

The man stayed a right skinflint and kept his nephew short. Never once offered Kevin a penny of what he'd inherited. Kevin said he had to borrow money to make the trip to England.'

Flora's smooth forehead puckered. She was on to something here, she knew. 'Why was Kevin so keen to come to England? To Abbeymead?'

'Reggie Anderson told him some tale about the place. About the Priory. His uncle visited here when he was a child, apparently, and heard this story. It was a kind of legend. He told it to Kevin as a joke, but Kevin took it seriously. He was fed up with his life in Australia. To be honest, Miss Steele, I think he owed a lot of money there – he did say once when he'd had a few that he'd been gambling. Anyways, he decided the story was true and he could make his fortune by coming here.'

'What was the story?'

'I dunno. Not exactly, except that it mentioned some kind of treasure trove.'

How desperately disappointing, Flora thought. It was like something from a child's story book. Kevin Anderson had been telling porkies, she was sure. The gambling debts were likely to be true – probably he'd come to England to escape his creditors. But the story of treasure to be found? Almost certainly he'd been stringing this young woman along, no doubt in the hope she'd succumb to his charms.

Out loud, though, she said, 'Kevin was looking for treasure? How exciting!'

'It would have been exciting, if anything had happened. But it didn't.' Polly had relapsed into dolefulness again. 'He turned funny the last few days before he died. Didn't turn up when we'd arranged to meet, and the next morning walked straight past the reception desk without a word. When I tackled him about it, he said it was none of my business. That was at first, but then when I did a little persuading… you know…' She gave Flora a coy glance.

'No, perhaps you don't. Anyways, I got him talking eventually. He'd telephoned his uncle in Australia – Kevin needed more money to stay on in Abbeymead. When he mentioned meeting me, Reggie Anderson told him to get on with what he'd come for and never mind stray girls. Stray girls, I ask you! If Kevin didn't get a move on, his uncle said, he wouldn't wire him the money and his nephew would have to work his way back to Australia.'

'The story wasn't such a joke to Reggie then? He must have believed there was treasure to find after all.'

'Seems like it.' Polly snorted. 'Sounded a bit Enid Blyton to me.'

And to me, Flora thought. Aloud she said, 'Still, a disappointment for you.'

'A real let-down. Whatever Kevin was supposed to find, he didn't. He went and died instead.'

Polly's heart didn't seem to have suffered too much of a dent. Was she telling the truth when she said that she'd no idea what Kevin had to find? Or had Kevin confided in her and she'd decided to search herself, after conveniently disposing of him? Perhaps they'd broken into the All's Well together and then quarrelled. There were so many possibilities.

'Hey, I better go.' The girl pushed her chair noisily back, dragging Flora from her reverie. 'Thanks for the bun,' she said, as Kate brought a newly dry cycling cape from the back of the shop.

'She's quite a character, isn't she?' Kate said, as the door shut behind Polly. 'Not exactly the Brains Trust but very beautiful.'

She was, Flora thought, on her way back to the bookshop. Beautiful and devious. Just how involved had Polly been in Kevin's exploit? The girl had a native shrewdness that would make finding out difficult. But at least Flora had her theory confirmed. Kevin Anderson had been looking for something that was valuable, a good enough reason to kill him. Mentally she gave herself a thumbs up. So much for blackmail, Mr Crime Writer.

But what treasure could Kevin have hoped to find in a library or a bookshop? There was only one kind and that was books. He was looking for a book or something in a book that would lead him to the fortune his uncle had spoken of. Buried treasure! Polly was right when she said it sounded straight out of Enid Blyton. If anyone other than that hard-headed young woman had said the words, Flora would have brushed them aside with a giggle.

She had to take it seriously, though. It must have something to do with the Priory, she thought, or with the Templetons. That's why Kevin had been asking Alice questions about the family and the house they had lived in for centuries. Kevin had asked Cyril Knight questions, too. Alice had mentioned how the retired gardener had been irritated by the young man's pestering. And Cyril was closely connected to the infamous cake.

Cyril Knight was likely to know the story of this supposed treasure, whatever it was. He hadn't just worked at the Priory for years, he'd lived in the village the whole of his life, and if Flora remembered Violet's words rightly, his mother had been a district nurse. Someone who, by the nature of her work, would inevitably hear any tales that were going. If Kevin had confided to Cyril what he'd discovered, in exchange for details of the legend Polly had mentioned, Kate's father could have decided the treasure would be best with him and taken his own action. He was definitely next on her list of suspects.

She was tempted to call on Cyril immediately, but then thought of Jack. She should tell him what Polly had said and suggest they visit the old chap this afternoon. Jack's idea of working together left a lot to be desired, but they were supposed to be partners in this. And she had enjoyed her day with him. She wouldn't mind spending a few more hours in his company, if only to see his face when she mentioned buried treasure.

CHAPTER NINE

Before she left for Overlay House, Flora needed to shop. The larder had looked particularly bleak when she'd stowed away the Frosties cereal this morning and now that the rain had stopped and the skies cleared, it made sense to get it done.

The greengrocer was first on her list. He'd had a fresh delivery that morning of potatoes and local cauliflowers, far superior to anything growing in Flora's back garden. Without her aunt's expertise, the vegetable patch was struggling. Boxes of Kentish apples had arrived, too, their shiny redness asking to be bought.

'How are you, Miss Steele?' the moustached owner asked, deftly twisting a paper bag full of apples and landing them in her empty basket.

'Well, thank you, Mr Houseman.'

'And that shop of yours? Doing better, I hope, now the kerfuffle is over.'

Flora gave the ghost of a smile. 'As good as can be expected.'

'It's a heavy burden for a young lady to shoulder,' he said. 'Always thought that.'

'The bookshop was a gift from my aunt,' she reminded him.

'I know that right enough. But sometimes gifts can turn into mill-stones, no matter how well they're meant. You're still young and you're not married. You should be out in the world going on adventures.'

It was very much what Flora thought herself, but to agree with him would smack too much of disloyalty to Violet.

'There are plenty of adventures to be had in Abbeymead,' she said lightly, then realised that she'd spoken the truth.

A quick goodbye and she hurried on to the butcher's. The butcher himself was new to the village, having bought his shop a mere five years previously, and knew little about Flora, other than she was a regular customer. He never regaled her, as so many of his compatriots did, with stories of how she had looked on her first day at school or how she'd eaten so much at the Sunday school party when she was eight that she'd been terribly sick.

'Two lamb chops and four slices of luncheon meat, please,' she said briskly.

'How's that book place of yours goin'?' the butcher asked, taking a large cleaver to a joint of meat. The All's Well, she thought, seemed a topic of fascination for her fellow shopkeepers. 'Found any more dead bodies?' A broad smile spread across his cheeks, shining beneath the artificial light.

'No,' Flora said brusquely. 'But you seem to have.' She gazed pointedly at the animal carcases hanging from a row of hooks behind the counter.

The butcher hastily wrapped her chops and luncheon meat. 'I've some nice chickens coming in at the weekend,' he said in a conciliatory tone. Flora ignored him, taking the parcel he handed her and marching out of the door and on to the baker's. She shouldn't get so upset, she knew, but it seemed as though there was no escape. The All's Well would always be the shop where a dead body had been found.

The bakery was situated at the far end of the high street, and her watch showed it was already long past twelve. Before she made her way to Jack's house, she would need to take her shopping home and, at this rate, she'd be lucky to get any lunch at all. Kate's iced bun would have to suffice. Briefly greeting a nurse she knew from the doctor's surgery and one of the waiters she recognised from the Priory, she sped along the road.

The bakery, unfortunately, was crowded. News must have circulated there were doughnuts today, she thought, resignedly joining a queue that stretched beyond the open shop door. She didn't want doughnuts, but why hadn't she learned to bake bread? Violet had tried to teach her more times than she could count, but she'd been too impatient. All that mixing, folding, resting, proving, before you even wrestled the thing into the oven.

In two minds whether to abandon her shopping and try later on her way back from seeing Jack, she was hovering in the shop doorway when she heard a high-pitched voice that she knew, cutting across the general hum of conversation. Vernon Elliot's. He was at the front of the queue, having almost reached the counter. Flora caught only snatches of what he was saying, although the women immediately behind him seemed to be hanging on his words. She thought she spotted Elsie, her bloodthirsty pensioner, standing close by.

The mention of All's Well had Flora's lack of attention transformed. Straining to hear what he was saying, other words bounced into her ears: *bad business, disaster, time to sell.* At that point, Elliot's voice dropped and she lost whatever else he was saying. It was the women who had been listening avidly, their heads nodding like energetic donkeys, who began talking more loudly. *Strange happenings, ghosts*, they said, sounding entranced by the words. The old story, Flora thought, her heart feeling like lead.

A woman in the queue two in front looked round at that moment and, seeing Flora behind her, gave her neighbour a nudge. The pair of them began to shuffle from one foot to the other, as though by doing so they could erase the comments they'd heard. Their discomfort appeared to transmit itself to Vernon Elliot himself, because he, too, looked around and saw Flora. She watched as he hastily turned back to the bakery assistant and placed his order.

Flora was left bewildered. It was horribly clear that Elliot had been talking about her, talking about the bookshop and spreading rumours that her business was dying on its feet. But why on earth would he do that? He might not like her, but neither had he reason to dislike her. As far as business was concerned, she was no competitor, so why slander her? It made no sense.

It did make her straighten her shoulders, though. She stood her ground in the queue, holding her head high, refusing to be intimidated. As every customer passed her on their way out of the shop, including Elliot, she was careful to smile cheerfully, until she, too, could grab a chunky farmhouse and flee, the loaf tucked upright in her shopping basket like a soldier ready to defend.

*

Jack pushed back the battered leather Chesterfield he'd bought from a London flea market and stretched his arms high above his head. He felt good. He'd written an entire chapter this morning, the words flowing through his fingers and onto the typewriter keys in a way they hadn't for weeks. A tiny nugget of confidence had started to grow that he might actually finish this project, though he preferred not to think of the looming deadline. It had been the books, he thought, the ones Flora had delivered a few days ago, that had pushed him back to his desk. One in particular, *The Juno Rebellion*, had been key. He'd flicked through the others, too, the ones he'd collected earlier, including the book on poisons, but had found nothing riveting. Nothing to interest Flora.

She had been strangely quiet – he'd heard nothing from her since yesterday's visits to the Priory and Katie's Nook. He realised with a jolt that he'd been hoping to, and wondered why. He should be grateful for the peace – it was what he craved after all, and what Flora most definitely disturbed.

Shuffling the typed pages into a small pile, he patted them with something that approached hope, and went downstairs to make himself the usual ham sandwich. Really, he should be more adventurous, but eating meat every day was still a novelty after so many years of rationing. He had swiped a smear of piccalilli across the buttered slices of bread when there was a bang on the front door. It was a bang he recognised.

'I can't believe what's just happened,' Flora announced, and darted past him into the drawing room he never used.

He followed meekly behind, bemused by her sudden eruption into his life again. 'Why don't you come into the kitchen?' he asked. 'It's a lot more comfortable.'

She turned to face him and he saw her doubtful expression. She must be remembering the horsehair sofa and reckoning that one of his kitchen chairs could be worse.

'It really is,' he promised, leading the way back to the kitchen.

Once ensconced in the room's warmth, with a cup of tea and a sandwich that Jack had whipped up in seconds, Flora's shoulders visibly untensed.

'Tell me,' he encouraged.

'Vernon Elliot,' she said with loathing. 'He was slandering me. Slandering my shop. Telling people that it was going bust, suggesting it was dangerous.'

'Are you sure? Why would he do that?' It sounded to Jack as though Flora might have mistaken whatever conversation she'd overheard.

'I've no idea,' she said, biting into her sandwich, 'but I heard him in the baker's not an hour ago. He was at the head of the queue and lording it over everyone, the way he does, more or less telling them my shop should be avoided.'

Jack was puzzled. 'It's an odd thing to do, unless it's some kind of payback for our invading the Priory yesterday. Elliot wasn't at all happy to see us there.'

'It's a spiteful thing to do. He must know the bookshop is teetering on the edge.'

'That might be the point,' he said gently.

'You mean he wants me to go bankrupt? What a truly horrible man he is.'

'There I can agree with you. Is that what you came to tell me?'

'Actually no. Something much more positive. I have news – in the shape of Polly Dakers,' she said proudly, and proceeded to recount her conversation with the receptionist that morning.

'Treasure trove,' Jack spluttered, spilling tea across the Formica table.

Flora beamed at him. 'I knew you'd like that.'

'It's ridiculous.'

'Yet a young man took it seriously enough to travel thousands of miles to come here. And fall further into debt as a result. *And*,' she emphasised, 'his uncle, who claimed the whole idea was a joke, was still willing to wire Kevin money so that he could carry on looking for this mythical treasure.'

Jack shook his head and munched steadily on. He took his time before he said, 'What on earth has this to do with Anderson searching the library at the Priory and breaking into your shop? That was your theory, wasn't it?'

'It's more than a theory. I'm convinced of it. Kevin was looking for something connected to this story. That's why he asked Alice all those questions. Why he asked Cyril Knight as well, the two longest-serving retainers at the Priory. We need to ask some questions ourselves. Find Cyril and grill him.'

'I've a book to write,' he protested, annoyed that his time had been annexed arbitrarily. 'Or haven't you noticed?'

'Oh, I'm so sorry,' Flora said, in a tone of mock distress. 'Am I unwelcome? Have I disturbed your writerly inspiration?'

She was enjoying teasing him, Jack could see, and he couldn't honestly say he was filled with inspiration. A workmanlike job on this book was all he was going to manage. He was intrigued, too, with the way this real-life mystery was developing.

'When do you want to go?' he asked, putting aside his reluctance.

'Now,' she said promptly. 'When we've finished these very tasty sandwiches.'

CHAPTER TEN

Cyril Knight lived in a row of terraced cottages tucked behind the grey stone bulk of the village church. It was evident he worked as hard in his own garden as he had at the Priory. A straggle of roses still bloomed even in October and a splendid display of chrysanthemums and winter pansies filled several flower beds. The house might need a lick of paint, but its garden was a haven.

'Cyril takes a pride in his home,' Jack remarked.

'Make sure you say that. We want him on our side.'

She greeted the old man with a smile, as he opened the door. 'Hello, Mr Knight. I hope we're not disturbing you. We'd love to have a chat, but if it's not convenient, we can come back later.'

She felt Jack fidget beside her at the mention of 'later'. He was thinking of his book, no doubt, and Flora felt a twinge of guilt, but work would have to wait.

'Now's fine,' Cyril said, adjusting a pair of corduroy trousers that, even with braces, seemed in danger of pooling to his ankles. He'd lost weight since Flora had last seen him and she wondered if worry over his daughter was the cause. He certainly looked poorly, his face pale and drawn.

Coughing badly, he led the way into the cottage's small sitting room.

'You're unwell, Mr Knight.' Flora was concerned for the old chap. 'We really shouldn't be here.'

'Don' matter. Mostly I'm fine – had a few bad moments back in the past, but I'm on the pills now and they keep the old ticker goin' 'cept I don' like these last ones I been takin'. Given me a fuzzy 'ead. Though mebbe it's just this darn cold. Had it for days and now it's gorn to me chest.' He waved them towards two fireside chairs. 'Sit yourselves down.'

The square-shaped sitting room faced onto the front garden and was surprisingly bright, despite the cottage's low ceilings. Flora looked around her. There was barely a surface in the room that wasn't covered with ornaments or photographs.

'You have your family to keep you company.' She nodded to the collection of frames on the polished side board.

'Photos is all I have these days.' Cyril gave a long drawn-out sigh. 'Dottie's long gone, even though she were six years younger'n me. One of our girls is up in Edinburgh and t'other over in Canada. Only my Katie's here. Our littlest. Gave us a surprise, that one, comin' so late.'

'It must be comforting to have her in the same village.'

'Course it is,' he said, but his expression was clouded.

'I called in at the Nook this morning for an iced bun and tea,' Flora went on. 'The café looked as lovely as ever.'

'The café's all right,' he said gruffly, 'but…'

Flora waited and when Cyril said nothing, she prompted, 'Alice told me you weren't too happy about Kate. She mentioned Bernard.'

'Him! That smarmy sod.' Cyril's lips twisted. 'The girl should never have married 'im. He had trouble written all over 'im from the start.'

'Is he being a problem?' she asked sympathetically.

'He's not good to her, that's what. He don' treat her right and I worry for her. The man has fists as big as—'

'Hams?' Jack offered, and received a cross look from Flora. Seeming mindful of his instructions, he tried again. 'You seem to be managing very well, Mr Knight. Your garden is beautiful and so is your house.'

'I love to garden. Always have since I was a little lad. It's peaceful-like. And Katie is a great help, a dab hand around the house. She's a good girl, she deserves better. And so do I,' he muttered.

'I expect you help her as much as she helps you. She told me how good you were other day at cake-making.' Flora tried to sound casual.

'Katie was havin' trouble stirrin'. She didn't say why, but I have my ideas,' he said bitterly. 'Anyways, I got hold of the wooden spoon and finished the job. It was for that bloke up at the hotel.'

This was her chance to explain their visit. 'He died in my bookshop, did you know?'

Cyril nodded.

'It still feels horrible that I found the man, and I wanted to ask you about him.'

'I don' know anythin' about 'im, 'cept Katie was thrilled to get the order. She delivers up there sometimes but she's always hopin' for something more reg'lar. She thought that mebbe a special cake for one of the guests would mean more business. Some hope. Not with Mitchell involved.'

'Bernie Mitchell got the order? That's good, though, isn't it? I thought he might have given up helping Kate when I saw him working at the Priory.'

'I don' know what he does up there. I don' trust 'im. And I didn't trust that Aussie either. Closeted together, they were, whispering.'

'Really?'

'Right spivs, the pair of 'em. They didn't like it when I appeared. Stopped talking immediately.'

'It seems a strange partnership,' Jack put in. 'I wouldn't think they had much in common.'

'Mischief. That's what they had in common. The Aussie bloke, Anderson, was after somethin'. He bothered me no end. And Alice, too. Questions about what I remembered. I soon got 'is number and sent 'im on his way.'

'I wonder what Kevin Anderson wanted with Mr Mitchell.' Flora looked questioningly at the old man. 'He couldn't have been asking about past times in the village. You've lived in Abbeymead all your life, but your son-in-law hasn't.'

'I dunno what they were up to. But they were plannin' somethin' together, that's for sure.'

Flora's mind was working at full stretch. Could Bernie Mitchell have been an accomplice? Could he have broken into her shop alongside Kevin, had a thieves' falling-out, and left Anderson dead? Mitchell had a criminal record, though not for anything too serious. Petty theft was what the village had been told, but Jack had been certain that a two-year sentence wouldn't have been handed down unless at least some violence had been involved.

'What kind of questions did Kevin Anderson ask you?'

''Bout the big house, the family. Did I know the legend?'

'And did you?' Jack asked, clearly intrigued.

'I told him what I knew, which weren't much, and the next thing he was knee-deep with that no-good son-in-law of mine plannin' somethin'.'

'A legend to do with the Templetons? It sounds fascinating,' Flora said. 'I don't think Aunt Violet ever mentioned it to me.'

'That's because the good woman had more sense. It's a daft story, always was. Kids loved it – you know, looking for treasure buried by some Templeton or other – but it was just a story.'

'Which Templeton? Not Lord Edward, surely?'

Cyril's face broke into a rare smile. 'That'd be worth seeing. Nah, it was centuries ago. When that chap with all the wives was around.'

'Henry the Eighth.'

'That's the bloke.'

'It *is* a long time ago.'

'That's what I said. Bloody stupid coming over 'ere from Australia lookin' for something buried – how many years ago?'

'Four hundred.'

Cyril snorted. 'If it were ever buried in the first place. The story's a lot of poppycock, I reckon. And if this Anderson had ever found somethin', it would have belonged to the Templetons, and if none of them were left, it should have gone to old retainers like Alice and me. Not to upstarts who've appeared out of nowhere. We'd have deserved to get somethin'. I dunno about Alice, but I could certainly do with it.'

Flora was shocked. 'I thought Lord Templeton would have arranged a good pension for you.'

Cyril pulled on the few strands of hair he had left. 'He were goin' to. He promised me he were goin' to London to sort it out with his man of business, but he never had time. Poor old chap went sudden-like. Then I was turfed out of my job by that posh scarecrow who thinks he owns the world. Paid to the end of the month, and that was it.'

'There was no gratuity? No gift?'

'A gift? I got nothin'. I draw the old age but that just about pays for me pansy plants. Katie wanted to sell the café when I was made to leave the Priory, bless her. I'd given her the money for the Nook, you see, and she felt bad, 'cause it was all my savings. But I said no, I'll manage, and if her bakin' business – not the café, mind – ever took off, then I'd have a slice of the profit. Or I would have if Mitchell hadn't poked his ugly mug into it. With 'im involved, no one will want to order anythin'.'

'Kate is such an excellent cook, she's bound to do well.' Flora felt a desperate need to reassure the old man. 'It may take time, but I'm certain her baking business will be profitable. She's doing home deliveries now and novelty cakes, too. They're great ideas – no one else is offering anything like it for miles around.'

'I hope you're right, Miss Flora. The girl is no better off than me. Never treats herself. That's why I take her flowers. I like to take them most weeks. Flowers are cheery creatures, though I'm a bit stumped today. It's fine in the summer – sweet peas is her favourite and I grow plenty of them at the back – but right now all I can take is chrysanths and Katie don' like those.'

Flora sensed Jack glance across at her. The speaking grey eyes were sending a message. He'd said very little, but she knew he'd been taking note and was feeling they'd gone as far as they could with Mr Knight. She was about to make her excuses when Cyril slowly got up from his chair. 'I just remembered. I promised Alice I'd drop in for a cuppa this afternoon, before I see Katie. Sorry, I have to get me suit on. Always wear the suit for Alice.'

'That's fine, Mr Knight. It's time we went,' Flora said hurriedly. 'Give my love to Alice, won't you?'

*

'Well,' Jack murmured, as they walked to Cyril's front gate, 'the old chap has motive. Motives, I should say. I lost count.'

Flora nodded. 'He hates his son-in-law who has been involved in something dodgy with Kevin, he wants to rescue his daughter from her horrible husband, and Lord Templeton's death and the sale of the Priory has landed him in a life of poverty.'

'The strongest is his need for money. It usually is.' It was a motive he most often used for the dark deeds populating his novels.

Flora was silent for a while, evidently turning over in her mind the recent conversation. As they reached the top of the village high street, she said, 'It was strange the way Cyril dismissed the legend, but was still keen to stake a claim to any potential fortune. Do you think he really believed the story, but was pretending not to?'

'Maybe he was hedging his bets. He's been treated abominably and, in the circumstances, he's likely to clutch at any straw going – even treasure buried centuries ago.'

'He's not the only one to hedge their bets,' Flora said thoughtfully. 'The uncle back in Australia, Reggie Anderson, supposedly treated the story as a joke, yet, according to Polly, the man was urging his nephew to get on with the job he'd come here to do. Why would Reggie say that, why would he be willing to send money so Kevin could carry on, if the legend was such a joke? There's a pattern here, isn't there? People rubbishing the story, but thinking to themselves that there might be something in it.'

'I'm not sure. The old man we've just met bears a deep grudge – understandable, I'm sure – and he's grabbing at anything that would make his life fairer, even if he knows it's an illusion. He seemed pretty vague: couldn't recall the legend, didn't know what his son-in-law was planning and didn't hear the conversation between Mitchell and Kevin.'

'Or was the vagueness deliberate? Cyril Knight looks a dear old man without a serious thought in his head, but I reckon he's a good deal cleverer than that.'

They had walked back to the green and were heading for the bookshop when Flora spoke again. 'For argument's sake, let's say that Cyril believed there was an outside chance that Kevin could uncover valuables from four hundred years ago, and considered he was entitled to them rather than a stranger from miles away. He'd want to know what was going on between Kevin and Bernie Mitchell, what they were actually looking for and where they were intending to look. That's why he eavesdropped. I don't believe for a minute that he just came upon them talking. I reckon he was deliberately spying.'

'You think he could have overheard something useful?'

'Why not? Something he could act on, something that would help him claim the prize for himself – as long as he got rid of Kevin.'

Jack took a while to consider. 'It's true that poison doesn't require physical strength, and it's true the old chap helped to bake that cake. It sounds plausible.'

'Except I've just thought that Cyril would have to get rid of his son-in-law as well. Mitchell would know as much as Kevin. He'd be as much of an obstacle.'

'Perhaps Mitchell is next on Cyril's list.' Jack's suggestion was light-hearted. It was difficult to imagine the old man they'd just met was capable of one murder let alone two.

'But the timing's wrong, isn't it? When Kevin broke into the bookshop, he must still have been looking for the secret. Why poison him before he could go any further? It would make more sense to wait for Kevin to find everything out, then kill him.'

'Not if Cyril has more knowledge of this legend than he admits, and he'd already learned enough by eavesdropping to put two and two together. He could have worked out what the treasure was and where he could find it.'

'It's a bit like Polly Dakers. Perhaps she's also put two and two together. I reckon *she* knows more than she said. She was as quick as Cyril to dismiss the story of buried treasure. She could be on the trail herself.'

'Polly Dakers as a suspect?' Flora's imagination was boundless, and he marvelled at it.

'Don't look that surprised, just because she smiled at you. Polly is a mountain of frustrated ambition – she thinks she's made for better things. And she works at the hotel. The cake would have been delivered to reception and you said yourself that anyone could have poisoned it at any time before Kevin ate the first slice.'

'You feel sorry for the old bloke and don't want to think he's guilty,' Jack teased. 'Polly's your stand-in.'

'Not at all,' she protested. 'Cyril may be guilty, but it's clear he's not been looking for anything since Kevin died. He's been unwell and he still looks pretty sick.'

'He could start searching at any time,' Jack reminded her.

'Which is why we need to know about that legend – in detail. Any ideas?'

CHAPTER ELEVEN

'I have a couple of books that might prove useful,' Jack offered unexpectedly. 'Histories of Sussex, though from what I can recall, they're pretty general. I'm not sure how much they'd tell us.'

'We won't know if we don't look.' Flora consulted her watch. 'Do you have time today? It's four o'clock already.'

Jack didn't respond immediately, standing quite still and gazing into the distance. She could see he was tussling inwardly: the need to finish a book that paid his rent or the excitement of a new discovery.

He gave in to curiosity. 'Walk back to the house with me,' he said at last, 'and we can split the books between us. There's a shortcut through Church Spinney. Do you know it?'

A shortcut sounded good. Flora was feeling weary and a long walk was not what she'd had in mind. It had been an extremely busy day with a lot of thinking and a lot of talking – first Polly, then Cyril Knight, trying to ask the right questions, trying to untangle the truth. Jack's house lay over a mile outside the village and on her previous visits, Betty had done the honours. Today, though, she'd be on foot both ways and she had promised to be back at the All's Well by early evening. Glass for the broken window had finally arrived and Michael was coming to do a proper repair, along with fitting extra locks and a new alarm. Until the shop was made as safe as possible, she couldn't feel entirely comfortable.

'I bought the books on Sussex when I was writing *Death at Devil's Dyke*,' Jack said, turning down one of the narrow lanes that ran off the high street. 'The hero of the book unearths a secret that since the Civil War has lain hidden in a dew pond at the bottom of the Dyke. I found the history of the area fascinating and I got to learn a lot about dew ponds.'

'The books sound promising.'

'Maybe, though I don't recall the name of Templeton coming up. Here, we take this alley.'

'How strange. I know the spinney, but I don't think I've ever gone this way.'

'You'd have no reason to, I guess. It leads out onto farmland, but just by the first farmer's gate, there's a pathway into the woods that winds itself round and about and emerges a few yards down from my house. It's a pleasant walk on a good day.'

'Why did you choose to live so far out of Abbeymead?'

Flora thought she knew the answer, but she wanted to hear from Jack himself. She still hadn't fathomed him out. He had lived in the house for at least five years, and during that time most of the village had seen nothing of him. Yet, since Kevin Anderson's death, he'd seemed happy enough to accompany her, to meet people, to take part in actual conversations. Which one was the real Jack? she wondered.

'Why did I choose it? The house had space and the rent was cheap. It needed a whole lot of renovation, but the landlord was happy for me to tackle it.'

'And have you?' She remembered the shabby drawing room and thought probably not.

'A bit,' he said defensively. 'I fitted a new bath and painted a couple of rooms.'

'When you get to the drawing room, you should dump that awful sofa. I'm sure the landlord won't mind it going.'

'Thank you, Miss Steele. When I need advice on interior decor, you'll be the first I come to.' She saw he was smiling. 'Watch your step,' he warned. 'There are rabbit holes everywhere.'

She looked down at the rutted path to check but, as she did, a rustle, a slight movement to one side, had her quickly raise her head. Those rabbits again, she thought. For much of the spinney, the path they were following was so narrow they were forced to walk in single file, a chance for Flora to absorb a landscape that, despite having lived in Abbeymead for most of her life, she hardly knew. Shuffling through fallen leaves and watching the shifting pattern of light and shade filter through thinning branches, she was entranced. The trees all around had lifted their heads to a new warmth, their autumn dress of red and gold glowing in the sun's afternoon rays, and somewhere a bird sang out its joy at the beauty of the day.

'It's pretty,' she said. 'Very pretty.'

'I think so, too. I walk here when the words get sticky.'

'Does it work?'

'Usually, though I have to confess that lately I've been doing a lot of walking.' He turned and grinned at her.

Why had this man become such a recluse? He was intelligent, friendly and very attractive. Best not to probe, she thought. Theirs was a business arrangement of sorts and anything too personal was likely to confuse the investigation. And it *was* an investigation that they'd embarked on – in the absence of proper detectives, she and Jack were doing their best.

After such a magical walk, the house they arrived at was bound to emanate disappointment. Looking at it anew, Flora found it difficult to understand what Jack had seen in the building, other than cheapness. It had been designed, if designed was the right word, as a kind of throwback to the Gothic, yet it possessed none of that style's grandeur. And flaking paintwork, rusting window frames – why had steel frames become so popular in the thirties? – left it looking even sadder.

She pushed her way through a ragged patch of grass to the front door. Jack was beside her and must have caught her disapproving glance. 'Don't say a word!' he warned.

'If you wanted, you could have a beautiful garden, front and back. You have so much space.'

'I'll sort it out in time.' He sighed, pushing the front door open with a thump. 'When Charlie Teague is out of quarantine, I'll give him a spade.' He strolled across the hall to the staircase. 'The books are in my work room. It's upstairs.'

Flora followed him, bracing herself for the inevitable chaos, but was surprised to find that, apart from a scattering of papers on the large oak desk, the room was impressively tidy. Books had been lined up military fashion on shelves that covered two of the walls, the window sill had been left uncluttered, the paper bin emptied, and a filing cabinet shut tight.

'Professional,' she said.

'A word of praise, I'll treasure that.'

He was joking, she was sure, but the expression in those astounding grey eyes was warm.

'So, the books…' she said quickly.

He walked over to the far wall and reached up to the top shelf where a line of leather-bound tomes sat smug and majestic.

'I picked them up from a market stall. I think it will be the second and third volumes that could prove useful. Let's see. Yes, volume number four is Georgian Sussex – a bit late for us. Here, you take this one and I'll buzz through book three.'

Flora looked around for a chair. The only one was at Jack's desk, a deep buttoned Chesterfield. That might fit him when he was typing, but it was far too deep for someone nearly a foot shorter. She settled herself on the floor, cross-legged.

'I can bring you a chair from the kitchen.' He sounded concerned.

'It's fine. I'm not so ancient that I can't still sit on the floor and enjoy it, and the rug is softer than your sofa.'

'Can we forget my sofa?'

'I think it would be best if you did.'

With that rejoinder, she opened the book he'd given her. It was a weighty volume with close-printed text. Mercifully, there was a sprinkling of images to leaven it. She flicked to the back to check for an index and found none.

'No index,' she said glumly.

'I rather thought not. We'll just have to skim and scan.'

'And hope we don't miss anything.'

It took them well over an hour of skimming and scanning, flicking forward, backtracking over pages, before they were satisfied they had covered the whole of both books.

'Nothing here,' Flora said unhappily.

'Nor here. Disappointing, but not unexpected. I wonder… could we be looking in the wrong place?'

'I don't see how. We're after a part of Sussex history and these books write about nothing else.'

'Yes,' he said slowly, 'but I'm thinking that maybe we should start with the king himself, with Henry the Eighth.'

Flora was startled. 'Henry the Eighth? Must we? He was a tyrant and what's the connection? There's not even a passing mention of him here.' She tapped the book cradled in her lap.

'Lateral thinking,' Jack announced. 'One of the tyrannical things Henry did was to ransack the monasteries and destroy their buildings. He wanted money but he also wanted to ensure that everyone accepted that this country had broken from Rome. The Priory could have been a monastery once – the name suggests it.'

'It doesn't look as though it was ever a monastery.'

'It could have been rebuilt. Derelict religious buildings were sometimes rescued after the furore had died down. I'm pretty sure Edward Templeton was a Catholic. That's likely to mean the Templetons as a family would have been.'

Flora blinked. 'You should know. I've no idea.' She thought for a while. 'I don't attend church regularly but at the few services I went to with Aunt Violet, Lord Templeton wasn't there. What are you thinking?'

'Only that if the Templetons were a Catholic family in Tudor times, the legend might have something do with that. There are a lot of stories about the persecution Catholics suffered, rumours about how they tried to protect their property. I have a book somewhere…'

'Don't tell me. You bought it because another of your heroes rescued the Pope?'

'No, but it's not a bad idea. I bought the book I'm thinking of on a whim. It looked interesting, but I never got round to reading it. Now, where would I have shelved it?'

'You have a system?' The room was neat, but Flora was still surprised.

'Naturally. Why do you think I wouldn't? Don't judge me on the garden.'

He got up from the Chesterfield and did a circuit of the bookshelves, then retraced his steps, stopping beside his desk and reaching up to the nearest shelf. 'This is the little beauty. *The Suffering Faith*. And it doesn't weigh as much as a baby elephant.'

He flicked to the back of the book, running his finger down one page after another. 'It actually has an index, Flora! Here are the Ts: Taylor, taxes and… Templeton.'

Flora jumped up and walked over to him. 'What does it say?' she asked eagerly.

He flicked to the page he needed. 'My hunch was right. They were a Catholic family, and a persecuted one at that. Accused of holding Catholic services in secret. Lady Ianthe Templeton, it says, was imprisoned in the Tower where she died several years later – it's thought from consumption. The house doesn't appear to have been forfeit, though. That would explain why the Templeton family still owned it this century.'

'Poor Lady Ianthe. But how could she have held secret services? There's no chapel at the Priory.'

'There doesn't have to be. Quite often Catholic families would set up makeshift altars in whatever room they deemed most safe.

They'd post a lookout who would sound the alarm if they spotted a stranger approaching. Any incriminating evidence would be whisked away before it could be seen.'

'Does the book mention the Priory?'

Jack scanned the paragraph he'd been reading. 'The original building *was* a priory, but for some reason the Catholic Church sold it to the first Lord Templeton. Perhaps a lack of monks? That particular Templeton refashioned it as a family home. It would have been in the late fifteenth century and probably explains why the building was left untouched during Henry's reign. No monks by then to oust.'

Flora leaned over his shoulder and peered at the open page. 'It doesn't say anything about a legend, though. Probably too silly for a serious book to recount.'

'Could be. If Lady what's-her-name, Ianthe, died a martyr's death in prison – presumably her husband was already dead – all kinds of stories could have flourished. If we want to be sure it's a nonsense, we'll have to look further.'

'Where do you suggest?'

'Fancy a trip to the seaside? We could go tomorrow while the weather holds.'

Flora's eyebrows rose. 'We're going paddling?'

'Not unless Hove museum has suffered a flood we don't know about. If there's a bus around ten, will that be all right?'

'Fine by me, but…' She gestured to the covered typewriter.

'I'll take another day off and then I'll get back to it.' Jack gave a quick glance through the window. 'It's already nearly dark. Time you were getting home. I'll walk back with you.'

'There's really no need. I'm a big enough girl to walk alone.'

'I'll come,' he said firmly.

And big girl or not, she was glad of his company.

*

Now they were in the wood, she wished she hadn't dragged Jack from home. The moon was full and riding high in the sky, silvering the trees and showing the path clearly ahead. She would have been quite safe, she thought, and began to fret over what to do with Jack when they arrived at her cottage. Should she invite him in? Cook him supper? He looked as though he could do with a home-cooked meal. Or simply leave him at the garden gate with a promise to meet at the Brighton bus stop next morning?

You must deal with it when you get there, she told herself, and, in the meantime, savour the beauty of this evening. And enjoy walking with Jack. The thought jolted her from her calm. That was definitely a feeling she needed to suppress. When Violet had fallen sick, men had dropped out of her life and she'd no intention of reinstating them. Jack Carrington was at least ten years older than her, a misanthrope, or so he appeared, and goodness knows what baggage he carried with him.

'How did you know Edward Templeton?' she asked, wanting as much to distract her thoughts as to answer the question that had been in the back of her mind for days.

'I didn't really. It was my father who knew him. They were old chums from their days in the army.'

'They fought in the First War?'

'They did. They were too old for the Second. That was my generation's reward. My father ventured back into uniform but strictly as a non-combatant.'

'Did you ever visit the Priory with your father? Is that why you came to Abbeymead?'

'I came because I remembered this part of the world as quiet and beautiful, but I never saw the Priory until I arrived five years ago and then only from the outside.'

'You didn't think to call on Lord Templeton? He only died two years ago.'

'I had no reason to call. He was my father's friend, so unlikely to be mine.'

Flora heard the sharp note in his voice. It seemed it wasn't the discrepancy in their ages that had stopped Jack calling at the Priory, but the fact that he disliked the company his father kept. Or disliked his father. She wondered just what kind of relationship he'd had with his parents.

'Once the war was over and their ways parted, I don't think they saw much of each other,' Jack went on. 'They may have met occasionally in London. I know my father got in touch with him when he decided it was time I shaped up and went to boarding school. Templeton pulled strings to get me into St Bartholomew's. I imagine he thought he was helping, though it was help I could have done without.'

'How old were you?'

'Around eight, I think.'

He must know exactly how old he'd been, Flora thought. She was beginning to understand a little the shadows in Jack's life. 'I take it that it wasn't a good experience?'

'You could say that. Certainly one that's best forgotten.'

They were halfway back to the farmer's gate and the path that led them into the village, when Flora became certain they were not alone. A crackling of leaves, a rustle between the branches. Then, a flock of starlings rising into the sky, disturbed from their roosting.

'A murmuration,' Jack said, looking skywards. 'I love that word.'

Flora hadn't followed his gaze. In the moonlight, her eyes were fixed on what looked like a flash of steel. A weapon of some kind? She spun on one foot, turning with arms outstretched, and gave him a hefty push as something sped towards them, towards Jack.

'What the—!' he shouted, falling heavily onto the tree-rooted ground. His hand went to his shoulder, grasping it tightly. Flora could see that the sleeve of his jacket had been torn apart and the shirt beneath gashed. Blood was pouring from what looked to be a deep wound.

She paled but then pulled herself together, yanking a thin scarf from her pocket and binding it tightly around his arm to staunch the bleeding. Crouching low over Jack's prostrate figure, her eyes skittered from tree to tree, trying to see what was coming. Who was coming. Nothing stirred but from the corner of her vision she sensed something looming high above her and looked up to see a steel bolt wedged deep into a nearby trunk. It had stripped the bark and exposed the naked white of the wood beneath.

A bolt from a crossbow? It couldn't be. Yet that's what it looked like. She felt her hands begin to shake. A madman with a crossbow, loose in these woods. Crouching lower and pulling the tourniquet around Jack's wound as tightly as possible, she waited for the inevitable.

It didn't come. The pair of them stayed immobile for what seemed hours, though in reality it could not have been more than a few minutes. No one came near, the birds returned from their flight, and stillness once again filled the spinney.

Flora lifted the edge of the blood-soaked scarf and peered at the mess that was Jack's arm. 'I think it's only a flesh wound, but I need to get you to a doctor.'

Jack shook his head, sufficiently recovered to say, 'No fuss, no doctor. I'll wash it. Disinfectant. I think I've got some.' In the stark light of the moon, he looked ashen. Haggard.

'We're no more than ten minutes from my cottage and I *do* have disinfectant.'

It settled her dilemma, at least. There was no question now that Jack could be left at the garden gate.

CHAPTER TWELVE

She managed to divest Jack of his coat without causing him too much pain, but removing the torn shirt was a more delicate business. She was worried the bleeding would start again and held her breath while, slowly and torturously, she peeled back the bloodied shirt and bundled it into the sink.

'Both ruined,' Jack mourned. 'My jacket. My shirt. They cost me every one of my clothing points for a whole year.'

'Which means that you bought them ages ago,' she reasoned. 'Time for a change, Jolyon. Now let me see this wound.' She bent down, a bowl of water and a bottle of disinfectant beside her. 'You have another,' she said, surprised. 'An old wound, by the look of it.' A deep, dark hollow had been gouged from Jack's upper arm. 'How did you get that?'

'German sniper,' he said briefly. He wouldn't say more, Flora knew. People didn't speak of the war, particularly men who had fought their way across Europe. They barely mentioned what had happened to them in those long years of struggle. No one did, really. It was as though a huge schism had broken the country apart – a second appalling conflagration within thirty years – and everyone was now silently trying to knit the edges together.

'I'll have a go at bathing your new acquisition,' she said, 'but if it's too deep, you *will* have to go to the doctor. You'll need stitches.'

Fortunately, it proved to be the flesh wound Flora had originally thought. The bolt had broken through two layers of clothes and ripped the skin from the top of Jack's arm, leaving in its wake a frightening gash and a large and rapidly darkening bruise. A half-naked Jack Carrington had a fine figure, she decided, then felt her cheeks flush. Concentrate, she scolded herself. Soap and water first, then a thick pad of disinfectant.

Jack flinched as the pad hit the wound.

'I'm sorry,' she said, 'but it has to be done. You don't want to develop a nasty infection.'

'I don't want to walk around with half an arm either.'

'Don't exaggerate. I can see the wound is painful, but it's not that bad.'

'Not for you,' Jack murmured. 'But thank you for the rescue.'

When she'd managed to help him dress with what was left of the jacket, she sat him down with hot tea and three spoonfuls of sugar.

'What the hell hit me?' he asked, cupping the mug between his hands.

'I don't know much about weapons, but I'm almost sure it was a crossbow.'

'Really? In the spinney?'

'Maybe someone out hunting who had a rotten aim?' she said hopefully.

'What would you shoot in the spinney – apart from me? Rabbits, I suppose.'

The country girl reasserted itself in Flora. 'You don't shoot rabbits with a crossbow.'

'It's unusual,' he admitted, 'but what else could it be? Whatever the reason, I'd like to get my hands on the man who let that bolt fly. It was unbelievably reckless of him.'

'Perhaps he wasn't being reckless.' The suggestion was cautious, but the fear she'd felt as she'd tried to protect them from what she'd believed was coming was still vivid. 'Perhaps the shot was deliberate?'

Jack drew himself up as straight as he could, his grey eyes stern and fixed on her face. 'You think someone actually shot *at* me?'

'At both of us maybe, but you most likely. The path through the spinney is one you take regularly to go home. If someone has been watching you, they'd know that. If they saw us walking to your house this afternoon, they could have waited for us to walk back.'

'It sounds a nonsense.'

'I didn't mention it before,' Flora said diffidently, 'but when we walked through the woods earlier, I felt there might have been someone close by. I was conscious of a movement and heard the leaves rustle.'

'Why didn't you say something?'

'I thought I was being fanciful and it was probably rabbits,' she confessed. 'I don't now, though.'

Jack sipped his tea, his forehead creased into small lines of worry. 'But who would have targeted me? Or you, for that matter?'

'It has to be whoever murdered Kevin Anderson. He or she is getting worried. They know we've talked to Alice, seen us go into Cyril's cottage, and decided we're getting too close to the truth.'

'But we're not.'

Flora fetched the kettle from the gas ring and refilled the teapot. 'They don't know that,' she pointed out. 'If you've killed someone, you're going to be jumpy, suspicious of everyone and everything. The last few days, you've been seen around the village and that's unusual. Together we've been conspicuous enough for this person to judge that we're a threat.'

'My fault then. It's only right he set out to kill me first!'

'It's obvious he'd kill you first,' she said practically. 'What kind of fight could I manage against a crossbow?'

'And you think I could?'

She sat down again, noticing how drawn and white his face was. 'Not at the moment, but you'll come round.'

Jack was about to reply when there was a bang on the front door. Their two figures froze instantly.

'Don't answer it,' he advised.

'It won't be crossbow man,' she said, moving towards the door. 'Or crossbow woman, for that matter. Neither of them would shoot us here.'

'How do you know that?' Jack called after her.

Flora was already at the front door, peering through the small square of glass set high in the wooden frame.

'It's OK,' she called back. 'I can see who it is. Michael. He's been mending the window at the bookshop. I promised to meet him there and didn't.'

'I'm so sorry to have messed you around, Michael,' she said to the man standing on her doormat, a rough canvas satchel slung across his shoulder. 'Something unexpected happened and it's stopped me getting to the shop.'

''S'all right, Miss Steele. All done and dusted. A nice job, though I say it myself. I took the old blackout blind down at the same time. Hope that was all right?'

'Brilliant. I've been meaning to do that for years. Let's hope we'll never need them again. Wait a second and I'll fetch my purse.'

'No worries about the money. I'll call by tomorrow. Just thought I'd let you know I'd mended the window, so you'd sleep easier tonight.'

'That was a kind thought. It's one problem off my mind, certainly.' She glanced over his head at the road beyond. 'You're in your van, I see. I wonder, could I ask you for a little more help?'

'Anything, Miss Steele, you know that.'

'I have my friend, Mr Carrington, in the kitchen. He's had… a slight accident, and isn't really up to walking home. It's a fair way back to his house. Do you think you could give him a lift?'

'Nothing easier. I'll wait for the gent in the van.'

Flora retraced her steps to the kitchen. 'Your carriage awaits, sir. Michael will give you a lift.'

Jack got awkwardly to his feet. 'Is Hove still on tomorrow?'

'Only if you're well enough.'

'I'll pick you up at the shop,' he said stoutly. 'Say ten o'clock?'

Flora sat for a long time that evening, gazing blindly into the fire. She felt overwhelmed, worries coming at her, one after another. Cowering in that wood, she had been truly terrified, certain they were both facing death. Jack almost had – he'd been amazingly lucky to escape with nothing worse than a gashed arm. Once she'd realised their assailant had disappeared, she'd dealt with Jack's injury as practically as she could, but now with time to think, she was filled with fear. The attack signalled a decisive shift in the investigation. Until now, neither of them had made any secret of asking questions, had been almost cavalier in whom they'd spoken to. There had seemed no need to mask their intent. Now they must think again, be a great deal more careful in how they went about things. A crossbow attack! Flora shuddered at the image of that lethal weapon splitting the trunk of the tree. It could have split Jack just as easily.

To distract herself, she made plans. Tomorrow she would go to the shop early, spend an hour or so cleaning before Jack arrived, and if he felt too unwell to make the journey, she'd open her doors to whatever business was going. A strong sense of guilt niggled at her. For the past week, she had given the All's Well virtually no attention and the bookshop was beginning to look uncared for. When her aunt had been alive, a regular routine of dusting, polishing and floor sweeping had been in place. The shop had sparkled, and in its newly dull state, Flora felt acutely that she was letting Violet down.

Deep within, she recognised that at the bottom of her malaise was her reluctance to continue with the way things had been. The escape that had never materialised was the problem, the disappointment that there was no longer a chance to take that precious year off, to travel, to explore. Uncomfortable to admit, the feeling that she was forever trapped.

CHAPTER THIRTEEN

Betty was particularly grumpy the next morning, her pedals groaning and, as they came to a halt at the crossroads, her brakes emitting an annoyed squawk, Flora was relieved to reach the high street at last and glimpse the All's Well in the distance. Pulling up a little short of the shop, she realised there was a figure already waiting outside her door. An agitated figure, by the look of it. Alice Jenner. Shouldn't she be at the Priory, or at least making her way there? She'd said nothing of calling on Flora today.

'Alice, good morning,' she greeted her. 'What brings you here so early?'

Alice turned at the sound of Flora's voice. Her face seemed to have aged twenty years and tears were in her eyes. Flora took one look and threw the bike against the wall, rushing over to the motherly figure and putting her arms around her.

'Whatever's wrong?' she asked gently.

Alice was crying in earnest now but, between the sobs, Flora heard the name Cyril.

'Cyril? Cyril Knight?'

Alice nodded and pulled a large handkerchief from the wicker basket she carried, blowing her nose noisily.

Deeply puzzled, Flora opened the door of the bookshop. 'You must come and sit down and tell me what's happened.'

Once Alice was perched somewhat precariously on the counter stool, Flora asked, 'What's happened to Cyril to upset you so much?'

Alice raised a tear-drenched face. 'He's dead,' she stammered.

'He can't be.' Flora looked at her visitor with incomprehension. 'I saw him yesterday. He was fine.'

Alice blew her nose again. 'I saw him yesterday as well. I didn't think there was anythin' wrong with him.'

Flora reached out and took the cook's hands in hers. 'Now. Tell me what you know.'

Alice took a deep breath. 'Cyril came to see me yesterday afternoon,' she began. 'We were havin' tea together. I'd finished cookin' for the day so had plenty of time. I made him his favourite eclairs.'

The thought seemed likely to set Alice crying again and Flora stepped in. 'I saw Cyril just before he came to you. When I left his cottage, he was about to change into his suit. He was looking forward to his tea.'

'He loved his teas,' Alice said fondly. 'Always dressed in his suit. It was the only one he had, but he said I deserved that he looked as smart as he could.'

'Cyril did arrive?' Flora asked cautiously, aware that at any moment Alice could collapse into tears.

'He did. We had tea straight away – he had a cuppa with a couple of eclairs.'

'He seemed well?'

'He were talkin' fit to bust. Laughin'. Enjoyin' his food.' Alice twisted her hands together so tightly the wrinkles in her skin melted one into another. 'I'm that upset, Flora, I can't work. Poor, poor man. He was treated so bad when Lord Templeton died, and now look…'

Flora felt desperately sad – she had very much liked Cyril – but suspicions were gathering in her mind and she needed to know exactly what had happened.

'After Cyril finished his tea, what did he do?'

Alice thought for a while. 'He didn't stay too long,' she said at last. 'Said he'd best be off. He was calling on Kate on his way home. She'd have shut the café by then.'

'Do you know if he got to the Nook?'

'That's the point. Kate was expecting him but he didn't turn up. She was on my doorstep at six this mornin'. She'd been up all night. Yesterday, after she'd shut the café, she waited for him and when he didn't come, she thought he must have decided to go home instead. She wasn't that worried, but after supper she went round to his house to see him. When she got there, he wasn't home. At least, no one answered the door. She thought mebbe he'd gone for a walk – it was a beautiful evening – and she let herself in with the spare key she keeps and waited. But Cyril didn't come back. That's when she started lookin' for him. All night she's been wanderin' round the village, and walkin' way out, too, even as far as Chidworth.'

'Then she came to you?' Flora prompted.

'She was desperate. She knew he was comin' to tea with me yesterday and had I seen him since? I told her, last time I saw Cyril, he was on his way to her.'

'Where was Mr Knight found?' Flora asked carefully, feeling the eggshells beneath her feet.

'At the Priory.'

'The Priory?' Flora sounded as incredulous as she felt.

'He never could have left the place, poor man.'

'Where was he found? And why didn't he leave?' Flora was bewildered.

'He was in the yard and it was me that found him.' Alice gave a muffled sob, then cleared her throat to say, 'I began work early. I'd been up and about ever since Kate called, so thought I'd get a good start, then call on Kate later to see if her dad had come home. I'd gone to dump some rubbish in the bins – and there he was. It was terrible. I thought I was goin' to have a heart attack, too. I went straight to Mr Elliot and told him he needed to call a doctor, but I had to leave right there and then and find Katie.'

'You said a heart attack, too. Is that what Mr Knight died of?'

'Mr Elliot telephoned Kate when I was with her to tell her what Dr Hanson had said. The poor man had been dead for hours, apparently. Cyril must have gone to the yard after he left me and died there.'

'It was definitely a heart attack?'

'That's what the doctor said and I s'pose he should know. Cyril was on pills for it, you know. It could have happened any time, mebbe, but I feel so guilty. I keep thinkin' it could have been those rich cakes.'

'That can't be true, Alice. He only ate a couple and cake has never affected him badly before, has it?'

Alice shook her head, the deep lines on her face seeming carved as though in wood.

'Heart attacks are funny things.' It was the only comfort Flora could think to offer.

Very funny, she thought to herself, and particularly prevalent if you were unlucky enough to be associated with the Priory. 'Why would Cyril have gone to the yard, do you think?'

Alice shook her head. 'I dunno. Old times' sake, perhaps. That's where he kept all his tools and gardenin' stuff. He had a little garden there – he used to plant unusual flowers, experimenting, you know, every now and then. Something a bit exotic.'

'It still seems strange of him to visit the place.'

They fell silent, each absorbed in their own thoughts, until Alice said mournfully, 'The lass is in pieces. Her father was some dear to her. I must go to the Nook, see what I can do. I wanted to tell you first, though.'

'I'll go and see Kate,' Flora promised. 'You must go home and rest. You've had the most awful shock and Mr Elliot can't expect you in today.'

Alice looked uncertain. 'He's a bit of a taskmaster—' she began.

'You're not to worry. I'll go up to the Priory myself, tell Mr Elliot that you're unwell and can't work. Come on.' She helped the older woman off the stool. 'I'd lend you Betty to get home, but she's not in a good mood today.'

That brought the inkling of a smile to Alice's face. She had walked to the shop entrance when the door opened and a man wearing a battered fedora appeared in the doorway.

'Mr... Carrington?' she said uncertainly.

'The very same, but don't forget, the name is Jack.'

Alice turned to face Flora. 'You'll go and see Kate?'

'Of course, I will. And I'll call by later and let you know how she is.'

*

The pain in his arm meant that Jack had slept badly. It was still throbbing when he stumbled to the bathroom early the next morning, ensuring that shaving, dressing and toasting bread for his breakfast took much longer than usual. Before he put on his shirt, he peeled back the bandage Flora had fixed, and could see the wound was still clean and tidy and already beginning to heal. He was unlikely to need further treatment. All to the good. The incident, though, had left him worried. At the time, he'd said little to Flora, but he was fearful the attack marked a new chapter in what she insisted was their investigation.

The crossbow could have been an accident, he supposed, and the perpetrator too frightened to make himself known, particularly if he believed he'd done serious damage. In his heart, though, Jack had dismissed the idea of an accident almost as soon as he'd floated it. The stakes had suddenly grown higher, the project escalating into dangerous territory, and he doubted it would be wise to continue. Yet he felt considerable anger that he could have died at the hands of whatever villain was hiding in plain sight. It would be some payback to expose them. There was a less praiseworthy reason, too – his writer's brain was enjoying the puzzle.

With no idea of how frequently the local buses ran, he'd suggested meeting at ten o'clock and, as Flora had agreed, he'd presumed they would get to Hove that morning. Walking along the high street towards the All's Well, he noticed her sturdy bicycle propped against the wall. He smiled to himself. Was she thinking of cycling to Hove with him riding pillion? The smile disappeared, though, as he opened the shop door. The plump figure of Mrs Jenner met his gaze and she looked very much as though she'd been crying, and crying badly.

He had time only for a brief greeting before Alice slipped past him, disappearing down the main road and out of sight.

'What's going on?' he asked Flora, who seemed to be almost as tearful. 'Mrs Jenner looked really upset, and why have you to call on Kate Mitchell?'

'Come in.' She didn't give him time to protest, pulling him by his good arm into the shop. 'Something awful has happened.'

'More awful than being shot by a crossbow?'

He was half-joking, trying to lighten the atmosphere, but Flora's face remained set.

'Cyril Knight is dead,' she said baldly.

Jack blinked. 'The chap we saw yesterday?'

'Yes, the chap we saw yesterday. Alice found his body in the Priory yard this morning.'

'What was he doing there?' It seemed an incongruous place to die, then Jack recalled how Cyril was planning to put on his suit. 'He was going to tea with Alice, wasn't he?'

Flora nodded. 'He went to tea and seemed perfectly fine, but then after he left Alice, he must have walked round to the yard and died. He never left the Priory, in fact. When she went to dump rubbish this morning, poor Alice saw him. According to Dr Hanson, Cyril must have lain there all night.'

Flora's voice, as she'd recounted the news, had been without expression, but when Jack looked into her face, he saw a deep sadness. He wanted to put his arms around her and hug her tight, but common sense told him that would be stupid and common sense triumphed.

'Did the doctor give any idea of the cause of death?'

'A heart attack, he said. Another heart attack. Just a little too convenient after we'd talked to the old man.'

He gave a low whistle. 'I know what you're thinking, and I agree that it sounds suspicious. But Cyril mentioned several scares in the past, and he took pills, didn't he?'

'Jack,' she said urgently, 'he was fine when we saw him yesterday. Fine when Alice gave him tea and cakes. Then he goes round to the yard and he isn't fine.'

'Why go? What would interest him there?'

'I asked Alice that, and she had no idea, except that it was where he spent a lot of his time when he was head gardener.'

Jack passed the brim of his fedora through his hands, his mind grappling to find a clear path in what was becoming an increasingly hazy landscape.

'Our trip to Hove is off, but what are you thinking of doing?'

'I must visit Kate some time today. Alice said she is distraught. I suppose her husband will be with her – Bernie Mitchell should be good for that at least – but she'll need friends, too. I'll call on her later, tell her how sorry I am and offer any help I can.' She paused, then said quickly, 'I'm sorry, Jack. I haven't asked you how *you're* feeling.'

'A little battered, but still standing. I don't mind that we're cancelling Hove, though. I wasn't looking forward to the bus journey.'

Flora fell silent, then seeming to brighten a little, she said, 'We might not be able to go to Hove, but we could go to the Priory.'

CHAPTER FOURTEEN

'Where are we actually heading?' Jack asked, as once more they walked together through the Priory gates. He'd agreed to Flora's suggestion on the spur of the moment, but was doubtful this visit would prove as useful as she expected.

'The yard, of course, at the rear of the building. It's where Cyril died. There might be a clue as to what happened.'

He tried to temper her enthusiasm. 'The doctor believes Cyril died late yesterday, doesn't he? If the old chap *was* murdered, the killer would have removed any clues hours ago.'

'You never know. We might find something and it's certainly worth looking.' Flora's voice was determined. 'It has to have been murder. There have been two unexpected deaths in just over a week, and both were connected to the Priory.'

Jack admired her stubbornness, but had to remind her that Cyril could easily have died from natural causes. 'He was an old man with a heart problem,' he said, and before she could protest, went on, 'There's something else to consider. *If* he was murdered, he's no longer a suspect. Kate Mitchell comes off our list, too. I can't imagine she would kill her own father.'

'Of course she wouldn't. She loved him dearly and Cyril adored her.'

There was a long silence as they trod up the gravel driveway. 'You know what else changes, if Cyril's death was a murder?' Jack asked, an unwelcome thought forcing its way into his mind. 'The idea of cake as a deadly weapon. Both men ate cake, true, but Kevin's was his birthday treat and Cyril's?'

'Chocolate eclairs.'

'Made by Alice Jenner, who had absolutely no motive for killing either Cyril or Anderson.'

'They could have been killed by the same person, but with different methods.'

He took some time to respond. 'From my research, I'd say that if a murderer is successful with the first killing, most often he or she will use the same method for any others they plan.'

'Then perhaps it wasn't the cake that killed them after all. What I can't understand is why anyone would want to get rid of Cyril.'

'He might no longer be our suspect, but he could still be involved in the business in some other way,' Jack said thoughtfully. 'You believed he might know more about the legend than he was telling us, and remember, he considered himself entitled to a share of any fortune that might be unearthed. If he did know more and was trying to strike a bargain with the killer...' He left the sentence unfinished.

'So Kevin Anderson looks for treasure,' she mused. 'In some way the killer learns what he's discovered and gets rid of him, but there's still information missing and it's Cyril who has the answer. It's plausible, I suppose, but I hate to think of Cyril making any kind of bargain.'

There was a pause before she burst out, 'It's so frustrating. We have just a small part of the picture, while everything else is foggy.'

'That's detective work for you.'

'Will it ever become clearer?'

Jack gave a shrug. 'Who knows? Just let's hope we're not wasting our time.'

Hope *I'm* not wasting my time, he thought, seeing in his mind the covered typewriter waiting balefully for him. He looked up, noticing for the first time where Flora was leading them. 'I thought we were going to the yard – we seem to be heading back to the kitchen.'

'It's to one side of the kitchen, directly opposite the main door of the Priory. There's access to the yard from either the house or the gardens. It's where Cyril had his base.'

'And where he ended. That's ironic – in a particularly nasty way.'

'I know.' Flora gave a small, sad sigh. 'Alice suggested that when Cyril left her, he went to the yard for old times' sake. I suppose it's possible.'

'It's also possible that we'll be spotted where we shouldn't be. After the crossbow, I'm a tad nervous. If the killer is roaming the Priory estate, I'd rather not spend too much time here.' He said it with feeling. His arm was still throbbing nicely and he really didn't want any more of his anatomy punctured.

'We have to be careful, sure, but there's no one around at this time of day. The maids are busy cleaning, the waiters are in the restaurant, Polly Dakers will be at her desk, Vernon Elliot in his office, and there's no head gardener now. Elliot pays an outside firm to keep the estate tidy.'

'And if their employees are in the yard?'

'They won't be interested in us. If they think anything, they'll think we're part of the staff. Although,' she looked at him critically, 'you don't look much like staff.'

'And you do?'

She didn't answer, but instead steered him round a last corner, keeping close to the red brick screen that had been built proud of the main building. A few yards ahead, a gap appeared in the wall.

'Here. We can go through here.'

They approached the yard cautiously. Cobbles, Jack noticed, and swept clean. Several waste bins were lined up against the far wall and a number of empty cardboard boxes were stacked together, awaiting collection. A narrow gravel path, laid across the cobbles, led to a locked inner enclosure. The path was there, perhaps, to make the trundling of garden equipment easier than over the cobbles. Jack's eyes fixed on the padlocked gate ahead, then switched back to the gravel.

'Where exactly do you think Cyril was found?' he asked.

Flora looked puzzled. 'Is that important?'

'Look at the gravel. Something has been dragged along it.'

She looked down to where he was pointing, then, tucking untidy waves of hair behind her ears, she said slowly, 'You think it was Cyril who was dragged?'

'I'm wondering. Everything else is neat and tidy, but the gravel hasn't been raked over. Which means that whatever disturbed its surface must be fairly recent.'

'If he was dragged, then he didn't die in the yard. But where?'

Jack looked again at the padlocked gate. 'The tracks come from there. Was that his old territory? Perhaps he went in to look around, though it's well and truly padlocked.'

Flora went up to the sharp-pronged fence, trying ineffectually to peer over it. 'He could have kept a key. See if you can see anything. You must be tall enough.'

Even straining, he could only just see over the top of the barrier. 'There's a shed,' he began.

'That's where Cyril kept his tools.'

'A wheelbarrow to one side. Some bags – it looks like they're full of leaves. Waiting to be burnt? Something has been burned, though. There's a small circle of ash on the ground and...' he stood on tiptoe, peering hard, 'it looks very much as though it's still smoking slightly.'

'Evidence! The murderer has burnt evidence!' He could feel Flora close beside him, bouncing with excitement.

'Steady on – we can't jump to conclusions.'

'What else could it be? Is there anything more to see?'

'I don't think so.' His eyes roved around the square space. 'Hang on, yes. On the other side, it's half hidden by the shed, but it looks like a flowerbed. No flowers now, but the earth has been disturbed. There seems to have been an attempt to smooth it over, but there's a definite dip in the soil.'

'Something's been dug up. Plants, do you think?'

'It looks like it.'

'So a plant is dug up and burnt.'

'It's a reasonable conjecture.' He turned away from the fence to face her. 'Why would anyone do that on a morning when a dead man has been found just a few yards away?'

Flora's eyes were sparkling. 'Because the plant was evidence. We're closing in,' she said, then spun around at the sound of footsteps.

'Miss Steele? And Mr Carrington?' Vernon Elliot's voice had an edge to it. 'What on earth are you doing here?' His spindly figure seemed to elongate with the strength of his annoyance.

'Mr Elliot, good morning.' Jack heard the false warmth in Flora's voice. 'We've just heard about poor Mr Knight. Alice told us.'

Vernon Elliot's cold eyes stared at them and she went on, sounding more flustered, 'Alice was the one to find him, I believe. She thought she'd dropped her glasses in the yard, but couldn't bear to come back to check. She's very upset. Quite ill, in fact, and has gone home to rest. I said I'd come here and look for the glasses.'

Jack was impressed. That was quite a story to concoct in a few seconds, as long as Alice Jenner did wear spectacles. He wasn't sure this Elliot bloke had bought it, though. His thin form was as stiff as a sheet of cardboard. Despite his West End tailoring, the man *was* a bit like a scarecrow, Jack thought. Cyril had been right.

'Did you find them?' Vernon asked, his thin lips tight, his mouth no more than a narrow slash.

'No.' Flora gave an uncertain laugh. 'Poor Alice, she was in such a state that she probably had them in her pocket all the time.'

'Well, now you've made certain, I trust you won't mind my asking you to leave. The Priory has suffered a sad event this morning. One of its oldest servants has died right where you're standing. I think we should respect that.' The ice in his eyes had barely thawed.

A hypocrite as well as a scarecrow, Jack decided.

'We were just off,' he said quietly. 'Very sorry to have intruded on what is a bad day for you all.'

'Thank you.' Vernon gestured to the gap in the brick wall, and more or less shuffled them out into the estate grounds.

'I don't trust him,' Flora said savagely, as they walked down the drive towards the Priory's wrought-iron gates.

'Would anyone?' Jack retorted.

A sudden growl of an engine behind them had them jump to one side, seeking refuge on the grass verge. A white van sped past, churning the gravel as it rushed to the exit. It was the van from Katie's Nook, and Bernie Mitchell was driving.

'How many people involved in this mad business do you trust?' Jack asked, watching the vehicle disappear through the gates.

Flora followed his gaze. 'You have a point.'

*

It was noon before they got to Katie's Nook. The blinds were drawn and the café clearly shut. Flora knocked gently on the glass door. A blind was inched to one side, Katie's tear-stained face clear through the glass. There was the sound of bolts being slid back and a key turning. Without saying a word, they walked in, Kate locking the door behind them.

'Katie,' Flora began, and put her arms round the young woman, hugging her tight. 'I am so sorry.'

There were tears and more tears before Kate recovered sufficiently to offer them tea.

'You sit down. I can make it,' Flora said quickly.

'It's OK. I prefer to be doing things.' Kate bent to retrieve cups and saucers from beneath the counter and, as she did so, Flora saw what she was certain was a new blemish on Kate's other arm.

'Is Bernie around?' she asked, incensed by this new evidence of brutality. Just where had Mitchell been going in the van?

'He had to go out, but he'll be back. I was best left alone for a while. I've been trying to grasp what's happened – it seems so sudden. Dad was fine, I thought he was fine. He didn't deserve to die like that.'

'It's dreadful for you,' Flora said quietly, sipping the tea Kate had brought to the table. 'I can't imagine…' Her voice trailed off.

Imagining wouldn't help Kate, and it was something she'd no wish to do herself. She tried never to think of her own parents who had died far too young. Flora had no memory of either of them. Occasionally a smell – tobacco smoke or the scent of jasmine – triggered a hardly recognised longing in her, but otherwise it was as though the couple had never existed. As a small child, she had faced an abyss. Until Violet had swooped to the rescue, she had been left completely alone in the world, and that was a fear the mind had always to suppress.

Jack had moved silently to stand beside her, and she saw he was looking at the counter. Kate had noticed his glance as well.

'Dad's suit,' she said with an effort. 'The undertakers have just come over from Steyning and brought it back. The funeral will be a week on Tuesday, but I'm not having any kind of wake. I don't think I could cope with it.'

'Undertakers?' Jack was wearing what Flora had decided was his inscrutable face. 'Won't there be a post-mortem?'

'Dad was an old man. He took pills for his heart and he'd had a few scares in the past. The doctor said he suffered a massive heart attack.' There was a long silence, several minutes ticking by. 'At least,' Kate said at last, 'he died instantly. I can't bear to think of him out there alone on a cold night…' She stuttered to a close, unable to finish.

'The authorities haven't asked for a post-mortem then?' Jack repeated.

Kate shook her head, looking over at the counter. 'Somehow I've got to get his suit clean. The undertakers want to dress him properly, you know, and this was the only one he had. He always wore it to go to tea with Alice.'

Flora walked across and lifted the suit to what light there was in the café. 'I see what you mean. Some kind of juice has dripped down the front, and there are yellow smudges on one of the sleeves.'

'Goodness knows how I'm going to get rid of that.'

A jumble of thoughts suddenly coalesced for Flora, dizzying in their clarity and their sheer rightness. 'A dry cleaner's? We could take it for you, Kate. We're going to Steyning in the next day or so. I'll ask the cleaners there to have it ready by Monday. I'm sure they'll be happy to walk the suit round to the funeral parlour when it's ready.'

'Would you do that?' Kate was pathetically grateful. 'It's people, you see. I feel I can't face anyone I don't know at the moment.'

'It's no problem. Lock up the café and go home and don't reopen until you feel ready. And forget about making Jack's cake. None of us are going to want to celebrate.'

When they were once more outside the shop, Kate's thanks still ringing in their ears, Jack turned to her. 'Steyning?' he demanded.

'There's a dry cleaner's there.'

'I'm sure there is.'

'And several florists. If you were going to order flowers for a hotel guest, Steyning is the most obvious place to go to. It's the nearest town. Look at the suit, Jack.' She pointed to the bundle he was carrying. 'Those yellow marks on the sleeve are pollen and the juice marks – sap maybe. Remember the pollen that was trapped in Kevin's table? Could he and Cyril have died from the same thing? Could the murderer have used the same method, like you said?'

Jack walked on for a few minutes without speaking. Eventually, he said, 'Flowers as poison? It's been done before. But no florist would use anything they knew to be dangerous.'

'What if the bouquet was harmless when it left the florist, but by the time it reached Kevin's bedroom, it included a poisonous flower or flowers?'

'And Cyril?'

'The plant in the enclosure. A plant that's been newly dug up and burnt.' She was trembling with the excitement of this new knowledge.

'Yesss. Could be.' He rearranged the suit on his arm, then dug his hand into the jacket pockets, one at a time. 'And here we have a key. The key to the enclosure, do you think?' He waved the glinting steel in the air.

'You're right. It's the key to the padlock. Cyril must have used it to go inside. Do you think he picked the flowers?'

'I reckon so and died right there. If so, it was death by mis-adventure, not murder, but still a trifle inconvenient for whoever planted those flowers.'

'And that person was Kevin's murderer.'

'Quite possibly. Whoever it was must have dragged Cyril's body out of the enclosure and along the gravel path to where Alice found it. Then dug up the plant and burnt it, hoping to remove any trace, padlocking the door again behind him. Or her.'

They had reached the bookshop and Jack hadn't quite finished with the subject. 'I can understand, sort of, why Cyril might want to revisit his old haunt. But why did he pick those flowers? He was an experienced gardener. He would have known they were poisonous, surely.'

'He may have been confused. He mentioned how fuzzy the new tablets were making him, didn't he? And he wouldn't have expected to find poisonous plants, not somewhere he'd worked for years. *And* he was keen to get flowers for his daughter. Desperately keen. He picked them to take to Kate.' Flora's voice broke at the thought.

Jack waited for her to regain her composure before saying, 'Will you take the suit or shall I?'

'You.' Flora's voice didn't waver this time. 'When I offered to go to the dry cleaners with it, I wasn't just being a good friend. The jacket has evidence that the police need. Once it's buried with Cyril, the evidence will be destroyed for ever.'

'And this concerns me how?'

'You know the inspector in charge of Anderson's case. You could take the jacket to him, ask him to have it analysed. There's time before I need to take it to Steyning. The funeral isn't for another week.'

'All cut and dried, except that as far as the police are concerned, they've no need for evidence. Inspector Ridley is definite that there isn't a case to answer. Anderson died of natural causes.'

She smiled up at him, the hazel eyes spelling mischief. 'Then it's your job to convince him otherwise. This is where you use your charm, Jack.'

'I have charm?'

Flora stood back and considered him. 'I think you do. It might be distinctive, but it's there.'

Jack stifled a sigh and bundled up the suit into a tight grip. 'If I must, but I can't think we'll have any luck. If the jacket is to gain credit as evidence, it will need to be examined by a police pathologist which, as far as Ridley is concerned, means wasting precious resources – time, money and effort.'

She reached out and gripped his hand. 'Just try. It's important. The police have the results of Kevin's post-mortem. They need to do one on Cyril before he's buried. The suit will convince them.'

Jack quickly disentangled himself. 'I'll be in touch,' he said, and walked away down the high street.

CHAPTER FIFTEEN

Jack wasn't looking forward to contacting Alan Ridley, but he had promised and after yet another ham sandwich – he was beginning to tire of·them at last – walked to the nearest telephone box and made the call. When Ridley understood what Jack was asking, the protests began.

'We can't do that, old chap. The Anderson case is closed and I know nothing about this Cyril Knight. Presumably the doctor was happy enough to sign a death certificate. It's a wild goose chase, Jack, and I'd be using police resources unnecessarily. Juice on a coat – I mean!'

'And pollen,' Jack reminded him. 'There was pollen in the crack of a table in Anderson's bedroom at the Priory. The flowers these men encountered are poisonous and someone is using them to murder.'

'You're suggesting that someone deliberately poisoned the old man who died at the Priory?'

'No. I'm suggesting that he may have picked the flowers, not realising they were dangerous, but whoever was growing them *did know*. They were growing them for a purpose. Cyril Knight's death was a tragic accident that forced the perpetrator to get rid of the evidence. They dug up the plant and burnt it. I saw the aftermath for myself.'

'Sounds a little too far-fetched to me – even for one of your crime novels.' The inspector gave a guffaw. 'If you want to kill someone, there are far easier ways of doing it.'

'Like aiming a bolt from a crossbow at them?'

'Sorry?'

'It's what happened to me yesterday. I was attacked in the woods, on my way home.'

'Good lord! You weren't injured, I take it.'

'I have a ruined shirt and jacket, but fortunately most of me is intact. A flesh wound where the bolt grazed my arm.'

'It must have been an accident. Careless, though, very careless. But in the countryside… well, you know.'

'No, I don't. I thought crossbows were illegal.'

'Not illegal to own, unless you're under eighteen. Certainly illegal to hunt with. But like I said—'

'Yes, I know, the countryside. And since I can't identify who fired the bow, there's nothing the police can do.'

'Got it in one,' the inspector said jovially.

'Alan,' Jack imbued his voice with urgency, 'there's something rotten going on below the surface in Abbeymead. Going unnoticed, like Anderson's death. The police have decided that he died from natural causes, which is exactly what the murderer planned.'

'You're saying we've been duped?' Jack could hear the man's growing annoyance down the telephone. 'There's no motive for the chap's death. There has to be motive, else why go to all that trouble to kill?'

'I'm working on it.'

It sounded feeble, but he dared not mention buried treasure. He'd nearly said 'we're' working on it, but thought it best he kept Flora's name quiet. Something told him that Ridley would be even less sympathetic if he knew the girl whose bookshop had been broken into was involved. He'd suspect collusion, which wasn't far from the truth.

'Working on it? Have to do better than that, old chap.'

The 'old chap' was beginning to grate on Jack, but he tried to keep a neutral tone. 'If your pathologist could take a quick look before the jacket goes to the dry cleaner's…' He tried as a last ditch attempt. 'I could catch the bus, bring it over to Brighton today.'

'No need for that. You're pretty het up over this, I can tell, and I suppose I could squeeze expenses to cover an extra half hour with the pathologist. I'll motor over to Abbeymead and pick up the jacket myself. Nothing much doing here this morning. But only if we can go to that great little pub. What was it called? The Cross Keys, that was it.'

Jack resigned himself to eating his second lunch of the day. He hoped that Flora would be suitably grateful.

*

Several days of waiting and wondering followed for Flora. She tried to put it to the back of her mind and get on with her life. It was difficult, though. The bookshop still attracted few customers, incoming orders were only a trickle now, and she had cleaned and polished the All's Well until she was almost blinded by its shining perfection. Beneath this determined activity, she was fretting. Did the delay mean that something was happening, that Jack had persuaded the police to accept Cyril's jacket as evidence, and were even now investigating? Or did it mean that Jack hadn't managed to speak to the inspector or, even worse, he had and been refused, and felt too uncomfortable to call and tell her?

Today, once she'd put away the dusters, she cast around for distraction, eventually trundling Betty from her shelter. There was only one book to deliver, but Miss Lancaster had remained a faithful customer, and the journey meant fresh air and a steep hill to use some of Flora's pent-up energy.

Energy or not, she was still forced to dismount as she reached the summit. With only three gears to her name, Betty was little help. As Flora wheeled the bicycle forward, a van came into view, parked awkwardly across the road. The van from Katie's Nook and it was Bernie Mitchell changing a wheel. He looked up as Flora pushed her bike past, but made no attempt to greet her.

She walked on for several yards but then stopped abruptly and retraced her steps. Mitchell was on his own, there was no one to overhear their conversation, and she couldn't walk past this horrible man without saying something.

'Mr Mitchell, can I speak to you?'

'Can't stop you, can I?' he said in a surly voice.

He looked unkempt, Flora noticed, his khaki overalls needing a good wash, and the straggle of hair emerging from his cloth cap in similar need.

'It's about Kate. Your wife.'

'I know who my wife is.' A pair of grimy hands continued to unscrew the vehicle's wheel nuts.

'You must know she's desperately upset. Her father's death has been a terrible blow and she needs sympathy. Kindness. Kindness from you, and I don't think she is getting it.'

Mitchell got to his feet, a sturdy wrench in his hand. 'And what's it gotta do with you, ezackly?'

'I'm Kate's friend and I don't like to see her so distressed. She's floundering, Mr Mitchell.'

He grunted and bent down again to the job in hand.

'She is being hurt, too. Physically injured.'

Mitchell straightened up and walked towards Flora, the wrench swinging from his hand. 'And?'

She felt real fear. This was an isolated spot and the man's figure was tense with anger. She swallowed hard.

'Kate has bruises on her arms,' she said, trying to keep her voice steady. 'There was a new one when I saw her on Saturday. If she's hurt again, I won't hesitate. I'll report it. The police will be interested. Your boss, too, I imagine. Mr Elliot would take a dim view of employing a man who beats his wife.'

Mitchell advanced further and was now towering over her. He lifted the wrench and waved it in her face. 'Listen, little girl, you've no idea what you're talkin' about. Keep your beak out of my business or you'll be sorry, believe me.'

He turned back to the van, leaving Flora gripping Betty's handlebars for support. Her intervention seemed to have done little good. She had now made an enemy for herself. And Mitchell was an ugly customer, there was no doubt of that.

As soon as she arrived back in Abbeymead, Flora went immediately to Katie's Nook. She'd wanted to call on Kate yesterday, but the café had been shut and she hadn't felt comfortable visiting her at home. This morning, as she'd ridden past the Nook, she'd noticed the restaurant had reopened. With Mitchell out of the way, this was an ideal time to call.

Kate was behind the counter and there were just two customers, sitting together by the window. Empty plates and teacups suggested they would be leaving very soon.

Kate looked up as the door chimed. 'Flora!' She managed a wobbly smile. 'It's lovely to see you.'

'I would have come earlier, but I thought it best to wait until you reopened.'

'I'm always very happy to see you whenever. And Alice, too. She came round to the cottage yesterday, bless her, and she's calling in on her way back from work. Can I get you something to drink?'

'Nothing for me. I really just wanted to see how you were doing.'

'Come and sit down.'

Kate gestured to a table some distance from her customers. Flora noticed how straight she sat in the chair, and how tightly her hands were clasped, as though to allow them freedom might release a torrent of emotion.

'I can still hardly believe what's happened,' Kate began. 'I can't get used to the idea that Dad is no longer around.' Her eyes filled and Flora reached out to stroke her arm. There was so little she could offer in comfort.

Blinking back the tears, Kate said, 'It was kind of you to go to Steyning for me.'

'We've not actually been yet,' Flora confessed. 'Jack had work to finish – a deadline to meet,' she improvised. A white lie was surely in order. 'But we'll be going tomorrow. Plenty of time for the suit to be ready.' She had no idea if they would make Steyning tomorrow – it was down to Jack and the inspector – but she wanted to reassure Kate.

'It must be wonderful to be a writer,' Kate said wistfully, 'and Mr Carrington seems a really nice man. Are you interested?'

'It's not like that,' Flora said hurriedly. 'We stock Jack's novels and we order his reference books. That's the only way I know him.'

'Sorry, I probably spoke out of turn. But you seem to be spending a lot of time with him.'

Flora cast around for a reason that didn't involve investigating a crime. 'I've been trying to help with research for his new book. It's proving a bit sticky. But are you really OK?'

She needed the focus to be on Kate – it was why she had rushed here from Miss Lancaster's – and her relationship with Jack Carrington was not something she wanted to think too deeply about.

Kate hadn't answered her, and Flora said gently, 'You see, I noticed…' She reached out for Kate's arms, turning both of them to face outwards. The bruises had mellowed, but were still clearly visible.

Kate snatched her arms back. 'It was an accident,' she said quickly.

'Two accidents, I think. Does he hurt you often?' she asked in a whisper.

Kate's two customers had gathered their belongings together and were making for the door, smiling a thank you as they went. Kate waited until the door had clanged shut before she answered.

'Not often,' she said in a low voice, 'but lately he's not been himself.'

'In what way?'

'He seems frustrated, as though he's under a lot of pressure. It makes him lose his temper, but he doesn't mean it.'

Everyone became frustrated at times, Flora thought, without resorting to hurting a person you were supposed to love, but she bit back the retort she would liked to have made.

'What kind of pressure, Kate?'

'Money mostly. The café doesn't make much of a profit, you know. We're always scrabbling to pay our bills.'

'The job at the Priory, though – that pays well, doesn't it?'

Kate looked uncertainly at her. 'It does, but…'

'But?'

'I don't know how much longer Bernie will be working there. He isn't happy with the job. Something's gone wrong, but he doesn't tell me a lot.'

Was the something the death of Kevin Anderson? According to Cyril, they'd been planning mischief together, but whatever that was, Kevin's death was a signal that it had gone badly wrong. Then Cyril himself had died. Bernie's own father-in-law. Was it guilt over the deaths that was making Kate's husband angry? Her recent encounter with the man filled Flora's mind: the image of Mitchell, his arm raised, the heavy wrench in his hand, advancing towards her, made her stomach clench. Guilt seemed an unlikely emotion.

Kate stared gloomily down at the table top. 'Even if Bernie stays on there, I don't know how we're to pay the fuel bill come next quarter.'

'Is it that bad?' Flora was astonished. She was used to fighting hardship herself, but had no idea that the Mitchells were so badly off.

Kate continued to stare at the table. 'It's the gambling, you see,' she said in a half whisper.

Flora felt her eyebrows rising. Bernie Mitchell's gambling? Of course it was his. She couldn't imagine Kate had ever had a bet.

'The dog track. Brighton stadium,' the girl said miserably. 'Bernie has been going to the dogs on Friday nights for years, but just recently he's met up with some chap – through friends, I think – who seems to have pots of money and it's encouraged Bernie to bet too high. He's not a bad man,' she insisted when Flora said nothing. 'It's just that he's easily led. He's been trying to keep up with this chap, but of course he can't.'

'Bernie loses?'

'Almost always,' Kate said sadly. 'It's put the café in a very precarious position. I've been so worried that I'd have to sell up and maybe lose all of Dad's savings. That's why I've been trying to do different things. Set up a baking business and deliver cakes house to house. But I haven't managed to get it off the ground, and now with Dad dying like that… It's all so dreadful.'

'It has to get better,' Flora said rousingly. 'I'll make sure of it.'

'How?' Kate looked surprised, as well she might, Flora thought. She had no idea what she could do to help this poor girl. But help she would.

'I'll think of something. You're not on your own. Meanwhile, if that husband of yours loses his temper again and deliberately hurts you, you need to report it. Come and tell me and we'll go to Constable Tring together.'

Her friend looked unconvinced but, at least today, she had sown the idea in Kate's mind. And made Mitchell aware that other people knew of his misdoings.

CHAPTER SIXTEEN

It was on the fourth morning of waiting for Jack's news, just as Flora was setting off from her cottage to cycle into the village, that she spied his familiar figure loping along the lane towards her. He was carrying a string bag and she could just make out Cyril's suit, carefully folded in it. Her breath caught in her throat. Jack must have information, but what?

'Going to the shop?' he asked.

'I was, but—'

'Perhaps a detour to Steyning instead?'

'What's the news, Jack?' she burst out. 'Don't keep me dancing on pins.'

'An interesting image. Do you want to go inside? There's quite a lot to relate.'

She fumbled with her key, saying as she did, 'Inspector Ridley saw the jacket?'

Jack followed her into the kitchen. 'Not only saw it, but took it to the pathologist – after some persuasion and as a special favour to me.'

He deserved her thanks, but Flora was too anxious to hear more. 'And?' She felt her face go rigid.

'The pathologist was at a loss.' Jack dumped the string bag onto the scrubbed wood table.

Her hopes dashed, Flora slumped into a kitchen chair.

'But,' Jack went on, 'he was sufficiently intrigued to call in a botanist friend. An expert on plants. The chap didn't have much to go on, just some pollen and juice, but caught in the lapel – we didn't see it – was a small fragment of leaf. From that, and the colour of the pollen, he reckoned it could be one of two plants, one of which was extremely poisonous. Narrowing it down meant the pathologist could run tests to detect the presence of something called cicutoxin. And bingo, he struck lucky. Our plant is water hemlock. Here, I have a picture for you. The botanist supplied it, along with a description.'

Jack brought out a sheet of paper from his inside pocket.

She looked at it hard. The plant, when in bloom, threw out a profusion of small white daisy-shaped flowers, poised delicately on long green stems. 'It looks pretty,' she said.

'Pretty and horribly poisonous. Within a few hours of ingesting the poison, a person can suffer seizures, their heart rate badly disturbed and their blood pressure zinging merrily up and down the scale. There are other cardiac effects, too, which I couldn't follow – too technical. But it all adds up to a highly erratic heartbeat, resulting in blood not being pumped around the body. What that comes down to is severe wheezing, great difficulty in breathing and, in the end, respiratory failure.'

'How awful.'

Jack took a seat opposite her. 'Death usually occurs within a few hours of ingestion, the pathologist said, though it can be much quicker. Cyril already had heart problems so he probably died within minutes, whereas Kevin Anderson was young and fit, and the poison must have taken several hours to work.'

Flora was silent, absorbing all she had been told. To inflict such catastrophic harm on anyone, even your worst enemy, seemed to her an act of the greatest evil. If she'd ever been tempted to waver in her mission, to forget the whole business and go back to simply selling books, this new knowledge had put iron in her heart. It wasn't just a case now of saving her shop. The person who had done such dreadful damage to fellow human beings had to be caught.

'When Cyril walked round to his old yard, he must have peered over the fence into the enclosure,' Jack went on, 'though I wouldn't have thought him tall enough. But he must have seen the patch of flowers and used his key to open the gate. By doing that, he unlocked the door to his death.'

'The flowers would have looked pretty and he wanted so much to take a bunch to Kate that wasn't chrysanthemums. I reckon that when he picked them, he got sap on his hands – no post-mortem was done so we can't know – but it must have got into his system in some way and there was a smear of juice on his jacket.'

'Poor old chap,' Jack said. 'What a way to die. And to lie there all night before Alice Jenner found him. Someone else discovered him first, of course, but who?'

'That's the question, isn't it? Whoever it was, dragged him out of the enclosure, did the business with the plant, locked the gate and left Cyril to be found.'

Jack gave a slight shake of the head. 'It's all speculation,' he said. 'But it rings true.'

'What about Kevin Anderson? He didn't go picking flowers.'

'No, he didn't, so we have to assume that someone tampered with the bouquet that was delivered to the Priory, before it reached his room.'

'Adding one or two blooms of water hemlock to it.' Jack grimaced. 'It's grotesque.'

'Presumably wearing gloves and keeping the plant at a safe distance.'

Jack stretched in his chair. 'I'm sure. Knowing what the plant was capable of, you wouldn't want to get close to it.'

'The flowers must have almost finished blooming,' she said thoughtfully. 'The description you gave me said the plant flowered into August, but early October?'

'The climate is pretty mild here and the enclosure sheltered. But if they were on their last legs, it explains the dropping pollen. Kevin probably didn't notice. As soon as he left his room to go on his drive or off on his visit to the All's Well, whoever was responsible must have whisked away the flowers. They wouldn't want anyone else coming into contact with the bouquet.'

'But a whole cast of people could have tampered with them beforehand,' Flora said despondently. 'The bouquet would have been delivered to the reception desk, so Polly Dakers could be involved. But so could Miss Horrocks – she could have taken the flowers upstairs. And what about the chambermaids? One of them could have arranged the vase. Any one of them could be our villain.'

'Motive, Flora. They had to have had a motive,' he reminded her. 'I've been thinking of where we go with this. Steyning will be most useful. We'll buzz round the florists there on the off chance of finding the one that took the Priory's order.'

'And have the suit cleaned, too. It's getting urgent. The funeral is on Tuesday. But' – she hesitated – 'didn't the inspector want to keep the jacket as evidence?'

Jack shook his head. 'He was humouring me, a gift to a writer he knows. He thinks I'm planning a novel based on poisoning, hence my interest, but he's no intention of pursuing the matter further. As far as he's concerned, the case is definitely closed.'

'We're on our own then.'

'It looks very much like it. Do you have to open the shop today? If not, we could take the bus to Steyning.'

*

The green and cream Southdown bus was on schedule and took only twenty minutes to reach Steyning, rattling through lanes that bordered open pastureland and, for a while, hugging the banks of the river Adur. It was market day in the small town and, when they climbed aboard, the bus was already packed with passengers from the villages it had previously called at. Flora found herself almost sitting in a portly woman's lap, while Jack squeezed himself into an impossibly small space behind the driver.

Clambering from the bus in the middle of Steyning high street, they spent several seconds shaking their limbs free.

'Phew. After that, I think I'll need to stretch for a week,' Jack said. 'Definitely the wrong day to travel.'

'We didn't have much choice.' Flora swung her arms back and forth. 'The suit needs cleaning and time's running out. I went to see Kate yesterday and felt guilty that we hadn't got on with the job.'

'How is she coping?' He felt sorry for Flora's friend and his eyes held concern.

'Desperately unhappy about her father. But worried sick, as well – over money. And over Mitchell and his temper. I mentioned the bruises on her arms and she admitted it was him, but excused him by saying he was under a lot of pressure.'

'He's not under so much pressure that he doesn't try to cover up his violence. He hurts her where the bruises aren't so visible.'

'I tackled him about it yesterday,' she said, as they began to walk along the high street. 'He'd broken down on Fern Hill.'

'You were on your own?'

'I did have Betty with me.'

'Flora!' he exploded, running a hand through his flop of hair. 'You know Mitchell is capable of violence and you start berating him in an isolated place. What were you thinking?'

'He was a bit scary,' she admitted, 'and later I had second thoughts that maybe I shouldn't have tackled him in case he took it out on Kate. But I had to do it. I can't let my friend be hurt and say nothing, and at least now he knows that he's being watched. I've told Kate she must go to the police if it happens again, and I'll be with her. I wish I could help her, but she needs money to escape, and that's something that neither of us have.'

'All the more reason to find the treasure! OK, I'm joking. I don't know where we're walking but I saw a dry cleaner's from the bus. Down there on the left.'

It took only a short time to hand in Cyril's suit and make arrangements for the clothes, when cleaned, to be delivered to the funeral parlour a few doors along. With their first errand so quickly accomplished, they began the search for florists with lighter hearts.

'I only know one,' Flora said. 'Beautiful Bunches. Aunt Violet got a bouquet from them every year on her birthday.'

'Was that you?'

Flora pulled a mocking face. 'Not me. An admirer from my aunt's past! I could never get her to tell me any more, but whoever he was, he was faithful to the end. The bouquets kept coming until Violet died.'

'Did he attend the funeral?'

'I've no idea. There were so many people in the church. My aunt was much loved in the village – and beyond. She was one of those doughty Edwardian ladies who never flinched from their duty and were always there to help. Pillars of the community. Her admirer may well have been among the mourners, but he stayed anonymous. Beautiful Bunches did the flowers for the funeral – they do wonderful displays.'

'That was it.' He pointed back to the shop they'd just passed.

Retracing his steps, Jack had no idea how they were to tackle this. Flora, it seemed, had no qualms. She greeted the assistant with a bright smile.

'Good morning. I'm hoping you can help us. We're from the Priory Hotel in Abbeymead. We ordered a bouquet to be delivered – it would be around three weeks ago – and we've been unable to trace the paperwork we need. Internal accounting, you know,' she said vaguely.

The assistant looked puzzled, but seemed happy enough to help. 'Who was the recipient?' she asked.

'A Mr Anderson. Kevin Anderson. He was a guest with us and had an important birthday during his stay.' Flora beamed.

'I'll get the order book. The original order should be with the delivery note.'

The girl delved beneath the counter and brought out a large black rectangle of a book. Opening the leather-bound cover, she began methodically to flip through the pages.

'Three weeks ago, you say? And the Priory ordered it?'

'That's right. For Mr Anderson.'

'I can't see anything. The last delivery we made to the Priory was the twenty-second of September, that's over a month ago. And that was for a Mrs Latimer. Another guest?'

'Most probably.' Flora brushed the question aside. 'The hotel is very popular. I can't always recall names. All the orders you supply are in that book?'

The girl picked up the heavy tome and cradled it against her breast. 'This is our bible. If it isn't here, we didn't deliver the order. Sorry I can't help. You could try Flowers for You. It's across the car park and through the twitten.'

'Thank you for looking,' Flora said, and made for the door, Jack tagging after her.

'I'm beginning to feel decidedly surplus on this trip,' he said. 'You could have done this perfectly well on your own.' He was thinking he could have stayed home and worked. He'd reached the stickiest point of the book, his hero well and truly trapped, and Jack was flailing. Having landed the hero in this predicament, how was he to rescue him?

'You are not surplus. We need two of us here, to act as witnesses. Then whatever one of us discovers, the other can corroborate. Why don't you ask next time?' she offered graciously.

Flowers for You was not difficult to find and Jack, remembering Flora's words to the previous assistant, reproduced them verbatim. This time it was a large brown leather book that was heaved onto the counter, the assistant running her finger down the list of customers.

'I don't think…' she began, 'but yes… Anderson, you say?'

Flora, he'd noticed, had kept in the background, but at this, she was suddenly by his side. 'Yes?' she prompted eagerly.

'There was a bouquet delivered to the Priory on the seventh of October. The card was addressed to a Mr Kevin Anderson and read, "Birthday Greetings".'

Jack felt a spurt of relief. At last, some success. 'That's the order we were looking for,' he said. 'Do you record the make-up of bouquets?'

'We always note down special requests. This one mentions lilies, delphiniums and asters. And a spray of gypsophila.'

'What about this?' he asked, producing the picture he'd been given.

The assistant frowned. 'That looks like water hemlock,' she said knowledgeably. 'We'd never use that! It's highly poisonous.'

'I should think not,' Flora chimed in. 'As my colleague said, we've had a problem tracing this order in our records. It's wonderful you have a note of it. Do you have details of who ordered the bouquet?'

The assistant looked again, and shook her head. 'We usually have a telephone number and a contact name, but there's nothing here.'

'Isn't that a little strange?' Jack asked sharply. 'Without those details, how would you deal with any problems? If you weren't able to deliver the order, for example.'

'There was a request for specific flowers, so I'm sure we must have had some details, in case we had to make substitutions. We keep a filing cabinet and any additional paperwork is put in there.'

'Could you look for us?' He tried Flora's trick, flashing her a smile.

'Of course. I'll look now.' The girl gave him a warm glance and disappeared into an office behind the counter.

There was the sound of drawers being pulled out and slammed shut, a ripple of files being opened, the shuffling of paper. A minute or so passed, Flora tapping the counter with nervous fingers. After the initial euphoria of tracing the flower order, it looked as though they were about to hit a brick wall.

It was several more nail-biting minutes before the assistant reappeared, a piece of paper in her hand. 'This was the order,' she said. 'It must have been handed in rather than telephoned.'

'Do you recall who gave it to you?'

The girl's forehead creased in thought. She looked down at the typewritten sheet. 'Now that I'm looking at the order, I do remember something. It was a bit odd, actually. I opened the shop one morning and found a brown envelope on the doormat. It had been hand delivered by the look of it – there was no postmark. This piece of paper was in the envelope, together with several banknotes. I think there was one for a pound and another for ten shillings.'

'An expensive bouquet,' he remarked.

'Could we see that piece of paper?' Flora was still beside him and he could sense her breathing rapidly. The murderer was almost within grasp, she must be thinking.

The assistant laid the page flat on the counter, angling it towards them and straightening out the creases as she did. Immediately he could see that, typewritten and without a signature, the letter was unlikely to help them in their quest.

Flora must have realised it at the same time. 'Thank you,' she said to the assistant, trying, he thought, to keep the dismay from her voice.

'Not much use, I guess,' he said into her ear.

'Not much.' She put on a brave smile and began walking to the shop door, but then turned and walked back. 'Would it be possible to borrow that piece of paper?' she asked the assistant. 'We would return it.'

The girl's face registered surprise. 'We don't normally—' she began.

'I'm sure it's most irregular, but it would be a tremendous favour to us. We would only keep it until we managed to trace who sent it. Naturally, we've already asked the staff, but, so far, we've been unlucky. Seeing the order might just tip people's memories.'

'I suppose it wouldn't hurt,' the assistant said reluctantly. 'For a day or two. But we'll need it back. For our own records.'

'You'll have it back, I promise. I'll bring it myself.'

Before the girl could voice any further objections, Flora whisked the sheet of paper into her handbag, and was out of the door.

He found himself meekly following her, and again wondering why he'd come.

CHAPTER SEVENTEEN

'What possible use will it be?' Jack demanded, when he joined her on the pavement.

'You tell me. You're the crime writer.'

'So you keep reminding me. But it's typewritten. Typewriters are anonymous.'

'Maybe not this one.' She waved the order beneath his nose. 'See the "s" on Anderson, it's missing the top curve. If we can find a typewriter with an "s" like that, we'll find the perpetrator.'

He took the sheet of paper from her and squinted. 'I can't make it out. I don't have my—' he began.

'Glasses,' she finished for him. 'You wear glasses, Jolyon! Are they heavy tortoiseshell? They're what you need to be a real writer!'

He felt ruffled. She was a little too adept at teasing. 'You can forget the Jolyon,' he said grumpily, 'and the glasses, and tell me how we go about finding this mythical typewriter.'

'It's not mythical. It exists, and our murderer used it. They typed the note to disguise their handwriting, made sure there was no signature, no address, no postmark. He or she means business. If we can find that typewriter, we'll find them.'

'At the Priory, I take it?'

'Where else?'

She couldn't have considered what an impossible task she'd set them, searching for one particular typewriter in a building that housed several dozen people, constantly on the move.

'That should be fun.' He didn't try to keep the mockery from his voice.

Yet the excitement in edging closer to the truth was undeniable, and for the first time in many years, he had a strong sense of living in the world rather than through the characters he created.

*

The bus back to Abbeymead was mercifully less crowded and they were able to find seats together. Flora had heard her companion's mocking tone, but was unrepentant. Apart from a dubious legend passed down through generations and no doubt embroidered upon on the way, the florist's single sheet of paper was the only lead they had, and she was determined to pursue it.

Jack, though, was intent on the difficulties they faced in tracking down the guilty typewriter. According to him, they were insuperable. How would they get access to the Priory? Remember their last visit? That had ended with Vernon Elliot virtually ordering them off the premises. How many typewriters did the hotel possess? Neither of them had any idea. No idea either of where they'd be found. Who could have typed the florist's note? Polly Dakers at the reception desk? Miss Horrocks in the housekeeper's office? Vernon Elliot? Bernie Mitchell?

'The typewriter might not even be in the Priory,' Jack said, as they climbed off the bus at Abbeymead. 'Bernard Mitchell does office work for his wife, doesn't he? He must use a typewriter to send out orders, invoices, letters to customers. That will be in the café or in his own home.'

'He's at the Priory a lot,' Flora said defensively, 'and Kate told us that some of the time he works in Elliot's private office, and that has to involve the use of a typewriter. The Priory must be our first target. If we fail there, we can move on to Kate's.'

'How do you suggest we go about it?'

'I've been working on a plan. On the bus, while you were busy listing all the reasons we couldn't succeed.'

'You're beginning to sound smug.'

That was hurtful, Flora thought, though possibly true. 'If I am smug, it's for good reason. Alice is calling in tomorrow – she's promised me a blackberry and apple crumble. I absolutely love her blackberry and apple crumble. She has been at the Priory all her working life and she's bound to know where any typewriters are kept. Once I know that, I can plan a route through the hotel. And I'll have a reason to be there. I'll take back the pie dish as an excuse, but when I leave the kitchen, slip away into the main hotel.'

'Hoping you don't run into Miss Horrocks or Vernon Elliot.'

'That's where you come in.'

He shot a glance at her. 'Whatever it is, I'm saying no right now.'

'It will be easy, honestly. If Elliot and the housekeeper are around, I'll need them distracted, and I've thought of a brilliant ruse. You can walk into the Priory quite legitimately and say you've been asked to organise a writers' convention in Sussex and you'd very much like it to be at the Priory, but first you need to check out the accommodation and talk prices. Elliot will be thrilled at getting the business and he'll summon Miss Horrocks to go round the bedrooms with both of you. That takes care of two dangers in one swoop,' she finished triumphantly.

'I have to issue a string of lies so that you can whip in and out of offices, trying out every typewriter in the building? I won't do it.'

'Why not? It's so little to ask.'

'Because it won't get you anywhere. Let's say for argument's sake that you find the errant machine – what then? Anyone at the Priory could have used it. It's not the killer clue you think it is.'

'Not anyone,' she corrected. 'The machines or machine – and there may only be one – will be in an office to which most of the staff won't have access. I know it's not a certainty – several people could use the same typewriter – but it must help. If it only narrows down our list of suspects, it's got to be worth doing. What else do we have?'

'The legend,' Jack said unexpectedly. 'We still have the legend and Hove library is still waiting. We could go on Monday. It's a quiet day.'

'You don't believe in the legend.'

'I don't, but someone else does or they wouldn't be killing for it. It can't hurt to discover what's at the bottom of this madness and more likely to lead us to the killer than searching for a malfunctioning typewriter.'

It was Saturday morning and Alice Jenner arrived in a rush, a large basket on her arm. Her face was pink and her breath coming short.

'So sorry, Flora,' she said, as the bookshop clock chimed noon. 'I meant to drop this off on my way to work, but I called in at the Nook first – Katie was at the café very early – and that made me late. Too late to call here.'

'You shouldn't have come now. You look exhausted and I'm sure it must be your lunch break. I could just as easily have waited for my crumble until tonight. Do you have time for a cup of tea?'

'I won't stop, my love. You've got customers, I can see.'

Flora gazed around the shop. Half a dozen people were browsing the shelves, but so far none had made the journey to the till. 'It's the coach trip from Steyning,' she said in a low voice. 'I'm not too hopeful.'

'Still better than an empty shop.'

'Are the rumours still going strong?' If anyone knew, Alice would. She was deeply tuned to the pulse of the village.

'Afraid so. Leastwise, among some. But anyone with any sense squashes such talk flat. It will wither eventually, you'll see.'

'It's a matter of which lasts longer – the gossip or the All's Well.'

'Is it as bad as that?'

Flora nodded. 'I've been trying to send out the few invoices I do have,' she lied, feeling bad and hoping another white lie wouldn't count, 'but my typewriter has gone on strike. Somehow the carriage has got stuck. I won't get the engineer to come for at least a week. I suppose you don't know of a typewriter going spare?'

Alice looked concerned. 'I wouldn't have the need for one. Let me think… Kate has an old machine at the back of the café. I'm sure it still works. Maybe you could borrow that?'

'I don't want to bother Kate, not at the moment.' It was a possibility, but only once she'd searched the hotel. 'Perhaps at the Priory?' she prompted.

Her friend thought again. 'Mr Elliot has one in his office but I doubt he'd be too happy lending it. And Polly has one behind reception, though it's very well used. There's usually someone bangin' away on it.'

'Never mind, it was just a thought. It doesn't look as professional, but I'll have to handwrite them. Now, tell me how you found Kate this morning,' she said, eager to change the conversation.

'Copin', I s'pose you'd say. The funeral is frettin' her, and you can't blame the lass. It's a difficult day when it's for one you love. That Mitchell's no help either. He should be by her side, but instead he's gone off somewhere, goodness knows where.'

'Gone off?'

'Katie hasn't seen hide nor hair of him for three days now. Drunk would be my guess, though not on Cyril's account. There was no love lost between them. Still, Bernard Mitchell never needed an excuse to get drunk.'

The news that Kate's husband had disappeared set Flora's mind turning. It was three days ago that she'd seen him on Fern Hill.

'What about the van? Is that missing, too?'

Alice shook her head. 'He must have dumped it back at the café before he took off. If he's drinkin', he won't want to be bothered with a van.'

So… after she'd met Mitchell, she thought, he'd changed the tyre and gone on to do whatever he'd planned. That must have taken him some time. She'd spent at least an hour with Kate when she'd got back to Abbeymead and there'd been no sign of him returning. What had he been engaged in that morning? And was that the reason he was missing now? Or had it been her threat to tell Vernon Elliot he was a wife-beater? She couldn't think it.

'I'd best be off now,' her friend said. 'Oh, one more thing, though.'

Alice hadn't finished delivering surprises, her next words causing Flora to gape at her visitor open-mouthed.

'Polly Dakers is leavin'. Gave in her notice yesterday! She's goin' to London, would you believe. Goin' to be a model.'

'But…' Flora stuttered, 'she needed photographs, money.'

'So I understand. But she's a lucky girl. Her uncle Ted is payin'.'

Hadn't Polly said her uncle had given her five pounds towards her portfolio, but couldn't afford to finance the whole thing? Had Uncle Ted sold an heirloom? Come into an unexpected inheritance? Or had Polly discovered an unknown source of wealth? If so, it put a whole new complexion on treasure trove and the legend. Monday's visit to Hove was going to be more important than Flora had thought.

She had always suspected the girl knew more than she'd admitted. If Kevin Anderson had taken her into his confidence, told her what he'd discovered, she could have been clever enough to work out the rest. It was perfectly possible. Flora was pretty sure there was a shrewd mind behind the beautiful face. If Polly was financing her new career from digging up a secret hoard, it meant she was likely to be Kevin's killer. Once she had wheedled the secret out of him, he would most definitely be in her way.

'Polly's holdin' a goodbye party,' Alice was saying. 'She asked me to invite you. Said you were very encouraging when she talked to you about her future.'

Flora was about to refuse, when she had second thoughts. As a bona fide guest, she would have a golden opportunity to wander the Priory, as long as she was discreet. She wouldn't have to depend on Jack and his unwillingness to be involved. It would be ironic if, at the girl's own party, she found evidence that Polly Dakers was a murderess.

'She's havin' the do on Wednesday,' Alice went on. 'It didn't seem respectful to have it any earlier, not with Cyril being buried on Tuesday. You will come, I hope.' Her friend sounded anxious.

'I'll come,' Flora said.

It was a date she would definitely keep.

CHAPTER EIGHTEEN

It was Sunday morning and Flora was restless. For the last two hours, she had swept and polished the cottage and a roast lunch was in the oven with Alice Jenner's fruit crumble to follow. Away from the bookshop, she should be relaxing, but her mind was bursting with the news of Mitchell and Polly Dakers. News she desperately needed to pass on. She'd been tempted to call at Overlay House and confront Jack in his study, even at one point putting on her walking shoes, but, in the end, she talked herself out of it. He wouldn't be happy to have his work interrupted and she shouldn't get too close. Theirs was a professional alliance, not a personal friendship.

She liked him, though. He could be annoying when he pulled age and did the 'I know better than you routine', but she liked him a lot. And, grudgingly, she had to admit she found him attractive. The lanky figure, those startling grey eyes, the fedora – she had fallen in love with the fedora. But this wasn't the right time for personal emotions. She heard herself give a small sigh. Was there ever a right time? She'd had boyfriends – she was twenty-five and it would have been strange if she hadn't – but, except for one, they had been fleeting presences. Violet had been the single, solid pillar around whom she'd built her life.

The one exception had been Richard Frant. She'd met him in her second year of college. He'd been a history student, not a budding librarian, but a party thrown by a friend of a friend had them collecting drinks together from the makeshift bar. They'd hit it off immediately, Flora feeling that at last she'd met a kindred spirit.

Neither had siblings and both had been a little over-protected, Flora by her aunt and Richard by his parents living close by in Bristol. Both of them longed to travel, to experience new countries and cultures and enjoy a few adventures before the serious business of life began. All through their last year at college they had planned, deciding on routes, how they were to travel, what tickets they'd need, what visas, and crucially how much money. Flora had worked three shifts a week in a local bar to save for the trip, while Richard was being funded at least partly by his parents. Flora couldn't ask Violet – even then, the bookshop trod a fine line between success and insolvency.

It had been a hectic year. Evenings spent in the student bar were no more, impromptu visits to the cinema were rare, and any chance of a crazy weekend at the seaside, decided on the spur of the moment, was forgotten. For months, Flora was too busy pouring drinks in the evening to be around to chat, to exchange gossip, to help a roommate decide on a dress, a hairstyle. One by one, the friends she'd made had faded from her life. But it hadn't mattered. She had her sights set on the journey ahead and on spending every hour of it with Richard.

It was in the final term of Flora's last year at college that Violet began to feel unwell. At first, it hadn't seemed serious, but as the days and weeks passed, Flora became concerned. She'd asked Richard if they could postpone the trip until her aunt was feeling better and he had seemed happy to do it.

Lying on the bed one hot afternoon in late June, he'd twirled the long strands of her hair round his fingers – it had hung below her shoulders then – and kissed her firmly on the mouth. 'Flora, my lovely Flora, how could I ever go without you?'

Yet he had. Only two weeks later.

The first she'd known about it was a postcard from Dieppe. That Saturday, he hadn't turned up at their usual place, a park the other side of town, but she hadn't worried unduly. Sometimes the cycle shop where Richard had a casual job called him in to do extra hours and he wasn't always able to let her know. She'd even thought of walking along to the shop that day, but then decided on a lap of the park and going home. Twenty-four hours later, the postcard arrived. Richard had started without her.

It wasn't just the trip she'd lost, her dream of travelling destroyed, the hours of planning, of working, rendered futile. It was far worse. She'd lost trust and felt utterly betrayed. She had believed Richard loved her, that they would share a future, their travelling merely the start of a long journey together. He had smashed her self-confidence into tiny pieces and it had taken months, years, to come close to mending the damage. Flora had vowed then that she would never, ever, allow a man to make her that vulnerable again.

Her aunt, already quite ill, had asked after Richard whom she'd always liked. Flora wasn't to mind her being a bit croaky, Violet had said, she must invite Richard to stay with them during the long summer. Unwilling to upset her aunt when her health was so precarious, Flora was forced to invent a story to cover Richard's absence, while hugging the pain wordlessly to herself.

Luckily, she hadn't needed to concoct an excuse for the ruined journey – she'd barely mentioned the possibility of travelling abroad. Her aunt already ticked off the days until Flora came home on vacation. For Violet, to lose her niece for a whole year would have been difficult, and Flora had wanted to introduce her plans gradually. Even after Richard's abrupt departure, some small part of her clung to the hope that when Violet recovered – her aunt was such a stalwart, she must recover – she would still get to travel. On her own and not so ambitiously, but travel nevertheless.

Her aunt's illness, though, had continued, becoming more and more serious, until finally Violet received a diagnosis of inoperable cancer. For nearly three years, Flora had cared for the person who was dearest to her. Those years had passed in a daze, with no time ever to think, some days not even time to change her clothes or brush her hair, helping Violet stay on at the All's Well while running between cottage and bookshop: shopping, cleaning, serving customers, organising medicine, doing the hundred small things that had to be done for an invalid.

It had been a sad time, but Flora had never regretted it. She had been with Violet throughout the unequal battle and, when it was over, had felt so exhausted, so wrung out by sorrow and fatigue, that the idea of a journey had taken a long time to reappear, and then only to be dismissed as an impossibility.

She wondered if Jack had seen much of the world. She imagined he had, but she knew so little about him.

*

On Monday morning, Flora was at the bus stop well before nine, a raincoat draped across her arm. The weather in October had been unusually fine, but with a new month the sun had disappeared and dark clouds were threatening. When Jack quietly appeared at her shoulder – he really did move like a cat – she saw he'd come prepared for a downpour as well. The belted gabardine could have earned him a place in a Raymond Chandler novel.

She grinned at the thought. 'Philip Marlowe, I presume?'

He studiously ignored her joke, saying, 'It would rain, wouldn't it, on the day we're off to the coast?'

The bus arrived later than scheduled but in time to save them from a drenching, the first drops of rain beginning to fall as they climbed aboard. At any other time, Flora would have savoured the trip through the lush countryside and later, beside a sea that today was the colour of gun metal. This morning, though, she had news to impart and spent the best part of the forty-minute journey recounting what Alice had told her of the missing Bernard Mitchell and a newly enriched Polly Dakers.

'Enough money for a portfolio of very expensive photographs. What do you make of that?' she finished triumphantly.

'Her uncle might have scraped the money together,' Jack remarked mildly.

'It's only a week ago that I spoke to her. She had no hope then of money from anyone, including Uncle Ted. If there's been an inheritance he didn't know about, it wouldn't be sorted out that quickly, and how else could he have got money?'

'Borrowed it?'

'He's a painter and decorator. Alice told me. He'd be mad to go into that kind of debt.'

'Perhaps, but if he's fond of the girl?'

'You're being deliberately awkward, Jack. It's as though you always have to dismiss my theories.'

'That's not true, but what you're suggesting makes no sense. Think about it for a moment. The girl suddenly has money to pay for photographs. You think she must have got it by wheedling sufficient information out of Kevin Anderson, then finding the buried treasure. Say, for argument's sake, Polly did get information from him, what does she do with it? Whatever it might be, she's done it in just one week – you made the point yourself. Does she buy a spade and go out to dig? Unlikely.'

'She could,' Flora said stubbornly. 'If she knew where to look. She's young and strong enough… Don't we need to get off here?'

He gave a quick glance around. 'You're right. We're in Hove already.'

Together, they scrambled off the bus and onto the promenade, Jack still intent on his argument.

'I can't see Polly Dakers setting out with a spade and a map, but let's say for one unlikely moment that she does and that she uncovers this problematic treasure, it won't easily be pocketed, whatever form it takes. We're talking about stuff buried in Tudor times. If she discovers coins, they're not legal tender and can't be spent. The only thing she can do is report her find, wait weeks for it to be declared treasure, and then have to offer it for sale to a museum, its value determined by an independent body. Much the same applies to jewellery. If she tried to sell any items herself, she'd discover that no reputable jeweller would touch them. Given the timescale, Polly couldn't have obtained money in the way you suggest. Uncle Ted coming up with the goods is a much better option.'

'I still find it suspicious.' Flora wasn't going to give up completely, and looked stonily ahead.

Gradually, though, the beauty of sea and sky had her swallow her annoyance. 'Look,' she said, 'over there. The clouds have cleared and there's a streak of sunlight. Doesn't it look wonderful?'

It was low tide and a narrow beam of light had cut a swathe of gold through the greying surf, the tips of waves shimmering as though lit by a hundred small lights, a glittering pathway to the open beach.

Jack shielded his eyes against the shaft of brightness. 'I think you can see France, if you look closely. Just on the horizon.' He pointed to a smudge Flora could barely make out. 'That would be Dieppe.'

How strange the name should reoccur so soon after she'd been thinking of it. 'Have you visited the town?'

'Several times. There's an excellent ferry service from Newhaven. The Channel can be a bit choppy, but it's worth a few hours' discomfort. It lands you well into France. You haven't been to Dieppe?' He sounded surprised.

'No, not yet.' She made herself sound sprightly. 'One day, I will, and from there, I'll keep on travelling.'

'You have plans! Where will you go?' He turned an amused face to her.

'I haven't decided yet. Paris maybe. Or Rome. Somewhere that isn't Abbeymead.'

'Once you get to Dieppe, you'll have the whole of Europe to choose from. We need to cross here.' He'd swivelled round, his back to the sea. 'If we walk inland for a few streets, we should hit Hove library. It's one of the first buildings in Church Road.'

'I haven't been there either.'

'Then you're in for a treat!'

At first sight, the Renaissance-style building with its balustrade and classical cupola seemed out of place, as though by accident it had found its way to the wrong shore. The original façade must have been golden stone – there were still a few patches visible – but it had greyed badly over the years, and the pillars on either side of the entrance loomed heavy and forbidding. Flora wasn't sure why Jack liked the building so much.

'See.' Jack pointed to the top of the pillars. 'The knowledge of the world is contained within, that's the library's message – one cherub holding a book, and the other a globe.'

Refusing to be daunted, Flora walked through the dark wood doors. Inside, she found a transformation. Tall, oval-shaped windows had been fitted into every wall and beneath them, a row of round windows – like portholes, she thought, perfectly in keeping with a seaside library. Even more light streamed from the central cupola, the overall effect one of airiness and space.

'The reference library is pretty comprehensive. It's been open for fifty years,' Jack told her. 'We can look for ourselves or ask an assistant for help. What do you think?'

'You've forgotten I was a librarian,' she retorted. 'Let's see what we can turn up.'

They turned up three hefty volumes of Sussex history and one that recounted a hundred myths and fairy tales from southern England.

'Shall we take two apiece?' Jack asked, moving the books to one of the long-polished tables.

She nodded. 'Have you remembered your glasses this time?'

'Naturally.' He drew from his pocket a pair of black-framed spectacles. 'Sorry, not tortoiseshell, I'm afraid.'

'Very fetching, though,' she said approvingly, as he settled them on the bridge of his nose.

It took them much longer than they'd wanted, or expected, to plough their way through the four volumes.

'Did nobody ever index in the past?' Flora asked crossly.

'I'm not sure they would have been much use.' Jack had won the single volume that boasted one. 'I still need to go through this book page by page, in case I've missed something that's not indexed where I think it should have been.'

Library users came and went, the chairs at other tables filled and emptied, but on they went, silently turning the pages. At last, Flora slammed shut her second book. She looked at her watch.

'It's past twelve and I'm starving. Also cross-eyed.'

Jack looked across at her. 'It suits you.' It was his turn to tease. 'But I've had enough, too.'

'And we haven't found a thing.' She gave a small groan.

'I did find some interesting myths. The book is too general, but there was one based in Sussex. Did you know that the Devil's Dyke was formed by the devil himself? He was digging a trench to allow the sea to flood the churches of the Sussex Weald. Apparently, his digging disturbed an old woman who lit a candle – or, alternative story – his digging angered a rooster causing it to crow, either of which made the devil believe that morning had arrived and he'd better disappear.'

Flora went to say something but Jack was quicker, still quoting from his book. 'If you run backwards seven times around the Dyke whilst holding your breath, the Devil will appear.'

'You must try it someday. I did know about the Dyke, but it's not the right legend.'

'Pity. How about a sandwich?'

'I'd rather have a bowl of soup. I've got quite cold in here.'

'Fine, we'll find a café. Before we do, though, I'll mention our search to one of the assistants. She might come up with something we missed.'

'We went through the shelves with a fine-tooth comb.'

'I know, but…'

Flora shrugged. If he wanted to waste his time. It was lunch that was calling to her right now.

CHAPTER NINETEEN

They found a café just off the promenade and chose window seats overlooking the wide, empty beach. The sea was now a thin line on the horizon and a football match was in progress on the wet sand.

'Those children must be playing truant,' Flora said, looking down at the youngsters' boisterous game.

'Who wouldn't with a whole beach to yourself? It's onion soup, by the way. Is that OK?'

'Onion soup is fine.' She gazed through the window, her thoughts clearly elsewhere. 'What are we going to do, Jack?' she asked at last, turning towards him. 'We're making no headway. I'm as far as ever from proving that something criminal happened at the All's Well. Something human, without a ghost in sight. Whoever murdered Kevin Anderson and killed Cyril is still out there.'

'The legend was always going to be a long shot. Even if we'd discovered what it actually said, it might not have helped.'

'So what on earth will?'

'Talking?' A frown appeared on Flora's face, but he continued, 'Talking to everyone and encouraging them to talk to us. When people are relaxed, they can let their guard down, let slip something they shouldn't or something they weren't even aware of. My heroes are pretty adept at worming out information that way.'

'And that's it?'

'Don't dismiss it. It's Cyril's funeral tomorrow and the next day you're going to Polly Dakers' party. Plenty of people, plenty of opportunities to talk – or let them talk.'

'Plenty of time, too, to look for a typewriter with a wonky "s"!'

Jack shook his head. 'I don't think it's worth the risk.' He turned to the waitress who had arrived at their table with steaming bowls of soup and two large white rolls. 'That smells good.'

Flora dipped a spoon into her bowl. 'It tastes good as well. I really should find the time to do more cooking. Aunt Violet was a great one for soup making, but then she had green fingers. She grew the most amazing vegetables. I try to keep the garden tidy, but I'm not nearly as successful.'

'Did you live with Miss Steele a long time?'

'Most of my life. Well, from the age of six, and I don't honestly remember much before then. Sometimes I think I can sense my mother close by – maybe a scent triggers the feeling or a particular sound recalls something that's buried in my brain – but really, my early life is a blur. Both my parents were killed in a car crash. Good friends of theirs looked after me for a while, but they were moving abroad – the father had a new job somewhere in Africa – and they couldn't take me with them. I was about to be sent to an orphanage when Violet came flying to the rescue. Out of nowhere, like a guardian angel.'

Jack was intrigued, his soup spoon suspended. 'Where had she been?'

'Italy. She'd been living there for years teaching English, ever since she left school. She was my father's sister and when their mother died, he offered her a home, but Violet, being Violet, preferred to be independent and trotted off to Italy instead.'

'How did the bookshop happen?'

'It was a legacy. That also came out of the blue. Not that I knew much about it, I was too young. I do remember at the time I was living with Violet in a flat near where I'd lived with my parents when they were alive.'

'In London?'

'Yes. My aunt hated the city, but my life had been turned upside down and she wanted me to know at least something familiar. She managed to get a job teaching in a local college. Then a solicitor's letter arrived saying her godfather, whom she'd never really known, had died recently and left her his house. It was quite a windfall! Violet didn't have any attachment to the house and was happy to sell. She bought the All's Well with the proceeds, and the cottage I live in. She'd never run a business before and it was tough for a woman on her own. But she did it.'

'The thirties wouldn't have been the best time to open a bookshop for anyone, whatever their sex.'

'Things haven't moved on that much today,' Flora said, continuing her strand of thought. 'At least, not for women. They proved their worth during the war – as land girls, in munition factories, driving ambulances in the Blitz, flying planes to airfields under enemy fire – but all that seems to have been forgotten. Slowly and surely they've been shunted back to the kitchen and the nursery.'

'Not all women,' Jack remarked quietly, smiling across at her. 'You've escaped both. And so did your aunt. Violet never married?'

'She was like a lot of her generation. Her fiancé was killed in the First War and, after it ended, there was a dearth of marriageable men, but I don't think my aunt ever recovered from losing him. That sounds overly dramatic, doesn't it? Of course, she got over the immediate grief and went on with her life, but she never wanted to marry. As far as I'm aware, she never looked at another man.'

'Even the one who sent her bouquets? That's true love for you.' Jack supposed there was such a thing, though from his experience it was rare.

'Or simply self-protection. Once you've lost something precious, you become wary. You might even,' she hazarded, 'choose to become a recluse.'

He took time to break the bread roll into ever smaller pieces, while he gathered his thoughts and tried to make sense of his feelings. 'You're a little too perceptive, Miss Steele,' he said at last.

'You don't have to tell me about it,' she said gently, 'but I'd like to hear.'

'There's not much to tell.'

'However little, it must be important to you.'

'It is, or it was. I had a fiancée, too, and like your aunt, lost out. In my case, ignominiously.'

'There was another man.' It was a statement of fact, as though Flora already knew his history.

'Not just another man, but my best friend.' He crumbled a few more pieces of roll.

'How wretched for you.'

'The worst. I was working in New York at the time. I was a journalist then, on one of the posh papers.'

'Your fiancée was American?'

'Canadian, but eager to travel the world. Particularly eager to travel across Europe and soak up the culture, et cetera. We were going to be married in England. My parents separated when I was very young, but for the wedding of their only child, they agreed to bury their grudges and pull together. Or try to. I had a good job, a beautiful wife-to-be, and I'd just had my first success as an author – a short story published in a literary magazine no less, and another that had won a well-publicised competition. Life looked pretty rosy.'

'It can do, just before something ghastly happens,' she said sagely.

He wondered what unpleasant reality had hit Flora. She was pretty, highly intelligent and annoyingly good company, yet at twenty-five she was still single and looked set to stay that way.

Flora looked across at him. 'What happened exactly?' she asked bluntly.

'One of the chaps on the paper's features staff came from Liverpool. He had a dour sense of humour and we hit it off straight away. Over the months, we became very good friends, or so I thought. When I told the paper I was going back to England to get married, he was asked to take over one of the columns I wrote, so he shadowed me for a few months. It meant quite a lot of socialising – New York was a long party in those days – and inevitably he got to know Helen very well. Too well, as it turned out. The day before we were due to leave for England, she and I had lunch somewhere.' He raked his memory for the name, but found it had faded. 'An Italian place,' he said, 'one we often went to. Anyway, we were just leaving the restaurant and I'd paid the bill, but I didn't have enough change for a decent tip. Helen rooted round in her handbag for some small notes and out spilled two first class train tickets. I picked them up for her and saw they were tickets to East Hampton.'

'Where is that?'

'The Hamptons are where affluent New Yorkers go in the summer – long stretches of beach and a string of seaside communities. Very exclusive and very expensive. When I looked at the tickets, the date sprang out at me.' Even now, he could remember the sickening jolt deep in his stomach, an augury of what was to come.

'I asked Helen who they were for,' Jack went on, trying to keep his voice even. 'That's when she told me. She was staying in New York, she said, and taking a holiday in the Hamptons. She hadn't known how to break it to me and she was very, very sorry. She couldn't come to England, couldn't in fact marry me. She had fallen for someone else.'

Flora pursed her lips. 'That's some speech! And you had no idea until then that she had changed her mind?'

'I must have had, I suppose, deep down. For a start, I didn't have to ask who the someone else was. I guess I'd sensed it for weeks and hadn't wanted to accept the truth. If you ignore the signs, the problem will go away – that kind of thing. Except that it didn't. Helen had planned her getaway meticulously, I have to hand it to her. Cashed in her ticket for the crossing to Southampton and booked a new honeymoon in the Hamptons.'

'She sounds a bitch,' Flora declared, and Jack knew she felt every word.

'These things happen. People change, feelings change. She could have talked to me, though, and I think I'd have understood.'

'Well, I wouldn't. But why shut yourself away? It's Helen who should have gone into purdah.' Flora sounded angry and he wondered if something similar had happened to her.

'I needed time on my own. Time to come to terms with what had happened. When I took the ship back to England, I expected I'd be clearing up the mess – the church, the presents, the whole damn thing – but my parents were fighting again, this time about the costs they'd been landed with, and I couldn't stand any more noise. So I left them to it and came to Sussex. I remembered it from childhood. On weekends, we used to drive down from London and stay in a bed and breakfast on the coast. West Wittering has one of the best beaches, and my father had a friend with a boat at Bosham. He used to take us for a sail occasionally. Those weekends and one or two holidays in Cornwall are the only times I recall living in a happy family.'

'I can see why you settled here.'

'I thought it would bring solace, a balm to my heart. And it has.'

'You could have enjoyed the quiet of the countryside without cutting yourself off from people.'

'That's true. At first, though, I wanted to be completely alone and later it became a habit. Villages are nosy places and people would be asking why I'd come to Sussex, what my history was, then they'd enjoy passing judgement on me. I was in a brittle state and couldn't bear to speak to anyone. It was so much easier to have newspapers through the letter box, a bottle of milk on the doorstep, a box of groceries left on the pathway.'

'You weren't even tempted to visit the bookshop?'

'A little, but then I hit on the idea of using Charlie. He'd run a few errands for me and I'd found him surprisingly reliable for his age. Also fairly taciturn. He didn't want to talk, all he wanted was to earn money. Charlie was another way I could avoid engaging with people.'

'Or avoid trusting them. No betrayal ever again. I get it.' She reached out for his hand and he felt her fingers, slender and warm. 'You're not a recluse, Jack. Not a natural recluse,' she amended. 'The way you speak to people, the fact you're such good company.'

'Another compliment,' he said lightly, allowing her hand to slip away. 'You'll have to watch those.'

'I'm keeping count, don't worry, but I do think it's time you emerged permanently from your burrow.' She looked at her watch. 'We should be getting back to Abbeymead. The buses aren't that reliable and I need to call in at the bookshop before I go home.'

He reached for his wallet. 'Fine, but can we whip back to the library? Five minutes only, I promise. Just to check that the assistant hasn't come up with anything.'

He could sense her reluctance, but he had a hunch it might be worth the extra few minutes.

'Hello there.' The library assistant greeted them with a friendly smile as they walked up to her desk. 'I'm glad you came back. I've got something for you. I ventured down to the basement once my colleague returned from lunch. We store all kinds of books there, often those that are too fragile to be on the shelves, and I think this might interest you. It's another book on myths and legends, but one that's focused entirely on Sussex. It's possible you'll find what you're looking for there.'

She brought out a slim volume with a soiled and broken cover. 'I'm afraid I'll have to ask you to wear gloves – the book is old and very delicate.'

'Anything,' he agreed. 'And thank you for taking the trouble to look.'

The girl smiled warmly up at him.

He felt a nudge from Flora. 'See what happens when you stop being a hermit,' she whispered.

He ignored her and, squeezing his hands into the pair of gloves the girl handed him, several sizes too small, he carried the book over to the table they had used previously.

'It looks as if it might fall to pieces at any moment,' Flora said, plumping herself down on one of the chairs.

Every edge of the leather binding was frayed, as though a family of mice had feasted on it. The pages were little better, badly yellowed and thin to the point of transparency. Jack felt himself holding his breath as he turned them, one by one. A few chapters in, his finger came to a halt, pointing at the name they'd been searching for.

'We have a Templeton at last,' he said.

Flora drew her chair closer, leaning over his shoulder and trying to read the small print. 'I can't make out the words. Read it aloud.'

He glanced around, making sure there was no one to be disturbed, and began to read in a low voice.

During Henry VIII's ravages of England's religious institutions, a monk belonging to the Bosham monastery secreted an important manuscript. In addition to his duties at the monastery, the monk was priest to the local landowners, a Catholic family called the Templetons, though naturally this was not publicly acknowledged. When the Bosham monastery was attacked, the monk fled to the Templetons for shelter. At a time of religious persecution, their family home had been modified and the monk escaped capture by hiding in a priest hole. Lord Templeton died defending his house and his wife was arrested for supposed treason. She was kept prisoner in the Tower of London, but before she was captured, Lady Ianthe Templeton entrusted to her priest a casket of her jewellery. The monk managed to escape to France – he took a boat from Shoreham – but before he did so, he buried the casket on the estate, noting exactly where he had hidden the jewellery. It may be that he hoped to return one day and restore the casket to its rightful owner. It is said that the manuscript the priest wrote was placed for safekeeping in one of the numerous volumes in the Priory library. If one believes the legend, there it has stayed for the last four hundred years and no one has discovered the casket, if indeed there ever was one.

'So *that's* what we're looking for,' Flora said, her voice ringing with excitement. 'A document written by a priest. That's why Kevin trespassed in the Priory library. It must be why he broke into my shop, too, though I can't yet see the connection. There is treasure, though, Jack. Whatever jewellery the monk buried must be worth a fortune now and certainly worth killing for.'

'But where is this supposed manuscript? Kevin never found it and neither has anyone else, by the look of it.'

'Which means that the treasure is still out there.'

'Not necessarily. Don't forget, it's a legend we've been reading. The manuscript might never have existed. Kevin searched the library and found nothing. Others might have done so before him.'

Walking back to the bus stop, he could feel her dejection and tried to think of something to cheer her, but apart from the malfunctioning typewriter, they were bereft of any further clues.

'There are too many false notes to the story,' Flora said, once they'd clambered aboard the bus to Abbeymead. Her low spirits had vanished and she was back in determined mode, it seemed. 'I know you think the legend is fantasy, but there has to be some basis to it or it wouldn't still be talked about. Historically, the circumstances in which the manuscript was supposed to be written are spot-on. That suggests that the parchment did once exist. Yet it's never been found, even though in four hundred years the library must have been cleaned over and over again and the books brought down for dusting. To me, that means the document is still hidden. Still waiting to be discovered. Then there's the bookshop to consider.'

'What about the bookshop?'

'The legend specifically mentions the Priory library, so why was Kevin looking in the All's Well?'

Jack had no answer. The argument was going in circles and it seemed very much as though they had reached a dead end. Relapsing into silence for the remainder of the journey, they were still saying little when they waved the bus goodbye and walked towards the bookshop. He felt his companion slow and, following her gaze, saw the figure of a man waiting outside the shop door, his back towards them.

The man turned as he heard them approach.

'Miss Steele?' He raised his trilby. 'Pleased to meet you at last. May I introduce myself? Joseph Rawston. Here, have one of my cards.' He shuffled around in the pocket of a pair of voluminous grey trousers and brought out a handful of business cards.

'Rawston's Rare Books, bang in the middle of Worthing town centre and one of the best bookshops in Sussex, though I say it myself. There's not a rare book I can't track down.'

This could prove interesting, Jack thought. Rare books were turning out to be important.

CHAPTER TWENTY

Flora took the proffered card, feeling uncomfortable. What was this man doing here?

'Sorry about turning up unannounced.' He appeared to have sensed a frostiness in the air. 'I did give you a tinkle on Saturday but there was no answer.' He smiled broadly. 'So here I am.'

He was lying, Flora thought. She had been in the shop all day on Saturday and the telephone hadn't rung once. By why would the man lie? It added to her discomfort.

'How can I help you, Mr Rawston?' she asked crisply.

'I think we can help each other, Miss Steele.' He puffed out pudgy cheeks, as though congratulating himself. 'Nice little place you have here.' His gaze roved proprietorially up and down the building, taking in the solid brick and flint walls, the pretty latticed windows and the wide white-painted entrance.

It was as if he owned the All's Well, she thought indignantly.

Jack had imperceptibly moved closer. 'Jack Carrington,' he said, holding out a hand that Joseph touched briefly. 'You've come quite a way from Worthing.'

'No problem, squire. Got the old jalopy.' He gestured to a Morris Minor parked a little way down the high street. 'I knew your aunt, you know,' he said suddenly, his gaze once more sweeping over Flora.

'Really?'

'Oh, yes. Used to meet her regularly at the local auctions.'

'I don't recall her mentioning you, Mr Rawston.' Violet may well have mentioned Rawston's Books some time in the past, but

Flora was keen to unsettle her unwelcome visitor. She didn't like the way he swaggered.

Joseph gave a little smirk. 'Violet Steele knew me all right. I don't think I ever saw you at any of the auctions, but your aunt was a dab hand.'

'She enjoyed the excitement of bidding.'

'She certainly did. A keen bidder as well – a little too keen for me at times.' His cheeks seem to deflate at the thought. 'An auction is why I came.'

At last, they were getting to the nub of this man's odd arrival on her doorstep.

'There was an auction at Abbeymead a few years back. At the big house here.'

'The Priory?' Jack asked.

'That's the one. The owner had died and the chap who'd inherited – somebody told me he was from Australia – didn't want any of it. The house, the furniture, the books. They didn't put the whole library up for sale. A lot of it wasn't worth having, but I liked the look of one of the lots and then went on to bid for a second. I didn't get that one, though. Your aunt was after it, too, and she was the one who took the books home.'

'I'm sorry you were disappointed,' Flora said politely, 'but I don't understand what this has to do with me.' She was feeling increasingly chilled, wanting nothing more than to shut the door on Joseph Rawston of Rawston's Rare Books.

'I'm coming to it, young lady. All in good time.' The cheeks had inflated again. Flora watched, fascinated, though she would dearly liked to have taken a pin to puncture them.

'The thing is,' Rawston went on, 'I still want to acquire those books. I've tried to find other copies but never managed it. I thought I'd come to the horse's mouth. See if we can do a deal.'

'You know that my aunt died earlier this year?'

'I had heard. Very sad.' He shook his head, his bulky figure shaking alongside.

'Why didn't you ask her when she was still alive? She would have known whether to sell or not. And known the right price.'

'I heard the dear lady was ill and didn't want to intrude. I'm sure you're just as able to fix a price. I'm willing to pay generously.'

'If these are books you've wanted so badly, why come now?' Flora pursued. 'You could have contacted me any time during the last six months.'

He looked up and down the high street, as if for inspiration. 'I have a client now,' he said at last. 'A client who will pay well.'

'Then maybe you should put him in touch with me.'

Rawston gave a falsely jovial laugh. 'That's not how it works, Miss Steele. I'm sure you must know that. We all have to make a small profit, don't we, and I'll pay you a fair price, but I can't divulge the name of my client – that's a personal contact.'

'I see.'

'So what do you say?'

She felt Jack give her arm a small nudge. 'I'll think about it, Mr Rawston.'

The smile vanished and the man took a pace forward so that his face was inches away. Immediately, Jack stepped between them. 'Miss Steele will think about it,' he repeated.

Joseph Rawston's eyes were cold and so was his voice when he spoke. 'You've got my card,' he snapped out. 'Telephone me as soon as you've decided.'

They stood together, watching the man's plump figure roll down the road to his parked car. Only when the vehicle had swept past them, Rawston looking grim-faced, did Flora turn the key of the bookshop door.

Once inside, Jack turned to face her, his eyebrows raised. 'Singular, wouldn't you say?'

'If that means odd, yes. I really disliked the man.'

'Poor Joseph. He won't be getting his books, I fear, which is just as well.'

'Are you thinking what I'm thinking?'

'That it's strange he should turn up on your doorstep at this particular time, desperate to buy books your aunt has had for several years?'

'Do you think he's learned of the legend, knows there's a priest's letter, and is chasing the jewellery?' It was a big leap to make, but Flora's instincts were telling her she was right.

'The fact that he wants the books doesn't mean the legend is true,' Jack warned. 'He could be testing the water. It's how he heard the story that seems most interesting.'

'The legend must be fairly well-known, particularly among older people – Cyril knew it, for a start.'

'But Rawston?'

'I suppose it's possible that Rawston heard it only recently,' Flora conceded, 'and that sent him scurrying through the books he'd bought at auction, if he still had them. Then, when he found nothing, he came here for those my aunt bought.'

'Not all the books at the Priory were put up for sale, were they? What about those left in the library?'

'Nowhere near all. But it would be difficult for Rawston to get access to the Priory. Much easier for him to start with Violet's books and hope to discover what he was looking for.'

Jack looked unconvinced. 'Do you still have the books he wanted?'

Flora's heart was beating far too rapidly at the thought of what Rawston's visit might mean. 'As far as I know, they're still where Violet shelved them.'

'A win! What are we waiting for?'

Flora led the way towards the rear of the shop and the section reserved for second-hand books. They had walked this way together before, she remembered. If they turned another corner, they would be exactly where they'd found Kevin Anderson's body. Was that young man connected to Joseph Rawston in some way? If those books had been Kevin's goal, he'd collapsed only several yards short, and Flora could almost feel sorry for him.

She stood back to let Jack view the two huge bookcases that held Violet's spoils.

'Do you know which came from the Priory?' he asked. 'Or do we have to plough through five hundred volumes?'

'I can't be completely sure, but I think they fill the bottom four shelves of each bookcase.'

'That's still a good hundred books to look through. We'll have to do it page by page. If this manuscript exists, it will be fragile, probably stuck in the binding. It won't float free by simply shaking each book. I say it's too big a job for tonight.'

'We can't just leave it.' Agitation gripped Flora. 'We're about to uncover a secret. A very valuable secret. We should search for it before someone else breaks in and finds it for themselves.'

'Michael has fitted extra locks, hasn't he? And a burglar alarm. Whatever secret there is will be safe for tonight. Tomorrow, after the funeral, we'll come back and get stuck in.'

'The shop will be closed anyway,' she said slowly. 'I wasn't going to open, not tomorrow, not with Cyril being buried, so no one will think it odd.'

Flora felt badly disappointed, but she was tired and no doubt Jack was, too. They could well miss what they were looking for. And if it turned out there was no manuscript hidden in Violet's books, it would be better to discover the fact after a decent night's sleep.

The rain woke her, hitting her bedroom window with a ferocity that sent streams of water bouncing onto the red brick path below.

Parting the curtains, she saw a blanket of grey: sky, garden, road. What a day for a funeral. Violet had been buried on a bright April morning and Flora had been glad of it. Daffodils had bent their head as the cortège passed by, primroses smiling from the hedgerows. Her aunt would have liked that.

She took some time to decide on what to wear: a dark raincoat that covered a black skirt and a grey top. There was to be no social gathering after the church service, but Flora felt it right to be dressed appropriately. Rummaging in her wardrobe, she unearthed the umbrella she hadn't used for days.

The funeral was booked for eleven o'clock and by the time she left home, the downpour had dissolved into a drizzle, but bruising clouds still filled the sky and it was a good bet that the heavens would open at the slightest provocation. Her fellow parishioners, she saw, had come similarly armed, a procession of black raincoats and black umbrellas making its way through the lychgate and up the brick path to the porch of St Saviour's.

This morning the grey stone of the Norman church was hardly distinguishable from its surroundings, the outline of its square tower against the murky sky the only noticeable landmark. Inside, the building was cold, its ancient damp seeping through Flora's raincoat and into her bones. Seeing Alice Jenner sitting alongside Kate on the front pew, Flora took a seat towards the rear and waited for Jack. She presumed he would come, though he'd made no definite promise.

Although Violet had been a regular church attender, Flora had rarely accompanied her aunt, and this morning she took a while to absorb her surroundings, properly aware for the first time of the centuries-old smell of must, the dust motes floating in the grey light, the finely crafted stonework: panels depicting Biblical stories and capitals carved with impressive Norman-style heads.

A figure sweeping down the aisle interrupted her survey. It was Miss Horrocks, ramrod straight in flowing black cloak and a black wool cloche rammed tightly onto her head. She gave Flora a brief nod as she passed. The woman could have walked out of a Dickens novel, Flora thought. Her gaze wandered again, this time taking in the large congregation. The church was almost full. Cyril had been well liked by his fellow villagers and there was sympathy for his daughter. Almost everyone, Flora reckoned, felt sadness for Kate. She craned her neck to look again at the front pew where Kate was sitting. Alice might be there, but there was no sign of the errant husband. Surely even Bernard Mitchell wouldn't let his wife down on a day like today?

Vernon Elliot was sitting in the pew behind them, his long, skeletal form dwarfing his fellow mourners, and on the other side of the aisle, Polly Dakers, beside an older man. Uncle Ted, perhaps? Flora hoped she would have the chance to talk to the girl, talk to Alice and Kate as well, and Elliot, too. It was what Jack had advised.

With the thought, came the man. He slid into the seat beside her, cramming a very wet fedora between his knees.

'Sorry I'm late,' he said in a low voice.

'Don't tell me – you couldn't find the church.'

'I got held up. Stuff,' he said vaguely.

'Such as?'

'I'll tell you later.'

CHAPTER TWENTY-ONE

That morning Jack had received an unnerving letter from his agent. Arthur Bellaby needed to see him as a matter of urgency, and would Jack meet him in London on Wednesday that week. Lunch was on him – at the Ritz, no less. Wednesday was tomorrow and going to London was the last thing Jack wanted right now. He could telegram, he supposed, and put the meeting off, but he was sure that Arthur wouldn't let it rest. This was a big opportunity for Jack, the letter announced. Carrington novels sold reasonably well, certainly well enough to feed their author, but this could be the next step up. Arthur had been coy in his letter about the exact nature of what was being offered. Something about a crime series set in different counties. A marketing campaign would run alongside and be the responsibility of whatever local authority was involved. Working together, his agent proclaimed, they would make the beauty spots of England hum.

Jack wasn't happy. He suspected this new series would be dictated by others and he would lose any creative freedom. He could be forced into days of travelling – if his novels were to be used as marketing tools for a particular area, he would need to know the county intimately. Publicity teams would expect nothing less. Jack didn't want to travel. He'd had enough of travelling. He was happy where he was. In Sussex, in Abbeymead. And he didn't want to tell Flora that he might soon be off. He was enjoying this new friendship, looking forward to the days he saw her. It was true she could be infuriating, but she could also be a delightful companion. One thing she wasn't, was dull.

By the time he reached the church, he was extremely damp, even though the earlier torrent had abated. The drizzle infiltrated every inch of his raincoat, or so it seemed, and his hat had been reduced to a squashy mess. He spied Flora straight away and inched himself into the seat beside her. She was looking solemn. It was a funeral, after all, and she'd known Cyril Knight and liked him a lot, whereas he'd met the old chap only once.

It was years since Jack had entered a church, let alone sat through a service, but the hymns, the lessons, the readings from the Book of Common Prayer, were over in what seemed a blink of an eye. Was that it? Seventy years in the world and then shuffled out in a matter of minutes. It was a sobering enough thought to have him reconsider what he was making of his own life.

'I must speak to Kate,' Flora murmured beside him, as the congregation said a last amen. 'Have you noticed? Bernie Mitchell isn't here.'

*

As was the custom, Kate and Alice, as her supporter, were the first to walk up the aisle and out into the churchyard. Flora followed, with Jack a pace behind. Luckily, the drizzle had worn itself out and, though the air was still bleak and the sky overcast, people mingled, small groups of parishioners gathering on the brick path or getting their shoes wet as they stood between the gravestones. There might not be a wake to attend – Kate had crumpled at the idea – but the need to talk still flourished.

Vernon Elliot paused in the covered porch before joining the throng. His suit was even more sharply cut than the one Flora had seen before, his shirt a fine cotton and his tie an Italian silk. He stood waiting to be noticed, then turned to the closest of his audience.

'Miss Steele? Mr...'

'Carrington,' Jack supplied.

'Good morning. Though not, alas, for Mr Knight. Cyril was a good man. A fine worker.'

Flora didn't answer. She was filled with disgust. This was the man who had cut Cyril adrift without a pension, without any recompense for his years of hard work at the Priory.

She thought her silence must have penetrated even Elliot's thick skin, because he said nothing more, merely giving them both a tight smile, and moving on to more congenial company.

It was Kate Mitchell who took his place. 'Thank you for coming, Flora, and you, Jack. And for getting Dad's suit sorted out. It meant the arrangements have gone very smoothly.'

The girl's eyes were raw, her face blotchy in the uneven light. Flora gave her a hug. 'We wanted to be here, Kate, and it was a lovely service. Were they Mr Knight's favourite hymns?'

Kate nodded. 'I hope he enjoyed them,' she said tremulously.

'You did him proud. I'm sorry I didn't call in yesterday. I did mean to when I got back from Hove, but it was late and you'd already shut up shop.'

The excuse made Flora feel guilty. The excitement of discovering the legend, and then realising that she might actually possess the missing document, had allowed Kate's predicament to take second place in her mind. 'You'll want to be quiet for the rest of the day,' she went on, 'but I'll call in later tomorrow, if that's all right?'

She'd call after Polly's party, she decided, though she'd say nothing of the girl's good fortune. That would be horribly insensitive.

'It will be lovely to see you whenever you come.' Kate managed a wobbly smile. 'I may not open the café again for a while, but if it's closed tomorrow, come to the house.'

Flora was surprised. Kate had been serving customers the day after her father had died, so why the decision to close now?

'I'm not up to managing it at the moment,' Kate defended herself.

'Of course,' Flora said soothingly. 'But Bernie? Couldn't he work at the café for a while, until you feel ready to go back? Where is he, by the way?'

Kate looked down at her feet and didn't speak for some time. 'To be honest, Flora, I'm not sure.'

'Drinkin',' Alice said, overhearing Flora's question and bustling up to them. 'Under the table somewhere.'

'Alice!' Kate protested.

'No good beatin' about the bush, my love. That's what's happened, take my word for it.'

While they had been speaking, the vicar had glided up to them, ready to detach Kate for a private word.

'Poor Cyril,' Alice said. 'What a day to be buried on.' She held her hands open to the heavens. 'And poor Kate, so alone. The sister up in Scotland's broken her leg and can't travel, and t'other one can't afford the fare from Canada. As for that no-good son-in-law of his not even botherin' to turn up!'

'Most other people did,' Jack said. 'It seems like the whole village has turned out.'

Alice looked round with satisfaction. 'That'd be about right. Cyril deserved it. Though he could have done without some of 'em.' She glared at the figure of Polly Dakers, resplendent in a violet top coat and pink hat. 'Some people have no decorum.'

Jack shuffled his feet, his gaze fixed on Flora. Talk to Polly, his eyes were saying, while I keep Alice occupied.

'She does look a bit awkward,' Flora conceded. 'Perhaps I should have a quick word.'

'Polly,' she called to the girl, walking towards her, 'I wanted to thank you for your invitation. It was kind of you.'

'Why not? I'm drowning in happiness and I want to spread it around.'

'I heard you had some luck. I'm so pleased. Last time we spoke, you were very downbeat.'

'That's when I had no chance of going to London. No chance of escaping this place.'

'Then a fairy godmother came your way,' Flora suggested lightly.

'More like a fairy godfather.' Polly gave a hoot of laughter, causing the mourners gathered nearest them to turn and stare.

'Uncle Ted, I imagine. Did he back the right horse?'

Flora sounded frivolous, but inside her stomach was screwed tight. She had no idea how Rawston and his supposed customer fitted into this, but she was sure Polly had had some involvement in Kevin's demise, whatever Jack said. It was simply too fortuitous that a large sum of money had fallen into her hands shortly after the young man's death.

Polly moved closer, her voice little more than a whisper. 'Actually, Flora, I can tell you. You're not like these old biddies.' She gestured dismissively to the people around them. 'It's a friend of Uncle Ted's that's come up trumps. He's ever so rich, lives in a big house near here. Pots of money, would you believe?'

'Really?' Flora was thinking hard, wondering just what had been agreed between this lovely girl and a man who must be so many years older than her.

'He's going to sponsor me,' Polly said, a huge smile splitting her face.

'That is kind of him. What sort of work will you be doing?'

'Work? You can call it that, I suppose.' Polly smirked. 'He's my uncle's age, and I'm young – and beautiful.'

She left it at that, but Flora immediately understood the deal the girl had made. She felt genuinely sad that Polly had decided on such a future but, then again, she was a young woman who knew what she was getting into. She was sharp, determined and worldly. She had tried to enmesh Kevin for the same reason. That hadn't worked out, and this was another chance.

'I wish you luck. At least, no more sitting behind the desk at the Priory.'

'No more working for that pig.' Polly glared at the sleek back of her employer. 'I'm off now, but I'll see you tomorrow.'

She would, Flora thought, in between the search for a damaged typewriter.

'Well?' Jack had sidled up to her. 'Does she have the treasure chart tucked into her sleeve? A spade beneath her coat?'

'Don't mock – I was wrong and you were right. I'm still sure she was hoping to use Kevin, but she's found an easier way. Or so she thinks.'

'And what's that?'

'A sugar daddy – I believe that's what the newspapers call them. Polly's very own treasure map! Is it time to go looking for ours?'

CHAPTER TWENTY-TWO

Flora made tea for them both in the cupboard that her aunt had designated the bookshop kitchen. It had a sink so tiny it barely accommodated two hands, but there was water, a kettle and a gas ring, and what else did they need, Violet had argued.

The funeral might have been brief, but Flora had known the afternoon would be a long haul – there were four shelves of books to examine, some of them very heavy and very large – and she'd made sandwiches before leaving home, nursing them in her basket throughout the ceremony.

'Here,' she said, unwrapping a package in greaseproof paper. 'Cheese and pickle.'

'An unexpected treat.'

'We'll need fuel for the work. I'm already feeling daunted by the thought of it. I almost wish that horrible man, Rawston, had never found his way here.'

'You shouldn't wish it, if you want to uncover the full story. By coming, Rawston has helped fill a few blanks.'

Flora set two cups of tea down on her work desk. 'He alerted us to what the All's Well might have under its roof, but—'

'But… there's something else. I'm still curious as to how he'd learned of the legend. If he's been in Sussex as long as he says he has, he could have heard the tale at some point, but let it slide off him. It's the kind of story people smile at and then dismiss. So what made him suddenly sit up and take notice? Who made him take notice?'

'Kevin? You think it was Kevin?'

'I think it's likely. As a guest in – what was it, the premier suite? – the chap had the use of an Aston Martin. He could have zipped over to Worthing and back without anyone noticing. Perhaps after he failed to find what he was looking for at the Priory? By then, he'd already asked a lot of questions and would have known of the auction, if he hadn't been aware of it before. Known there were books missing from the present-day library that had been sold locally. This man, Rawston, specialises in rare books. If Kevin asked around, he wouldn't have had too much trouble finding the shop.' Jack waved half a sandwich in the air. 'These are delicious, by the way.'

'Good. I'm glad they survived.' Flora fidgeted on her stool, leaving her own food untouched. 'Let me get this right. Kevin goes to Worthing, finds Rawston's Rare Books and asks about the Priory sale. Rawston shows him the books he bought at the auction, hoping to sell him one, but then what?'

'Kevin wouldn't want to buy all the books, if Rawston's lot was as big as your aunt's, but he'd want to check every one of them thoroughly. I reckon he'd have no other option but to take Rawston into his confidence. Maybe they agreed some kind of split and searched through the books together, but found nothing. They're disappointed – until Rawston remembers that your aunt had been at the same auction and bought a part of the library, too. A whole other section.'

'So Kevin comes looking for them,' Flora finished for him. 'It's why he broke into my shop.' She thought a while, sipping her tea slowly. 'He could have been coming back from Worthing when he nearly ran me down.'

'The timing fits. It was that evening he visited the All's Well.'

'Why not simply come as a customer, as he did with Rawston? Try and broker a deal with me?'

Jack grimaced, his eyebrows shooting up. 'That would have happened? Somehow, I don't think so. I imagine he got the measure of Rawston pretty quickly. He was a bloke that Kevin could do a deal with. He could have asked around and realised you weren't going to be as easy. And maybe, by that stage, he reckoned he'd put in enough work to justify taking the whole of whatever treasure there was for himself.'

'How does Rawston fit in now?'

'He must have heard of Kevin's death – it's been in the local papers. He would have read how the chap died here in this shop and realised that Kevin had been going it alone. Maybe reneging on any agreement he had with Rawston. Our plump friend must have decided that it was his turn now to scour your aunt's books. As far as he was concerned, Kevin died from an unfortunate heart attack. That's the official line and there'd be nothing to suggest that Rawston should be wary, so why not pursue the search for himself?'

'It makes sense.' Flora emptied her cup. 'You're so annoying, Jack. You reason step by step and turn out to be right. Mostly.'

'We don't know that I am, and sometimes inspiration is more valuable than logic. It's simply the way my brain works. Don't forget I was a journalist. You put together facts after what can be painstaking weeks of research, and you make a story with them.'

'Do you miss it? Being a journalist?'

'It served a purpose,' he said laconically. 'Enabled me to be independent at a fairly young age.'

Flora wondered whether to broach what must be a difficult subject, and then decided to be brave. 'You said your parents had separated.'

Jack brushed the crumbs from his fingers. 'Divorced a good twenty years ago. But, yes, they separated when I was ten. I lived with my mother for a few years when I wasn't imprisoned in boarding school, then when I reached the dizzy age of fourteen, my father suddenly noticed me and invited me to move in with him during the holidays.'

'Did you?'

'He seemed marginally easier to live with. My mother either smothered me with kisses or screamed at me for looking too much like my father. It wasn't exactly a calm existence.'

'And living with your father was?'

'I wouldn't say calm, but it was interesting. Dad was always on the move. He made his living doing deals and either he had money flowing out of his pockets or he was having to do a moonlight flit.'

Flora tried not to look shocked, but didn't succeed.

'Most of the time he was very good at it, the deal-making,' Jack offered, as though in mitigation. 'I never spent a holiday in the same place. He was always on to the next opportunity – and the next woman. He was what I'd call louche. It got tiresome having to remember all their names. As soon as I landed my first job, I rented my own room. Dad gave me enough to see me through to my first pay cheque. I think he was glad to resume his old life and not have a surplus adolescent to consider.'

It explained a lot about Jack Carrington, she thought. He had wanted to build a home, never having known one. He'd tried to live a different life from either of his parents, carving out a respectable career, taking time before he married, only to have his dream broken apart by the woman he loved. No wonder he had taken cover.

'Where was your first job?' She was keen to know more.

'A local paper in a part of London where I'd once lived. *The North London Observer*. They took me on as a junior reporter. I was wet behind the ears, but it was a grand way to learn the job.'

'When you'd learned, did you stay?'

'You never truly learn. I was there for three years. Three years of attending court hearings, reporting on council meetings, following up petty crimes. Then I had a stroke of luck, not that I didn't like working for the *NLO*, but I was in my early twenties by then and keen to move on. By sheer good fortune, I hit the jackpot.'

Flora had started towards the cupboard to refresh the pot, but at this she turned, her face expectant.

'I wrote an exposé of a local gang. They'd started with small crimes but, by the time I was writing my article, they'd graduated to blackmail, protection, violent intimidation. My landlady's son was a friend of the gang leader's. It sounds unbelievable but this chap, the gang leader, led an outwardly respectable life, his wife belonging to the Mothers' Union, his son going to the local school like every other boy. Anyway, Terry knew him from school, they'd been classmates, and had stayed friends. My landlady couldn't have known what kind of company her son was keeping – Terry was the apple of her eye.'

'It was Terry who gave you information?'

'He did, without realising it. Information that, when written up in a suitably dramatic fashion, attracted the attention of a national newspaper and led to them offering me a job.'

'That must have felt like winning the football pools.'

'It did – for a few hours – but the day after I got the offer, I was called up, like a lot of young chaps.'

'The paper kept your job open, though? It was why you were in New York?' Flora brought fresh tea and refilled their cups.

'And Rome and Sydney before that. I became their senior crime reporter.'

'You've had more excitement in one day than I've had in my whole life.' She was wistful. 'Why didn't you stay with the paper? You could have asked for a different posting, rather than giving it all up for a woman who wasn't worth it.'

He grinned. 'You're a harsh judge, Flora. It wasn't only the business with Helen that led to my decision, though I suppose she was the catalyst. I loved my job but even jobs you love can pall. And it was beginning to. As a crime reporter, you see the worst of people and realise that justice is a blunt instrument. Innocent people get trampled on, the guilty can go free. I reckoned it would be good to turn the tables, if only in fiction, and when Helen humiliated me, I knew it was time to change my life completely. I'd been writing fiction in my spare time, no more than bits and pieces, but I'd had some good comments, published a story, won a competition or two. I decided to take the plunge and resigned there and then. I'd enjoyed a comfortable lifestyle, and if an author's life didn't work out, I had savings to live off. Though only until the big break arrived!'

'And that's how you ended up in Sussex.'

'If I was going to find an agent and a publisher, I needed to be reasonably near London, but I didn't want to live in the city. I had fond memories of Sussex – I think I told you – and it was on a day trip here that I found Overlay House. It was spacious, tucked away, and the rent was reasonable.'

'And near enough to London to find your agent?'

'Arthur Bellaby. He's sixty with the energy of someone forty years younger. I had a letter from him this morning. It was what held me up, in fact. He wants to meet tomorrow in London to discuss a new project.'

Flora was taken aback. If they uncovered anything this afternoon, Jack wouldn't be here for the next step, whatever it was. 'Tomorrow could be important,' she said. 'Do you have to go?'

'I think I do, even if it's to say no, though I'd much rather be staying. I'm not looking forward to the slow train from Worthing – but I do get lunch at the Ritz.'

'It must be quite some project,' she remarked drily. 'OK, if you're going absent without leave, we need to get on with this job. I'll be at Polly's party while you're away, and before I go to the Priory it would be good to know just what, if anything, is secreted in the books Aunt Violet bought.'

CHAPTER TWENTY-THREE

The shelving her aunt had chosen for the second-hand volumes she loved lay towards the rear of the building, at a point where the interior narrowed to little more than a passageway. Here, the shelves, instead of being angled as they were in the wider sections of the shop, had been crammed against one wall, to allow customers just enough space to view.

'We'll do this systematically,' Jack announced, arriving in front of the shelves. 'Strip each shelf one by one and we should end up with four separate stacks.'

Left to herself, she thought wryly, she would have pulled the books out in any order and then forgotten which ones she had looked at.

'Two piles for you, two for me,' he said. 'Once we've finished with a book, we'll put it back where it came from.'

Flora dropped to the floor and squatted cross-legged. 'Let's hope we won't have to trawl through every one of them.'

'Amen to that. You know what I think about missing manuscripts. If we find nothing, I'm hoping you'll give up the search.'

'Then all I'll be left with is a rogue typewriter, and you don't like that either.'

It was a wearisome task, the books heavier and dustier than Flora had expected. Her cleaning evidently wasn't up to her aunt's standards. The leather-bound volumes might have been fat, but their pages were thin, and a long time was spent trawling through each and every one of them.

By the time she was halfway through her first column of books, Flora was ready to give up. She desperately needed to find the person who had murdered Kevin Anderson and left her with a dying business, but she was losing heart. Perhaps she should trust to finding the damaged typewriter, either in Polly Dakers' room or Vernon Elliot's private office. And, who knows, she might strike lucky and uncover evidence that would point definitively to one or other of them having typed that note.

Reshelving a book she'd searched unsuccessfully, Flora hesitated before picking up the next, and thought about tomorrow's party. She was glad to be going. It would be an opportunity to chat with people who might know more than they'd previously admitted. It would provide cover, as well, for the clandestine activity she was planning.

Would Bernie Mitchell put in an appearance? He worked at the Priory, and Polly appeared to have invited everyone who had any connection with the place. Alice was convinced the man was lying drunk somewhere, but Flora wasn't at all sure. He had disappeared shortly after she'd seen him on Fern Hill. He couldn't have been drinking all that time, surely? If so, by now he'd be in a coma and lying in a hospital bed. Kate had seemed to accept Alice's view, but perhaps the poor woman was so worn, so sadly resigned to an unsupportive husband, that she was prepared to believe anything of him.

'Have you given up?' Jack asked. His pile, she saw, was considerably smaller than hers.

'Almost. It's very hard work, and I'm beginning to feel hungry again.'

'I'm nearly through my first column. I'll give you a hand when I'm done.'

She felt guilty. This wasn't the way anyone would choose to spend their afternoon, even with uninviting weather outside. Jack had work piling up, as well. Tomorrow he was meeting his agent, who would almost certainly want to know when he could expect the next book, a book that Jack had neglected to help her. He didn't even believe in the legend or in the missing manuscript or indeed in a malfunctioning typewriter. It was all down to her and, dejectedly, she wondered why she'd been so certain it was the answer to her problem.

Would it really make much difference to her business if she could prove Anderson had been murdered here? She straightened her aching shoulders. It had to. She was managing now to attract a small trickle of people to the shop, but they were mostly customers from beyond Abbeymead. It was the village that the All's Well depended on for the bulk of its trade, the village that Aunt Violet had assiduously courted as she'd built her business. And it was orders from Abbeymead that had dried up. Alice's friend, who worked in Steyning, had let slip that the bookshop there was doing particularly well, far better than they were accustomed to. Flora had to believe that this search would make a difference.

While she'd been daydreaming, Jack had cleared an entire stack, putting the last of the volumes back on the shelf. He reached over for one of hers, dislodging a much smaller book that she hadn't noticed before. A book that over the years would have been carried by many of the inhabitants of the Priory. She felt goose bumps rising.

'This one,' she said. 'Let's try this one. It's a Book of Hours. It must have got into my aunt's purchases by mistake.'

Jack looked across at the volume she was holding. 'A Book of Hours? I agree, it would be too precious to sell – one of the most coveted items a literate person could own. When life was regulated by religion, it would have been vital to own a collection of biblical texts and prayers to read throughout the day.'

'And a perfect hiding place for the manuscript! This could have been Lady Ianthe's own – the book looks very old – something she would have kept close to her.'

'Is that a coat of arms?'

Flora bent her head, looking down at the beautifully tooled cover and stroking its rich surface. 'It could be, though the symbol is very worn.' Carefully, she peeled back the first page to reveal a vivid illustration. 'It's quite lovely – masses of gold and silver, and lapis blue. It must have cost a fortune to produce.'

'So, a prized possession. No doubt handed down through generations.'

'Certainly, in a Catholic family like the Templetons,' Flora agreed. 'I think prayer books and family bibles superseded Books of Hours for Protestants. Shall I keep turning?'

'There's doesn't seem a lot to turn.' Jack leaned over to look more closely.

'They're usually in three sections, the church's feast days first, then passages from the gospels, then prayers and psalms.'

She began slowly to turn the wonderfully illustrated pages, through the calendar of feast days and saints days, marked in rich, gold lettering, and on to the second portion of the book. It was as she was moving between a passage from the Gospel by Matthew to one by John, that she stopped. She sat back on her heels, numbed, her breath caught in her throat and her stomach somersaulting.

'It's here,' she said in a strangled voice. Her fingers wrapped themselves around a folded sheet of parchment. 'It's actually here!'

Unfolding the paper, she spread it flat, seeing a page filled with the strong black strokes of a quill pen. Her breath did stop then, at least for a second.

'My God, you're right,' Jack murmured, huddling up closer to read. Together, they peered down at the close-written lines. 'Can you make the words out?'

'We need a torch,' she decided. Jumping up, she hurried back to her desk at the front of the shop. The bottom drawer held the torch that Violet always kept for emergencies.

Beneath the brighter light, Flora could just begin to make out the curls and loops of Tudor writing. 'Shall I read it?'

'You'd better. I'm still too stunned to speak.'

My Gracious Lady,

I write in haste. My friend and brother in God, Francis, has brought news of a ship that leaves for France tonight, whereby I may secure a passage. It gives me much sadness to leave my country but there is no safety for me here.

Many dangers lie ahead of me, My Lady, and I dare not take with me that which you entrusted to me. Fear not, I have buried it well close by and leave this letter in your most precious volume, which I hope will find its way to you wherever you may be.

Root out the devil, My Lady, and find sorrow and wisdom between.

Your servant in God
Anselm

Flora let her breath go. 'The legend *wasn't* rubbish. The priest *did* hide Lady Ianthe's treasure before he escaped to France and this is his message to her.'

Jack got to his feet, stretching his arms to the ceiling. For a few minutes, he paced up and down the narrow space, while Flora watched him uneasily.

'It's a wonderful find,' he said at last. 'But where does it actually get us? If this Anselm buried Lady Ianthe's jewellery on the estate – and I guess we can assume the rest of the legend is correct – it could be anywhere in the Priory grounds. There's no X marking the spot, is there? That's an awful lot of grass to dig up. And you'd have to, more or less, if you want to prove to the police there was treasure and that Anderson was killed for it.'

'Anselm must have left a clue for Lady Ianthe to follow. He had to have, or there would be no point in his writing.' Flora picked up the parchment again and read silently through it.

'So where is the clue?'

'There's only one part of the letter that's unclear and that must be it. What did he mean by finding sorrow and wisdom?'

'What did he mean by rooting out the devil? Anselm, old chap, you talk in riddles.'

'To us, maybe, but it would have to mean something to Lady Ianthe. Lead her to discovering the hiding place. But how?'

Jack shook his head. 'You've done brilliantly, but I reckon this is the end of the trail.'

She scrambled to her feet to stand beside him, her mouth stiff with annoyance.

'Why are you always such a naysayer? It isn't the end,' she said stoutly. 'It could be just the beginning. We need to find what Anselm was referring to.'

Jack took a while before he responded. 'How do you propose to do that?' She heard the deliberate calm in his voice. 'It's time to admit it's a dead duck, Flora – why pursue it any further? How is it going to get more customers through your door?'

'I don't know if it will,' she said honestly, 'but I do know that something wicked has been going on in Abbeymead and I need to expose it. I'm surprised you don't feel the same. The triumph of good, the defeat of evil – isn't that what your books are all about?'

'Yes, but—'

'How is there a "but"?'

'Look, I understand the commitment you feel, but it's become impossible. We looked for a document, we found it, and though it's fascinating and historically hugely interesting, it doesn't get us any closer to where we need to be.' The grey eyes fixed her in a steady look, willing her to agree.

'It will if I can work out what Anselm meant,' Flora said defiantly. 'And it won't require me to dig up acres of grass!'

'I'll take your word for it.' Jack sounded cynical. 'Where do you propose to start this monumental search?'

'It's obvious. The Priory library.'

He stared at her. 'Kevin would have searched all the books that are still there.'

'He didn't have the benefit of this letter, did he? He was unsuccessful, but I won't be.'

'You expect to find… what, exactly?' She could tell he was humouring her.

'I've no idea. Something that has to do with the devil and sorrow and wisdom.'

'Quite a tall order. You intend to go through every book in the library on the off chance that those words have some kind of meaning? Always providing you can get access to the room. Come on, Flora, be realistic.'

'I can get access. I'm going to the Priory tomorrow. I can easily slip away from the party.' She bent down and ran a finger along the spines of the books they had reshelved. 'You know,' she said suddenly, a flash of inspiration emerging through the murk. 'I don't think I'll have to look far after all.'

'You've had one of your hunches?'

'Not just a hunch, but a crushing, mind-boggling revelation.' She clasped both his hands and danced him around in a circle.

'Whoa! Tell me,' he said, laughing.

'Anselm mentions rooting out the devil. Have you noticed the titles of the books we've been looking at?'

Jack frowned. 'I've been too busy turning pages.'

'Look now,' she urged. 'Most of them are books on witches. Aunt Violet bid for this particular lot because she loved really old books *and* was fascinated by witchcraft.'

Flora bent down to the bookshelf and selected one of the thinnest volumes. 'This one is *The Discovery of Witches* by Matthew Hopkins. He was known as the Witchfinder General – that was his grim profession.' She turned to the title page and read aloud.

The discovery of witches: in answer to severall Queries, lately delivered to the Judges of Assize for the County of Norfolk. And now published by Matthew Hopkins Witch-finder, for the benefit of the whole kingdome.

Jack bent to flick through several more title pages, and when he spoke, he sounded sceptical. 'These books were published in the seventeenth century. Much later than the period we're interested in.'

'Witchcraft was a big topic then.'

'So a past Lord Templeton was into witches. Why is that important?' Jack's hands made a furrow through his thick hair. 'I don't see where this is leading.'

'Why was this Lord Templeton into witches, though? It could be that it was a burning topic of conversation in Sussex at the time or… something closer to home. A book he found on his library shelves that prompted his interest. I've remembered what Aunt Violet once told me. The Priory library holds a copy of the *Malleus Maleficarum*. There are several still in existence – one is in the British Library. It's the earliest treatise on witchcraft. I don't think the Priory copy was one of the first to be printed. If it were, it would be too valuable to leave on the shelves unguarded, but it is old and it's perfectly possible that it was there in Anselm's time.

Our monk could have read it and chosen it as a resting place for his final clue.'

'That's pretty tenuous.'

'I don't think so. The *Maleficarum* would be a book that a Catholic priest would be sure to read. The Pope had already acknowledged a belief in witchcraft and sent inquisitors to Germany to prosecute so-called witches. This book, *Malleus Maleficarum*, helped popularise the belief that witchcraft was heresy, a crime against God. A priest would need to arm himself against such terrors. Anselm could have been reading it as he planned his escape and slipped whatever clue he'd come up with between its pages. Lady Ianthe would be familiar with the book. She and the priest may have discussed its contents together. Rooting out the devil? She would know where to look.'

'It's not just a long shot. It's out of sight.'

'Maybe, but you're the one who said inspiration can sometimes be more valuable than logic.'

'If this book is the archetypal treatise on witchcraft, why isn't it here among the books your aunt bought?'

'To be honest, I've no idea. When Lord Templeton died, his solicitors chose the books they thought would make the most money, along with the best paintings and the best pieces of furniture. Whoever put the lots together may have thought the *Maleficarum* was too scruffy to sell, not realising its importance. I've seen it and it was shabby. Or it simply got left behind by accident, in the same way as the Book of Hours was included in Violet's haul.'

'Or it may no longer be in the Priory library.'

'That's true,' Flora said calmly. 'But until I look, I won't know.'

Jack silently replaced the remaining volumes on the empty shelves. For a long time, he didn't speak. Finally, he said, 'I still have to go up to London tomorrow.'

Flora pulled a small face. 'You don't sound too enamoured.'

'I'm not, particularly at this moment, when I should be keeping an eye on you. At least I'll be back by early evening. Go to Polly's party, but go there to have fun. No gatecrashing the library for this book. Or darting in and out of offices on the hunt for a faulty typewriter.'

Flora felt ruffled. He was laying down the law to her but dipping out of the investigation himself, and at the most crucial time.

'If you weren't haring off to London, you could have come with me to the party and we could have worked together. We're so nearly there.'

'When I get back, we'll talk about it. Find some other way to get into the library. I'll even ask for a guided tour of the hotel under the pretext of booking a conference, while you do your worst. Until then, promise me you won't do anything stupid, Flora.'

CHAPTER TWENTY-FOUR

Flora dressed for the party with care. Smart but unobtrusive, she thought, choosing a light wool dress that had been Violet's last birthday present to her. They had bought it in Hill's department store on a special shopping trip to Hove. Violet had been too weak to travel by bus, so they had raided the All's Well's till and booked a taxi there and back. They'd stayed on for lunch in Hill's restaurant, an even bigger treat. It had been a wonderful day, the last time Violet had ventured out of Abbeymead, and because of that the dress was particularly dear to Flora.

She checked her reflection in the mirror. Her aunt had been right about the colour – the deep green set off her reddish-brown hair to perfection, its A-line skirt skimming slim hips and pooling just below the knee. What could be more fashionable? Shoes were more of a problem. It was years since Flora had bought anything that could take her to a party and she was reduced to fishing a pair of strappy heels from deep in her wardrobe, a memento of carefree evenings spent at college hops. She prayed it wouldn't rain before she reached the Priory.

Polly's invitation had been vague, but Flora had learned from Alice that the party would begin at four that afternoon. Elliot apparently had agreed time off for the staff until their evening shifts. Waiters and chambermaids would return to work, but Alice would be free to go.

'I should think so, too,' she'd said to Flora, when she'd called at the cottage earlier in the week. 'By then, I'll have done a restaurant lunch, started the evening meal and prepared all the food for Polly's party, with only that lummock of a girl, Ivy, to help. And it hasn't been easy, mind you. Polly's been so finicky over the food – she's really pushed the boat out. The chap who's sponsoring her is paying for it all, or so she says. He's a mystery man, but he must have loads of money.'

The Priory grounds were a little shabbier than the last time Flora had walked up the gravel drive, the contract gardeners no doubt being between visits and Bernie Mitchell still officially missing. She'd asked Alice when she'd called whether any attempt had been made to look for him. Flora had heard nothing herself and it seemed the village in general had taken Alice's view that he was on some drunken binge and would return when he felt like it.

'Kate's filed a report at the police station,' Alice had said, 'though to my mind she'd be better off leavin' him missin'. Anyways, the police don't seem too bothered. They think he'll come back when he's run out of money, and so do I. Bad pennies always do.'

If the grounds were not looking their best, the entrance to the old house made up for them. The carved stonework of the square tower was garlanded with streamers and, looking up, Flora saw that each of the windows of the tower had been hung with similarly bright decorations. It was a wonder that no one had climbed onto the roof and hung baubles from the tall Elizabethan chimneys. She walked past the stone pillars into the large square hall that now functioned as the foyer of the hotel. Every wall had been covered in balloons, with bunches of what looked like glitter stuck at intervals along the wood panels. The cleaners would not be too happy with that. Hopefully, Polly had thought to invite them to her party.

A massive trestle table had been set up on one side of the room, the disapproving face of a long-dead Templeton glowering down at it from the panelled wall. Alice hadn't exaggerated when she'd spoken of the food. If the table had had a voice, it would have groaned from the weight, and several of the young men Flora recognised as waiters from the restaurant were already munching their way from one end of the trestle to the other. A few of their fellows carried trays of glasses filled with straw-coloured liquid.

Flora obediently took the glass that was offered. 'Champagne,' Polly announced, bouncing up to her. 'Only the best for me from now on! I'm glad you could come, Flora.' The words were said warmly, the girl sounding as though she meant them.

'It's good to see you looking so happy,' Flora responded.

'Why wouldn't I be?' Polly gave one of her sudden loud laughs. 'My dream's coming true – at last. I'm sharing it with friends, people who've wished me well. Though I had to invite the old misery,' she whispered in Flora's ear, 'or he'd never have let me use the hotel.'

Flora looked across the crowded space and saw a small knot of people, dressed in their finest, gathered beneath a picture of Edward Templeton as a young man. The tall, thin figure of Vernon Elliot stood out from the group, like a weed that had grown too tall to hide in the herbaceous border.

'Hopefully, he won't stick around too long,' Polly said. 'Then we can have fun. Plenty of people here who like a real party.'

Plenty of young people, Polly could have said. She had invited a number of mature souls – her mother, Alice, a group of villagers with whom her mother was particularly friendly and, of course, Uncle Ted. Otherwise, the company was made up of Polly's friends from the village and the youngest members of staff at the Priory. Of the secret sponsor, there was no sign. Pity, Flora thought. She would liked to have seen just what kind of future Polly was stepping into.

'My, you look lovely.' Alice had quietly joined them and was looking Flora up and down, her eyes bright with appreciation.

Flora saw Polly's lips begin to form themselves into a pout. The girl evidently didn't enjoy hearing praise for someone she considered hopelessly unfashionable, but her expression brightened when one of the more dashing waiters switched on a record player that had sat unnoticed on one of the hall's oak coffers.

Bill Haley's 'Rock Around the Clock' reverberated through the space, startling the older guests, but bringing smiles to younger faces. The waiter swooped down on Polly and began an energetic dance with her around the edge of the room, both of them laughing uproariously.

'I saw Kate this morning,' Alice said quietly. 'I wanted her to know where I'd be – she's so alone, poor lamb – and she couldn't face this party, though Polly invited her. She's at the café, trying to keep herself busy.'

'I'm not surprised Kate had no wish to come,' Flora responded. 'It looks as though it could get rowdy.'

As if hearing Flora's words, Vernon Elliot lifted his glass in the air, banging it with a teaspoon until he got the attention of the gathering. It took several minutes.

'I would like to propose a toast,' he began portentously. 'To Miss Polly Dakers who has been a valued member of staff at the Priory these last two—'

'Three,' Polly put in.

'—these last three years.' He glowered across the room at her, then remembered he should smile. 'Polly,' he continued, in a reedy voice, 'may be leaving us today, but I'm sure we'll be hearing from her in the future.'

I'm sure we will, Flora thought.

'Let us now raise our glasses to Miss Dakers, to Polly, and wish her well in her new life.'

There was a ringing declaration of 'To Polly' and a general murmur of good luck, followed by a good deal of swooshing down of champagne. While several of the older guests began to make their excuses, the waiters busily refilled the glasses of those who remained. It would become rowdy, Flora judged, but that was all to the good. The noise and distraction would provide extra cover for what she'd come to do.

Alice had stayed by her side and now nudged her towards the overflowing trestle table. 'You should try one of these,' she said, pointing to a plate of round golden whirls decorated with strips of icing. 'Lavender and lemon cakes. I'd never made them before, but I reckon they've come off really well.'

Flora had just taken her first bite when her companion was called to one side by a young boy. Was that Charlie Teague recovered from the mumps? It was, and he was once more playing messenger.

When Alice returned, she was white-faced. 'I'll have to go, Flora. Kate can't be on her own.'

'Whatever's happened? Why was Charlie here?'

'The police have been round to the Nook. They've found Bernie Mitchell. Leastways, they've found his clothes. A pile of them on Littlehampton beach. A dog walker said he noticed them there two days ago. Thought someone had gone swimming but then when he walked the same way today, the clothes were still there and he got worried.'

'And Mitchell?'

Alice shook her head. 'Not a sign. I asked Charlie. He was with Kate when the police called – she's a soft spot for him, always giving him an iced bun or custard tart. He heard Constable Tring say they were keeping an open mind, but that it looked like suicide, though there was no note. But there wouldn't be with Mitchell. He'd not have the thought to say sorry to the woman who loves him.'

Even in death, Alice couldn't forgive the man. 'It's possible,' Flora said, 'that he went for a swim, as the dog walker thought, and then got into difficulties.'

Alice gave a little shrug. 'Perhaps. Makes no difference. The man's gone and that lass is breakin' her heart, I'll make no doubt. After losin' her father, too – it's too much for the girl to bear.'

'I'll come by shortly,' Flora called after her companion's disappearing back. 'I'll call at the Nook on my way home.'

Alice hadn't lowered her voice and Flora was aware that several people close to them had stopped their conversation and been listening intently. Before her friend had collected her handbag and was halfway to the entrance, the murmuring began. At first it was quiet, whispering sibilants, but becoming louder and more confident as the story expanded to fill people's expectations.

For a while, Flora stood where Alice had left her, trying to make sense of this new drama. She had last seen Mitchell on Fern Hill, changing a punctured tyre and, to all intents and purposes, working his way through a normal day. Where had he gone from there and when had he returned the van to Katie's Nook? Alice had been clear that Mitchell hadn't been driving when he left. If so, how had the man got to Littlehampton beach? From Abbeymead, there was no direct route, and would anyone contemplating suicide wait around for a series of buses?

In any case, why suicide? Flora cast her mind over the times she'd seen Mitchell in the last few weeks, looking for any clue that might explain his behaviour. There had been that odd moment, she recalled, just after Cyril died. She and Jack had been walking down the Priory drive, having been more or less ordered off the premises by Elliot, when Mitchell had driven past them at a crazy speed, almost scraping the estate gates as he shot through.

Something had gone badly wrong for the man, that was clear, and his death was unlikely to be an accident, even though she'd suggested as much to Alice. Flora couldn't imagine anyone stripping off at the end of October and plunging into the English Channel for a leisurely swim. No, suicide was a far more sensible explanation, yet the question remained of why and why now? What had happened to make Mitchell determined to die? Or… maybe to fake his death and assume a new identity. That was always a possibility. Flora had heard of desperate men, and it was usually men, who had done just that.

Perhaps his gambling debts had become more than he could face. Or he'd acted out of guilt. If Mitchell had been involved in the murder of Kevin Anderson and the death of his father-in-law, it wouldn't be surprising that he'd taken his own life, or decided to disappear for ever. Or – Flora felt her heart beat a little faster – could it be another case of murder? Had the real killer seen Mitchell as a danger and disposed of him?

She felt overwhelmed by the questions, far too many questions. Right now, she was at the Priory for a purpose, and the message Charlie Teague had brought had made her job that little bit easier. She looked around. Every guest was talking, huddled together in groups, gossiping avidly. The music played on – The Platters' 'Only You' had replaced Bill Haley – but no one was taking any notice. This was a piece of news that wouldn't die easily.

It was time to make her move.

CHAPTER TWENTY-FIVE

Flora had set herself two tasks, to her mind each dependent on the other. They were two sides to the biggest question of them all: what was hidden and who had killed for it? She had Anselm's letter in her possession now, but the monk's instructions lay somewhere in the Priory library. If she could unravel their mystery, they would lead her to what had been hidden, what had provided the motive for killing. It wasn't simply motive she needed, though. She must find the murderer, or at least narrow down the likely suspects, and that was where the errant typewriter would play its part. Jack might dismiss her search as pointless, but she was convinced it was utterly right. The machine had been used to type an order for Flowers for You, leading to a bouquet that had signalled death.

She was standing a few feet from the reception desk, Polly's erstwhile home and, giving a quick glance around the foyer at the groups of chattering people, she edged backwards until she felt its hard wood behind her. It took only a slight shuffle to the right to whisk herself behind the desk and disappear into the office beyond. It was a much smaller room than Flora had anticipated, made even smaller by the litter of paper: a tall column of brochures and one of advertising leaflets, a stack of invoices, and ledgers piled so high they were in imminent danger of crashing to the floor. Polly, it seemed, had made no attempt to tidy the space. As far as the girl was concerned, she had worked her last hour at the Priory and someone else could pick up the mess.

It wouldn't be Bernard Mitchell, Flora mused, though he could easily have worked here. Could have used this very typewriter, sitting square on the old mahogany desk. Polly was no longer a suspect, but with Mitchell's disappearance, his role as a typist had assumed a new importance. Bending down, she opened the top drawer of the desk, searching for a sheet of spare paper. A collection of dead make-up and blunt pencils was her reward. The next drawer down had packets of chewing gum and a few tattered envelopes. It was only when she reached the final drawer that she struck lucky. An opened packet of typing paper sat beneath a scattering of cardboard files that looked as though it might constitute Polly's filing system.

Quickly, Flora inserted the paper into the roller and hit the letter "s". It came out perfectly formed. She made another attempt and found exactly the same. Then she tried with the shift key down. However she typed, the letter was never less than perfect. Tearing the sheet from the typewriter, she balled it up and threw it into the overflowing wastebasket. She would have to search further afield and that meant Elliot's own office.

Flora slid unnoticed around the reception desk and back into the party, still in full swing. Vernon Elliot, she saw, was by the huge stone fireplace, engaged with several of the village worthies, men who had influence in the district. Elliot had his head bent, as though trying to savour every one of his companions' words. Flora wasn't fooled. His was a false attention, good public relations, that was all, but it served her purpose in keeping him engaged.

Alice had said that Elliot's private office led off from the library. Having spent many happy hours in that magnificent room, when Lord Templeton had kept open house, Flora could have found her way there blindfolded. She would search first for the *Malleus Maleficarum*, she decided, and then move to the office to test the only other typewriter in the building. Hopefully, her search would prove swift and she would be back at the party within minutes.

Drink in hand, she weaved in and out of several small groups of people, a nod here and there, a smiling triviality on her lips, until she was close to the corridor that led to the library. In a few steps, she had ditched her glass and was walking swiftly towards her goal. No one had noticed her leave, she was certain. The news of Mitchell's likely death, while devastating for Kate, had kept people distracted and talking.

Flora had always loved the library. It was her favourite room in the whole of the Priory. Unhooking the rope that now guarded the room, she walked through its double doors. As always, it was a revelation of light, the high carved ceiling patterned a luminous green and cream and one entire wall taken up by a series of tall, arched windows. The shelving was dark – mahogany – but set within arches of white plaster, the higher shelves holding marble busts of an array of pompous-looking gentleman. She had once asked Lord Templeton who they were, thinking they must be his ancestors. He'd shaken his head. *No idea, Flora*, he'd said. *They're probably the spoils of an early Templeton's misspent youth, while he was on the Grand Tour.* A carved mahogany fireplace, a satinwood desk and Chesterfield wing-back chairs completed the room's tranquil beauty. She was relieved that Elliot's fell hand had not fallen on this wonderful room.

For a while, she stood motionless on the threshold, allowing its peace to wash over her. Then an overpowering urge took hold and she almost ran across the Persian carpet, past the thinly populated shelves that had once housed books sold at auction, to those lining the far wall. Flora knew exactly where she must look, grabbing the wooden library steps and trundling them to the section closest to the line of windows. This was where the books on witchcraft had always been kept. If the *Maleficarum* was still in the library, it would be here or hereabouts.

With so many volumes sold, the remaining books had been given a good deal more space, but a quick glance showed her they were a motley collection. She would need to work her way systematically through the section, from left to right, top to bottom, to find the one she needed.

The calm November day was coming to an end, its mellow light filtering through the window, splashing itself across the first few shelves. Running her finger along the spine of each book, she still had to bend close to make out every title. Many volumes were part of a series, identical in shape and colour, and these she could speed across, but for the most part it was a painstaking task. Halfway down the section, and close to a window, she found what she was after. The *Malleus Maleficarum* was still here! As she'd told Jack, it was by far the oldest book in the library, its leather cover roughened, the gold lettering faded, and the edges of its pages crinkled and occasionally torn.

Very carefully, she pulled the volume from its resting place and, scurrying down the library steps, took it to the window seat. One by one, she turned the pages, but had advanced only a little way before she felt the weight of the paper change. A rising excitement had her turn the page very, very, slowly and there it was! A narrow strip of parchment, seemingly at some point used as a bookmark. Extracting it with the utmost care, she put the *Malleus Maleficarum* to one side and laid the parchment onto the cushioned seat. The strip bore faded brown marks along its entire length, and as she looked more closely, she could see they were images that had been drawn in ink. Holding the sliver of paper to the light, she screwed up her eyes, trying to make out the outline of the first drawing. It appeared to be a statue. Puzzled, Flora concentrated on the next image. That seemed to be nothing more than a cross. The final picture was clearer – a tree.

She sat back, bewildered and deeply disappointed. Surely there had to be more. Yet this slip of parchment must mean something. Anselm had hidden the precious object entrusted to him, then left clues for his lady to follow. Delving into her handbag, Flora brought out the priest's letter, her eyes fixing on the strange line that neither she nor Jack had fathomed.

Root out the devil, My Lady, and find sorrow and wisdom between.

Flora had rooted out the devil, that was the *Maleficarum*, but sorrow and wisdom? Her gaze went back to the strip of parchment, alighting on the image of the statue. Wisdom? She looked again. It was the statue of Minerva, she thought, the goddess of wisdom, a statue that she'd often sat beneath in the Priory grounds. But the tree? There were an awful lot of trees on the estate. Was this one in any way special? A tree that meant sorrow. She'd read something. What had she read? Desperately raking her mind, it suddenly came. She jumped up, her arms almost punching the air. The dule tree, a tree *of lamentation or grief*, she'd read, once used as a gallows for public hangings. And between those two images, a large cross. She had done it! She had found the treasure's resting place. X did indeed mark the spot.

She smiled as she recalled Jack's words. He should be here right now, sitting by her side, enjoying their triumph. Battling a wave of guilt, she told herself that her visit today had been too good an opportunity to let slip. Jack should have delayed the meeting with his agent. It would have taken only a telephone call. He couldn't blame her for stealing a march on him, though he probably would.

She stayed for a while, curled up on the window seat, the light gradually fading, as she absorbed what had happened. She had actually found what Kevin Anderson had searched for. Maybe what Mitchell had searched for. Certainly what those writers of legend had believed existed. She picked up the strip of parchment, placing it gently within the folds of Anselm's letter, and slipped them both into her handbag. She must take the documents to the police, explain their importance, persuade them to dig where Anselm had directed. They would see then what had been at stake, why Anderson had broken into her shop and why he'd died before he could reach the book he sought.

The police would remain sceptical, Flora knew, which was why she needed a name, a name that would finally convince them that this was a murder case. The name of the killer. There was one last job to do, and for the first time she looked properly around her. She had been so focused on finding the *Maleficarum* that she'd barely looked at the library itself. Glancing towards the entrance, she saw now that an unobtrusive door had been cut into the wall just to the left, between two of the bookshelves. The space beyond must always have been there, but Elliot had accessed it with this new door. His private office was where she must go next.

After the beauty of the library, the room was a disappointment. With no natural light and only a small desk lamp to provide illumination, the gloom was depressing. Did Vernon Elliot really work here? There was a desk, certainly, an office chair and one of the wing-back Chesterfields from the library, presumably for any guest he might entertain. A small table stood in the corner, but was bare except for the stunted green of a plant only half alive. No wonder, she thought. How could any living thing thrive in this murk? There was a modern bookcase to her right and another older set of shelves on the wall adjacent to it. Neither, she imagined, would hold anything interesting.

The older bookcase, though, looked as if it had once belonged to the library. That seemed strange until enlightenment dawned. Of course, this space had once been a part of that magnificent room. She remembered now – why hadn't she before? There had been a square enclave at one end. Lord Templeton had liked to retire there, to read when his eyes grew tired of the bright light in the rest of the library. Elliot had hived this enclave off with a false partition and a door. It was an odd thing to do, but she wasn't here to ponder Vernon Elliot's foibles. She was here to find a typewriter.

Flora had taken the precaution of slipping a second sheet of typing paper into her handbag before she'd left Polly's office, but now she looked around the dimly lit space in vain. A rubber mat sat in the centre of the desk, seeming as though it should house a machine, but there was no sign of one. It made no sense. There must be a typewriter. Alice had been certain there was one here. Kate Mitchell had said as much, sounding proud that her husband typed Elliot's personal correspondence in his private office.

Flora walked over to the bookcase that had once belonged to the library. It was unlikely she would find a machine hidden among the row of business tomes, but if she viewed the room from this angle, she might work out just where Elliot chose to keep it. She leaned back to take stock, but her new position made no difference. It was hopeless. The typewriter must have been taken away for repair, it was the only explanation. To have come so far and be beaten at the very end! Dejected, she'd begun to move away when her foot found the curled edge of a rug and, tripping, she fell heavily backwards against the bookcase. She grabbed at a shelf to steady herself and her hand touched metal.

There was a loud click in her ear and suddenly, she felt herself falling further. The shelving behind her head began to move, swinging inwards so that she was catapulted into a dark space. A shard of light filtered through from the desk lamp beyond, but otherwise it was pure darkness and she could barely make anything out. Not that there was much to make out. Except in one corner, crouched in the gloom, was an upturned box and on top of the box sat a typewriter.

Flora's mind was skittering. What was this space and how had a typewriter found its way here? It had to have been deliberately hidden. Hidden because it provided a clue to where the florist's note had been typed and therefore a clue as to who'd typed it? That must be it. Pulling the spare sheet of typing paper from her handbag, she attempted to wind it into the machine, but her hands were trembling so much that the paper crackled and scratched against the roller, ending up at a lopsided angle. It didn't matter. Nothing mattered, but to try the keyboard. She struck the letter 's' and was immediately rewarded – it was missing the top curve! This *was* the machine. This was where that note had originated. But who had typed it? 'Mitchell, or Elliot himself?' she asked aloud.

'Elliot, Miss Steele,' came a voice from the doorway.

CHAPTER TWENTY-SIX

She spun round from the machine to see Vernon Elliot walking towards her. He came to a halt a few feet from where she stood, casting the secret room into complete darkness by blocking any light from the office beyond. Silhouetted in the entrance, his tall, stringy figure assumed a menace that Flora had never felt before.

'Mitchell?' he queried, his voice rising in incredulity. 'You surely can't think that clown would ever have contrived a florist's bouquet? The man was good enough for the common or garden stuff but—'

'Common or garden as in growing poisonous flowers?' Flora interrupted, finding her voice and trying not to let it waver.

'Exactly. I never rated him as a gardener. Leaf clearing was about his mark, but anything needing a careful touch, no. Still, he managed to keep the water hemlock alive for long enough and burnt it when its job was done. That's all I needed from him. You can buy plants from abroad, you know,' he said in a conversational tone, 'get them sent through the post, and no questions asked. I made sure to order from Holland. There'll be no trace, every scrap of paperwork destroyed weeks ago.'

'You ordered the plant?' Flora was mystified, even as she felt fear creeping closer. Had Elliot schemed to murder even before Kevin Anderson showed his face?

'Timing was of the essence,' Elliot said, as though anticipating her question. 'It turns out that buying plants from abroad is an unusually swift process. Everything comes down to careful planning, Miss Steele. Preparation and planning. It's what separates the clever from the dolts of the world. Dolts like Mitchell. He would never have devised such a strategy in a thousand years.'

'So why did you?'

It was a pertinent question. Elliot owned a prestigious hotel and clearly hoped to make it a financial success. Murdering his guests hardly seemed the way to do it.

'I had to – as soon as I knew why Anderson had come here. It was obvious there had to be a reason for his visit. You don't travel all the way from Australia to stay in a Sussex village without good cause. I didn't believe all that guff about wanting to see the house his uncle had inherited. I knew there would be something else and, once I found out why he was here, I had to get rid of him.'

Flora stared at the man confronting her, barely able to take in what was happening. Was this the same person who had welcomed her to the opening of the Priory, the same person who had greeted her today with the hope that she would enjoy Polly's party?

'How did you find out why Kevin was here? By encouraging him to drink with you?' She couldn't believe she was actually saying these words.

'So you heard about that? Miss empty-headed Dakers, no doubt. Thank the Lord, I'm rid of her at least. One less blabbermouth. Kevin liked a drink – I believe Australians are partial to beer, but Kevin was much more of a whisky man. He became quite loquacious when he'd had a few. Enough for me to realise that what appeared a ludicrous mission was, in fact, quite serious. I hadn't heard the legend myself – I'm not a native of these parts – and if I had, I doubt I'd have taken much notice. When Anderson first told me the story, I thought it was a joke, but the more he talked, the more I was persuaded that he was actually on to something.'

'Kevin seems to have done a great deal of talking.'

'He never stopped asking questions, which was suspicious in itself. The story he'd got from his uncle had been vague – Reggie Anderson had heard it as a child – but Kevin set about discovering details. And he did it well, I'll give him that. Learned about the Templeton family in Tudor times, how they had been persecuted and died. He even managed to trace the priest they'd employed. With what he discovered, I could see it was just the kind of thing that could have happened in troubled times. After he went to see that rascally bookseller in Worthing, I was convinced there was something to be had from it.'

'So you decided to use what Kevin had found for yourself? You decided to kill him?'

'I don't think the poor chap suffered – at least not much. And so easy, you wouldn't believe. Miss Horrocks arranged the florist's bouquet in his room, and all I had to do was add a couple of stems of water hemlock. Deadly stuff. I had to borrow Mitchell's gloves and mask. Of course, Kevin wouldn't have had that protection.'

'He could have disappointed you. He might not have touched the flowers.'

Flora heard herself sounding normal in what was an insane situation. How could she? This wasn't just a very bad dream; it was as though she had stumbled into another life.

'That was the beauty of the plant I chose. You don't have to touch it to be affected. It's sufficient merely to breathe close to it. The pollen isn't quite so toxic, but it gets everywhere, particularly when the blooms are almost finished. I had to be careful not to poison my staff, or there would have been questions. The flowers were whisked away as soon as Kevin went out for his drive in the Aston Martin. I was glad the poor chap enjoyed at least some of his birthday, though I did have a few qualms. He could have collapsed at the wheel and that was an awful lot of motor car to risk. But I calculated that he was young and fit and it would take some hours before the poison took hold.'

She had to escape, get past this dreadful man blocking her from the light. Even with his meagre frame, Elliot filled the entrance almost completely, and in any tussle he would be much the stronger. Her only means of flight was to lull him into thinking that she was no threat, that she meant him no harm, and when his guard was down, make a dash for it. It would be difficult – he'd caught her with the typewriter, trying to prove he was a murderer, but perhaps if she could distract him sufficiently, she could rush at him, hurl herself at his horrible scrawny body and break free.

'You made a sensible calculation,' she said, thinking flattery had to work since she had no other resource. 'It was some hours before Kevin died. But Cyril Knight? Was that a clever move, too?'

'Entirely his own fault, my dear. If he hadn't come nosing where he shouldn't, he would never have died. I can't say I was sorry to see him go. Cantankerous old man. Always complaining about the way he'd been treated. That was nothing to the way *I* was treated by that crooked uncle of Anderson's, selling me this place under false pretences. Ruining my life.'

Flora stared at him, not understanding. 'The sale must have been above board. Reggie Anderson inherited, the solicitors said so. The Priory was his to sell.'

'False pretences,' Elliot repeated. 'I had to borrow heavily to buy the place, couldn't afford a surveyor, then found out just what a pig in a poke the man had landed me with. Half the roof falling in, a hot water system that didn't work, rising damp in every ground-floor room. The list is endless. Anderson knew about the defects – his legal team would have told him – but he deliberately played dumb, hiding away in Australia. It's meant more money, more borrowing. I don't have a hope in hell of paying any of it back. Whatever is buried in the Priory grounds is mine. I need it. Why should I buy a useless house and not gain from its gardens? To think that crook's nephew thought to come here and benefit all over again. It makes me sick to the stomach.'

Hadn't Jack said there were very few reasons for people to kill – love, revenge, greed? She'd ascribed lack of money to Kate, to Cyril, to Polly, as a motive for murder, then found them all innocent. Beneath her nose, it was Vernon Elliot who'd had the most powerful reason.

'All would have been well, too,' Elliot was saying, 'if you hadn't interfered, with that idiot writer you seem attached to. The man with the stupid hat. He was lucky I was a good shot.'

Flora was startled afresh. 'It was you? It was you, who aimed that crossbow?'

'A warning, nothing more. You'd started to meddle. Kevin had been foolish enough to die in your bookshop and I could see your business was suffering as a result – I even tried to foment it a little in the hope you'd be forced to sell up and move away. But you didn't. You'd worked out that to save your shop, you had to discover why a seemingly healthy young man had died there. I watched you the afternoon you visited Cyril Knight and realised it meant trouble. It was only a matter of time before Cyril told you what he knew – Kevin had talked to him a lot – and you began to dig more deeply.'

'He did tell us. You were a little late with your crossbow.'

'There you are, you can't prepare for everything. I wouldn't have killed either of you. Not then. I simply wanted to frighten you away, send the fedora man back to his study and his books and you away from Abbeymead. In a way, I was being kind. You should have heeded my warnings. Cyril managed to kill himself and couldn't spill any more information, but that didn't stop you. You should have walked away, Miss Steele. If you had, this unpleasantness could have been avoided.'

He waved a vague hand at the dark enclosure in which he'd trapped her. Flora had slowly begun to realise what that unpleasantness could be, and her stomach knotted at the thought. For a moment, she lost the will to fight back.

'You've had more than one chance to save yourself, but you've been foolish. If you had sold your books to Joseph Rawston, I could have found what I needed and you wouldn't be here now.'

'You sent Rawston to me?'

'Of course, I sent him. Kevin told me he was going to meet a man who'd bought books from the Priory library. By then, Anderson and I had scoured every volume here and found nothing – we'd made an agreement, you see. It made sense that the document this priest wrote would be amongst the oldest books, but it turned out that they were the very ones that had sold at auction. Kevin died, poor chap, before he could tell me the result of his trip to Worthing, so after his demise, I thought I'd follow in his footsteps.'

'Wasn't Rawston suspicious? He seemed to me a man who wasn't entirely legitimate.'

'You're perceptive, Miss Steele. Joseph Rawston is no better than a barrow boy, but I made a deal with him, too. The books he'd bought at auction were useless – Kevin must have discovered that – but then I learned from Rawston that at the same sale your aunt, too, had bought a large number of very old books. I commissioned Rawston to buy them back from you.'

Flora had gradually edged closer to the entrance, keeping to the deep pools of darkness that lined the edges of the small enclosure. She didn't think that Elliot had noticed her movement, but she couldn't tell for certain. His eyes were narrowed, his gaze sharp, even as he was speaking.

'Kevin learned about your aunt's books on his visit to Rawston, which is why you found him in your bookshop the next day – so clumsy! And dishonourable. He'd evidently decided to cut me out, to double-cross. Pathetic, really. He should have died in his room, that was my plan. Instead, by stupidly breaking into your shop, he managed to arouse suspicion.'

Elliot gave a deep sigh. 'Water under the bridge now, of course. I couldn't be sure the books you owned would be any more use than the ones Rawston bought, but I had to have them. I paid him well and ended up getting nowhere.' Elliot's face darkened at the thought.

'Why pay him? Why not follow Kevin's example and break in?' She had shuffled a few more inches forward.

Elliot looked shocked. 'I couldn't do that. Such a risk, apart from being so very uncivilised!' He gave an exaggerated shudder. 'Another break-in would certainly have alerted the police that something untoward was going on. They were happy to accept that Kevin had died from a heart attack and, from the beginning, I made certain they kept thinking it. The minute they contacted me to identify my unfortunate guest, I had Mitchell get rid of the flowers, Horrocks dump the cake and the cleaners scour Anderson's bedroom. It's what's called making sure.'

'Not that sure. The room wasn't completely clean. There were pollen grains left in the crack of the table. Pollen that led directly to flowers grown in a padlocked enclosure at the rear of the Priory.' Flora edged a little closer.

'Really? I didn't have time to check – I was too busy getting to the morgue. Cleaners are so slapdash these days. You should have accepted his offer, you know. Rawston's. If you had, you wouldn't be here now.'

'So you've said. And Bernard Mitchell? What offer should he have accepted?'

'You think I killed him? You can't know the man. I'd no need to kill him. He was a bully and a coward. Threats were enough to make him turn tail and run.'

'You threatened him because he knew too much.'

'He always knew too much. I threatened him because he was going to the police. Such ingratitude. All the money he took from me to keep his mouth shut, and then to renege. I could have killed him, true, but I really didn't want another murder on my hands. The hemlock was easy, gentle. For Mitchell, it would have had to be something more gruesome. In the event, all I had to do was threaten murder, and off he went.'

'He didn't go that far. The police believe he committed suicide from Littlehampton beach.'

'Maybe. Who knows? He could have survived. It's not a matter that keeps me awake at night. If he's still alive, he won't come back. He's far too scared of ending in the churchyard. Even if he finds the backbone to return, I won't be here. But you, Miss Steele, you are another matter. You're not a coward and you're highly intelligent. Such a shame. I've been watching you for some while, watching you solve the puzzle for me. I know you have the priest's letter in your handbag, along with the strip of parchment you found in my library. Luckily for me, your handbag is on my desk, while you, unfortunately, are in the priest hole.'

Stupefied, Flora gazed around her. 'This is what this room is?'

'Absolutely. Neat, isn't it? And such a neat ending. I've no doubt that the man who wrote that parchment spent time just where you're standing. Time waiting in the dark, hoping the Catholic hunters had searched the Priory and failed. According to the legend, the priest escaped. That, I'm afraid, won't be happening to you.'

Flora raised her head at that, and said in as steady a voice as possible, 'What will be happening to me?'

'You'll be staying just where you are. There's only one way to access the priest hole and that's from a small lever in the bookcase. I discovered it when I had the library partitioned to make an office for myself. An office with possibly the most romantic secret in Sussex.'

At that moment, Flora couldn't think of anything less romantic.

'I wasn't sure what I'd do with it, but everything has its uses. For one thing, it can house a typewriter for which I have no further use. And it can house you.'

The air around Flora suddenly felt thick, a heavy layer pressing down on her, making it difficult for her to breathe. She had known all along that this was his plan, but somehow hadn't brought herself to believe he would actually go through with it. Another murder on his hands. And it would be murder. But why hadn't she believed it? Elliot was cold, unfeeling, and quite possibly insane.

'You're going to shut me in here?' she asked, knowing the answer, and bunching her muscles into a tight ball.

'Best not to fight it, Miss Steele. I've read that in such circumstances it's easier if you simply lie down and accept your fate. There's little point in yelling and screaming, since no one will hear you. No one even knows where you are. I doubt that anyone even noticed you had left the party. As far as the other guests are concerned, you ate and drank and went home. No, much better to go quietly. I must leave you now. I have an appointment with a shovel and some rudimentary directions.'

For a split second, he looked away and Flora, every fibre of her body tensed with new strength, hurled herself forward in an attempt to push him aside and throw herself into safety. She hit him flat in the chest and, for an instant, he staggered back, seeming to lose his balance. But, in another instant, he had regained his feet and was thrusting her backwards with such force that she stumbled and fell. From her prone position, she saw his hand reach up, her ears catching the click of a lever. The bookshelf swung back into place and she was plunged into total darkness.

CHAPTER TWENTY-SEVEN

Jack left the train at Worthing station a contented man. It had been a good meeting with his agent – a slap-up lunch at the Ritz, the usual fulsome praise for his work which Jack discounted as no more than encouragement, but far better news of the new project. Arthur was hugely enthusiastic. These days, an increasing number of people were taking holidays, he said, and there were several English counties eager to persuade visitors to come to them. An exciting story based in that county – crime was seen as the very best option – would work wonders. Each authority would appoint someone to oversee the scheme and arrange publicity, leaving Jack free to write whatever he chose. A trio of places had been suggested – not the entire country, Jack thought gratefully – ones that would lend themselves most readily to the kind of crime he wrote. Cornwall was the first name to emerge.

The county held happy memories, some of the few Jack possessed from his childhood. A business contact of his father's had owned a cottage in a small fishing village near Padstow and, for two summers running, the three of them had spent several weeks enjoying what in retrospect seemed endlessly long days of sunshine. The village itself was little more than a hamlet, lacking any kind of shop or even a church, but there were several farms to buy from and a pub just a mile or so along the Padstow road. His father had spent a lot of time there, Jack recalled, while he and his mother enjoyed days on the beach, a delight of rocks and seaweed and saltwater pools.

He would have to reacquaint himself with the county, Arthur told him, research the area in some depth, but his expenses would be paid and he could choose where to base himself. Early summer had been suggested as a date for his arrival.

All in all, the offer was sounding better than he'd first thought, particularly as, despite a few hopeful days, he was still struggling with the current novel, not much closer to completing it than when he'd first met Flora. He wondered how she'd fared at Polly's party and whether she'd learned anything new. In a burst of financial madness, he ignored the bus stop outside the station and hailed a taxi, and was on his way to Abbeymead before the train had left for Chichester.

Jack had missed her today, missed seeing her slim figure walking towards him, the mischievous smile when she teased, her caustic comments that demolished any pretension. After spending the afternoon with Polly, she was bound to have plenty in reserve.

He looked at his watch – seven o'clock. She would be back from the Priory by now. He couldn't see Vernon Elliot allowing the party to go on for too long. Leaning forward, he tapped on the cabbie's screen and asked the driver to drop him at Flora's cottage.

The last of the Michaelmas daisies provided a guard of honour, as he walked up the cottage pathway to beat a tattoo on the front door. When there was no answer, he knocked again. Walking across the grass to the sitting room window, he shaded his eyes and peered in, hoping to see Flora dozing in a chair. The room, though, was quite empty. He walked around the house to the kitchen door and knocked again.

He was puzzled. It was plain that Flora was away from home, but where? Out delivering books? From the corner of his eye, he spied Betty standing proudly beneath her shelter – Flora was definitely not on a delivery round. For a moment, Jack felt deflated, but rallying his spirits decided she must have gone to the bookshop after the party, and for some reason was still there. He was tired and thirsty from a day spent in the bustle of London, but the beer he'd been looking forward to would have to wait.

Ten minutes later, he was outside the All's Well, looking blankly at window blinds that were firmly closed. The shop was clearly shut. Could Flora be at the back of the building, he wondered, in the yard that she found so annoying? It was a fleeting hope and one that was soon dashed. Walking back to the high street, he tried to think sensibly. She had to be in the village somewhere. She had been at the Priory most of the afternoon and, with the evening drawing in, she would hardly have ventured far afterwards.

He slapped a hand against his forehead. Of course, she would be with Kate Mitchell. It was only yesterday that Kate's father had been buried and Flora would naturally want to lend her support. Why hadn't he thought of it earlier? He had no idea where Kate lived, or Alice Jenner for that matter, but Katie's Nook was just over the road and he'd try there first.

He turned to go and found Charlie Teague at his elbow.

'I'm back,' Charlie announced.

'So I see. And feeling better, I hope.'

'I wasn't really ill, but my mum wouldn't let me out. She said I was infecshus.'

'Your mum was right.'

The boy beamed up at him. 'I can do your orders now, Mr Carrington. For this place.' He jerked a thumb towards the bookshop.

'That's good to know, Charlie. The thing is that I've met Miss Steele now and I may as well collect my books for myself, but if I can't for any reason, I'll certainly let you know.'

Charlie's face dropped, causing Jack to say rousingly, 'I'm sure there are plenty of other errands you can do for me. Finding Miss Steele for one,' he joked.

'She went to the party,' Charlie offered.

'I'm aware, but she should be back by now. When did you last see her?'

'Walkin' up to the Priory. She looked nice.'

'But not since then?'

Charlie shook his head.

'Well, if you do see her, can you tell her that I'm looking for her?'

'OK.' Charlie kicked a loose stone along the pavement. 'You could try the caff. She could be with Mrs Mitchell. There's a lotta trouble goin' on there.'

Jack didn't ask what kind of trouble – he would learn soon enough. 'I was just about to call,' he said.

At the Nook, there was no sign of Flora. Through the glass door, he could see Kate Mitchell sitting at one of the small, round tables, nursing an empty mug, and Alice Jenner sitting opposite. It was Alice who jumped up when he rang the bell.

'Mr Carr... Jack. The Nook's closed, my love.'

'I'm not looking to eat. I'm looking for Flora.'

'Come on in. We've been waitin' for her to turn up. She said she'd come by after the party.'

'You saw her at the Priory?' He took a seat at the table, noticing how pale Kate looked.

'She was there all right,' Alice said. 'We were talkin' together when...' She trailed off. 'When Charlie arrived with the message.'

Jack frowned. 'The boy mentioned to me that there'd been trouble. What's happened?'

'Bernie...' Kate began, but then stuttered to a close.

'The police have found a pile of clothes on Littlehampton beach,' Alice continued for her. 'Constable Tring got a telephone call and came round to tell Kate while I was at the party. They think the clothes belong to Bernie. Kate's been asked to go to the police station tomorrow to identify them.'

Jack took a while to absorb the information, then reached out and grasped Kate's hand. 'I am so sorry.' There was little more he could say.

'Anyways,' Alice went on, 'Charlie Teague brought me Kate's message and I left the Priory straight away to come here. Flora was quite definite she'd call in afterwards. "I'll come by shortly," she said. Perhaps, in the end, she was too tired and went home.'

Jack shook his head. 'She's not at her cottage and she's not over the road. The bookshop is shut up.'

'Then she must still be at the Priory. I must say I'm surprised. Mr Elliot isn't one for a party, but perhaps Polly twisted his arm to let it go on later.'

'Can I offer you a cup of tea?' Kate asked suddenly, as though only just realising that Jack was there.

'No, but thank you.' He got up hastily. 'I think I'll walk up to the Priory. I'll probably meet Flora on her way home.'

'Give her our love,' Alice said. 'Tell her to forget the café this evening. I'm going to walk Kate back to my cottage now. She's staying with me for the night.'

Jack nodded and let himself out of the door. A traipse to the Priory was not what he'd had in mind, but his need to see Flora had grown rather than lessened, and there was the beginnings of a worry that had always been in the back of his mind. He'd warned her to go to the party and simply enjoy it, but what if she'd gone in search of that blessed typewriter, or worse, ransacked the library, and was now in some kind of trouble?

CHAPTER TWENTY-EIGHT

Jack gave himself a shake – he was being unnecessarily dramatic – but he still set off at a spanking pace. It began to drizzle before he'd walked even halfway, the wet seeping deep into what was his best pair of trousers, and he arrived at the front entrance of the hotel damp and uncomfortable. The bunting decorating the stone arch, that had once looked so cheerful, was now in a sad droop. Stepping into the main hall, Jack saw wilting flowers and a mass of balloons, most of them slowly deflating. Several women in maids' uniforms were wielding brooms, while a lone waiter danced between them, collecting the empty glasses abandoned by Polly's guests. The party was plainly over, but where was Flora?

'Can I help you, sir?' The smart young waiter had stopped his dance, a loaded tray balanced precariously on his shoulder.

'I'm looking for Flora Steele. I believe she came to Miss Dakers' party.'

'I'm new here,' the boy confessed. 'I don't know many of the villagers yet.'

'She was here,' one of the maids chipped in, overhearing their conversation.

'Did you see when she left?' Jack asked eagerly.

The maid shook her head. 'I was busy handin' round plates, tryin' to get people to eat up the buffet, so we didn't have too much food to clear.' She pointed to the now empty trestle table. 'I saw her earlier on. She was with Alice Jenner. She's the cook here.'

'Alice left early, I believe.'

'That's right,' the second maid chimed in. 'It was when the message came – that Mr Mitchell had drowned. That caused a right stir.'

'But Flora, Miss Steele, stayed on after that?' he persisted.

'As far as I know.'

'Then she must still be here.'

Surprise was written across all three faces, and he said quickly, 'Miss Steele isn't at home and she isn't at her shop. Mrs Jenner was expecting her at Katie's Nook, but she never arrived. Something must have happened to her. We need to search the hotel.'

'What could have happened to her here?' The waiter sounded mystified.

'I don't know,' Jack said a little desperately. 'She might have got locked in somewhere. A bathroom perhaps?'

One of the maids stifled a giggle. 'Locked in the lav!'

Jack looked at her. 'You could come with me. Help me look for her,' he said.

'Anythin' to stop clearin' up this mess.' She looked down with disgust at the pile of crumpled serviettes, cigarette ends and cake crumbs that littered the polished wood floor.

'Upstairs first?' he suggested.

It was a swift search. They checked every bathroom on the first floor and looked briefly into every bedroom that wasn't occupied.

'There's a public lavatory downstairs,' the maid said. 'Mebbe we should have tried that first.'

Why didn't we, Jack thought, feeling flustered and irritated, but he said nothing. He would need the girl to check the toilet cubicles for him.

When she did, though, it was to draw another blank. Jack stood in the corridor, thinking hard. Was he making a fool of himself? Had Flora gone for a walk after the party, maybe to get some fresh air, clear her head, and he'd missed her when he'd called at her cottage?

But then, why would she go for a walk when she'd promised Alice she would call at the café? And knowing what devastating news Charlie Teague had brought, she surely would have called if she'd been able.

'The library,' he said suddenly. 'I bet she's in the library.' Of course she was. He should have realised – it was so obvious. She'd gone to the library, looking for the *Malleus Maleficarum*. He'd told her not to, but when did she do anything he told her? She'd slipped away to the library and was still there, still searching, and risking discovery at every moment.

'It's at the end of this corridor,' the maid said. 'I'll leave you to look for yourself, sir. I best get back to the rubbish.'

'Thank you for your help,' Jack said over his shoulder, hurrying along the corridor to where the maid had indicated.

The library, that was it. And wasn't Elliot's office nearby? He had a vague recollection that Alice Jenner had mentioned it. When he saw Flora... he was getting the words ready to tell her how stupid she'd been, exposing herself to goodness knows what danger, but reaching the open library doors, the words died on his lips. It was immediately obvious that this stunning room was deserted. He did a brief walk around the space, taking note of the empty window seat, the empty occasional table. Not a book lay open. He glanced across at the run of bookcases. Not a shelf disturbed, every volume standing to attention. Flora could never have been here.

Badly worried, he walked out of the library, passing another open door to his right. Elliot's office. He stopped and, retracing his steps, walked in. What a dreary place it was. Not a vestige of light, other than the desk lamp. He switched it on and looked around. A desk, a couple of chairs, two bookcases – one old, one modern – but... He paused. No typewriter. There had been a typewriter, it was clear from the indentations on the rubber mat, now sitting bare on the desk. What had happened to it? Had Flora been right to think the florist's order had been typed here? If so, the machine that had typed it was missing. Along with Flora. Jack needed to call the police.

Galvanised into action, he rushed back along the corridor and into the hall, dashing behind the reception desk to grab the hotel's telephone. It felt oddly light in his hand and, with a churning stomach, he realised that the line had been cut, the cable dangling uselessly in the air. Slamming the receiver back onto its rest, he sped past the maids still at work and out into a drizzle that had now become heavy rain. Jack hardly felt it as he ran at full tilt down the Priory drive, through the black iron gates and along the lane to the village. There was a telephone box on the corner between Katie's Nook and the baker's. He would call from there.

He had Inspector Ridley's home number in his pocket diary and was lucky to get through almost immediately.

'Hello there, Jack.' A cheery voice crackled down the line. 'Any more poisoned jackets to offer me? Or have you suffered a shotgun pellet in an unmentionable place?'

'Neither,' Jack said curtly. 'Flora Steele is missing, Alan. She went to a party at the Priory Hotel this afternoon and hasn't returned home or gone back to her shop. No one saw her leave the hotel. I've searched it as best I can but I need the police to do it thoroughly, and to search further afield. The Priory has extensive grounds and she could be anywhere. She might have slipped out of a side entrance, or been forcibly taken from the building.' His heart gave a sharp kick at the thought.

'You want me to send chaps up to the Priory? All the way from Brighton? I can't do that, old chap. Wasting police resources again. You're a devil at it.'

'She is a missing person.'

'Not yet she isn't. Wait twenty-four hours and if she's still not back this time tomorrow, give me another bell. I'm sure you'll find she's trotted off to see a friend or gone shopping. You know what women are.'

Jack didn't, but he did know when the shops shut. 'There are no shops open,' he said sharply, 'and Flora doesn't have any friends except the two I've just spoken to, women she was supposed to meet.' He realised as he said the words, how true they were. He'd always assumed he was the loner but Flora, for all her bubbly nature, was just as solitary.

'Please, Alan. I have a very bad feeling. Flora was intent on finding Kevin Anderson's killer. You won't accept the man's death was murder but, believe me, it was. Whoever killed Anderson could have kidnapped Flora – or worse – if she's got close to exposing him. The chap who owns the Priory appears to be missing, too, and the hotel's phone line has been deliberately cut. Like I say, I've a very bad feeling. Surely, you could send a couple of constables?'

Ridley sighed deeply. 'It sounds a pretty rum do, but for you, Jack, I'll ask Tring to send a couple of the new recruits he's training. We'd have to have a warrant to search the house, but they can look around the parkland as long as they're discreet. They need some exercise and, if the grounds are as extensive as you say, they'll get it.'

'Thank you. I'm grateful.' And he was, profoundly.

Emerging from the telephone box, he found Charlie Teague once more kicking stones down the street.

'You again,' he said.

'Have you found her?' Charlie looked up at him, a cheeky smile on his face.

'No, I haven't,' Jack said shortly.

'Who were you phonin' then?'

'That's none of your business, Master Teague.'

Jack stood irresolute, not knowing where to go, what to do.

'You went up to the Priory, though?' Charlie, it seemed, was not going away.

'Are you spying on me, young man?'

The boy shrugged his shoulders. 'What did the hotel say?'

Jack gave up. Charlie Teague was determined to be his confederate. 'They said they hadn't seen Miss Steele leave.'

'Then she must still be there.' Charlie kicked a larger than average stone into the gutter and watched it roll away.

'That's what I thought, but I searched the whole of the building. Both floors.'

'Did you look in the library?'

'Yes, of course,' he said, impatiently. A frown creased his forehead. 'Did you mention the library for any particular reason?'

'I 'membered the priest hole, that's all. Did you look there?'

Jack felt his mouth drop open. 'What priest hole?'

CHAPTER TWENTY-NINE

For what seemed minutes on end, Flora lay frozen into immobility, her body seemingly embedded into the stone floor. Then panic kicked in. The air was growing heavier by the second, its taste damp and cloying. Her throat seemed to have closed and her breath began to come in spasms. Blindly, she stumbled to her feet, staggering forward and groping along the wall, first to the left and then right, feeling for a lever, a handle, anything that might set her free from this dungeon of death. Rough plaster was all she could feel.

It was plain the mechanism could only be set in motion from the bookcase beyond. Why had she thought otherwise? Hadn't she read of priests dying of starvation or from lack of oxygen before they could be released? Simultaneously gasping and crying, she groped her way back to the door that had cut her adrift from the world and began first to claw at the barrier, and then to hammer against its unforgiving surface until her fists bled.

Flora could see nothing, but when she felt the sticky wetness on her hands, she realised what she had done and came to her senses. She could hammer until she had reduced her body to a pulp, but the shelving was immovable and there was no one to hear her. Except for Elliot, no one would venture into his office. She shuffled back a few paces and fumbled her way down onto the floor of cold stone. How many times all those centuries ago had Anselm been forced to take shelter in this way? He would at least have had a candle to light him and a book to while away the hours, but for his sake, she hoped it had not been often and not for long.

Sitting cross-legged, the cold slowly seeped through her body. Her limbs might be numb, but she was struggling hard to keep her mind alive. How was she to escape this dreadful fate? Think, Flora, she urged herself, but in truth, there was little to think about. The situation was all too clear. Elliot had the papers he'd killed for and even now would be somewhere in the Priory grounds making use of them. Would he return to the house, to the office, in order to gloat? If so, and he were to flick that lever, sending the bookcase swinging open, she must be ready for him. But in her heart, she knew it for a forlorn hope. She had already tried to rush the man and failed and, as the minutes passed, the hours passed, she would grow only weaker.

It was far more likely that Elliot would never return, but simply leave her here to rot. Very soon he would have what he'd killed for. Jack had been right. The murder had been committed for money. On the surface, Elliot exuded success: he owned an historic mansion and a country estate, employed a large staff, wore Savile Row suits and handmade shoes. But beneath this carapace of wealth, he was as hunted, as desperate for money, as Bernie Mitchell struggling to escape his squalid gambling debts.

No more struggling for Elliot, though. Once he'd retrieved the jewellery, he'd be on his way to London to search out a shady dealer, if he hadn't already found one. Whatever he unearthed from the Priory grounds, he'd not receive its true value, but still he would pocket a good deal of money, certainly sufficient to disappear from Abbeymead and leave his dreadful secret behind. Only if some future owner of the Priory were to fall heavily against that bookcase would the secret come to light. What would that new proprietor make of it, she wondered, a door swinging open to reveal a decomposed body and an ancient typewriter?

The image had her shudder. Death suddenly seemed very close, her mind pivoting to Kevin in his final moments, to Cyril in his agony, and then to her aunt. How distraught Violet would have been if she'd known what the future held for her beloved niece. There would be no waking now to a bright morning in Montmartre, no throwing coins in a Rome fountain, or walking the hill to the Acropolis. And no All's Well. What would happen to her aunt's beloved bookshop? The thought made Flora cry again.

She had let Violet down so very badly. If she'd not persisted with this investigation, she would still be safe. The affair had begun rationally enough with her desire to save the All's Well from debt and eventual closure, but she could see now that rationality had gradually been lost. An absolute determination to bring the killer to justice, shop or no shop, had taken over.

Jack had warned her to be careful, but she hadn't listened. He'd asked her not to take risks today, to wait for him to get back from London and together they would work out their next move. But she had stupidly barged ahead and fallen into the most dreadful trouble she could ever have imagined. Why? Her pride? Her refusal to take advice? Or a wish to show that women, patronised, infantilised even, as they so often were, could do as well as any man?

What would Jack do, she wondered, when he discovered her gone? He would be coming off the train from London any time now, full of news from his day in the city. He might even go looking for her and, when he didn't find her... what would he think? That she had walked out on him, walked out on the bookshop and the village that had nurtured her all these years? He must know that she wouldn't, and he'd search, if not tonight, then tomorrow. But no matter how hard he looked, he wouldn't find her. He might try to run Elliot to ground, hoping the man could tell him more, but Elliot would be long gone from Sussex and, if ever Jack caught up with him, it would be far too late.

Flora's eyes filled with tears again, and she brushed them angrily away. She was too full of self-pity, she told herself. If she was to die, she must do it with dignity. She must resign herself to whatever was to come. Maybe she would fall into a coma and know no more. That would be the easiest. Spreading herself to lie flat on the cold floor once more, she hoped that was how it would be.

*

'A priest hole?' Jack repeated, hardly able to get the words out.

'It's where blokes used to hide when they were being chased. Relig'ous blokes.'

'I know what a priest hole is, but what's it got to do with the Priory?'

'There's one in the library. Old Lord Templeton used to let us kids see it. Real spooky it was. One of the bookcases swung out and there was this horrible black hole. We used to play a game, say we'd pull the lever and shut our mates in. But the old chap never let us play there alone. He said it was too dangerous.'

'I'm not surprised.' Jack's heart had begun to thump loudly. Was it possible that Flora had gone to the library after all, discovered the lever Charlie spoke of, and found the priest hole? Then by accident shut herself in. Or… been shut in.

'Could you locate it, this lever – if we went back to the hotel?' Jack was praying hard.

'I reckon so.'

'Then, c'mon, Charlie. If you open that priest hole, you've a big treat in store.'

'What kinda treat?'

'Never you mind. It will be big, that's all you need to know.'

Charlie gave a soft whistle. 'I'll find it,' he said, striding ahead of Jack and already on his way to the Priory gates.

Jack was unsure how he was to explain a second visit to the hotel within an hour, but when the two of them walked through the square stone of the entrance, there was no one to be seen. The foyer had been cleared of every scrap of rubbish and the reek of floor polish stung Jack's nose. He reckoned the maids must have finished for the day and the waiters were now working in the restaurant at the other side of the building. No one had replaced Polly Dakers at reception, and, crucially, Vernon Elliot was still absent. Hopefully, the formidable Miss Horrocks would remain above stairs, supervising the evening routine of turning down beds.

'Quick,' Jack said in a low voice. 'Make for the corridor on the right before anyone puts in an appearance.'

Charlie was before him, already halfway to the library, but when the boy walked into the magnificent space and looked around him, his young face was perplexed.

'It's not the same,' he said.

Jack caught up with him and put an arm around the boy's shoulders. 'Places you've been to when you're young can look very different when you see them again,' he said encouragingly. 'Take a minute to remember.'

'I 'member all right,' the boy said stoutly. 'But it don't look right.'

Jack felt despair rising. 'Think,' he said urgently. 'How does it not look right?'

The boy turned slowly in a circle, his gaze sweeping the room. 'That was there.' He pointed to the wall of windows, 'and them, too.' He gestured to the walls on either side, filled floor to ceiling with books. 'But the bookcase that moved – it was here in the corner, and there in't a bookcase there now.'

To have got so far but face defeat was beyond bearing. 'Are you sure, Charlie?' Jack asked, anguish in his voice.

'Yeah. Absolutely. The room looks kinda smaller now.'

'That's because you're bigger yourself. Places always shrink...' Jack stopped. 'Or because the room has been altered,' he said slowly.

Charlie looked hopefully up at him.

'When you used to play here, was there an office off the library?'

'Nah,' Charlie said. 'Old Lord Templeton wouldn't have known what to do with an office.'

'Come.' He grabbed Charlie's arm, dragging him out of the library and into the adjoining room. The place was in darkness and he switched on the desk lamp.

'Cor, this is new,' Charlie said, looking around him.

'And the bookcases?' Jack held his breath.

Charlie looked. 'Not that one.' He pointed to the modern shelving unit at the other side of the room. 'I never saw that one. But this one. This looks like the one that was in the library.' He moved closer. 'There was a nick in the wood, like someone had taken a penknife to it. Yeah. It's still there.'

Jack tried to still a heartbeat so loud he could hear it thrashing through his ears. 'The lever, Charlie. Show me.'

'It was up there.' He pointed to a shelf above his head. 'I couldn't reach it. Old Templeton had to lift me up so I could pull it.'

'You probably still can't reach it, but I can. Tell me where.' Jack's hand floated uncertainly in the air.

'It was a bit higher than that. Right in the corner, near the last book.'

Jack fumbled, his hand groping along the shelf that Charlie had indicated, but finding nothing. 'I'll try the next shelf up.' He reached up once more and suddenly his hand touched metal. 'I've got it,' he said tersely.

'You gotta pull hard.'

Jack pulled hard and stepped back quickly as the entire bookcase began to swing open. It was a moment of excitement, a moment of dread, and his senses were acute. The bookcase had swung open smoothly, easily, he noted. Whatever the mechanism, it had recently been oiled. Which meant that Elliot knew about the priest hole.

Then he saw her. A crumpled body lying in the dark cavern beyond.

'Cor!' Charlie exclaimed again. 'In't that Miss Steele?'

Jack rushed forward and scooped her from the stone floor, holding the girl's limp form close to his chest as he brought her out into the lamplight. She had lapsed into unconsciousness, but the warmth of his body seemed very slowly to wake her.

Flora's eyes half opened and she struggled to speak. 'Is that you, Jack?'

'It is, and you're safe.' He hugged her even closer.

She gave a wan smile. 'What kept you so long?' she asked. Then fell unconscious again.

CHAPTER THIRTY

When Flora finally woke properly, it was to find Jack Carrington sitting in a chair by her bedroom window. She blinked at him.

'What—' she began.

'Alice is downstairs,' he said soothingly. 'You've been in and out of consciousness for hours and she's been keeping watch. She's been here since I brought you back from the Priory. Kate Mitchell, too – at least, for the first night.'

'The first night?' Flora tried to sit up, but her head was doing unpleasant things and she subsided back on her pillows. 'How long have I been asleep?'

'On and off for a couple of days. We called Dr Hanson. He poked around with his stethoscope and decided you were healthy enough, that it was simply your body repairing itself after a shock and there was nothing to worry about. I must admit I'm glad to see you open your eyes.'

She'd had a shock, Jack said, but what had that been? Her memory stirred. At first, it was only a trickle – fragments of images, snatches of words – then the trickle turned into a torrent. 'That place,' she whispered. 'The dark. The air. Suffocation.'

Jack walked over to the bed and took her hand. 'It's OK to feel scared. I wouldn't blame you if you had nightmares for days to come. But you're going to be fine.'

'Of course I am,' she said stoutly. 'It was just… I'm being feeble, and I need to get out of bed.'

'Absolutely not. For the moment, you're to stay just where you are.'

'But the shop. It's been closed all this time. How many days did you say I've been here?'

'Two, and the shop has been open, at least for part of every day. I snaffled your keys – sorry – and opened up. The All's Well is being run by Charlie after school hours, with Kate watching over him from the café.'

'Charlie Teague?'

'The very same.'

'He's just a child.' Flora scrabbled at the counterpane as though she was about to fling back the bedcovers and rush to the bookshop.

'He's twelve years old, going on forty. Charlie will do well. He's been told to write down any orders that come in and hand over any books ready to be collected. I brought up the few packages I found from the cellar. If anyone wants to buy a book off the shelf, he knows how to take the money.'

'There won't be many customers anyway,' Flora said miserably, turning her head into the pillows. She felt utterly exhausted and, despite hours of sleep, her body was pummelled and aching.

'Well, no, but I didn't like to mention that.'

She lay, eyes half closed, her mind roaming over that last afternoon at Polly's party. 'Is Kate all right?' she asked suddenly. 'There was terrible news about Bernie Mitchell.'

Jack lowered himself gingerly back into the tiny bedroom chair, his frame long and awkward. 'I wouldn't say she's in the best of health,' he replied, 'but she's managing to keep things together. Just. When, and if, they find her husband's body, it might be a different matter.'

'There's no news of him yet?'

'The lifeboat was scrambled and the coastguard has put out an alert, but it's all a bit late. Mitchell's clothes had been on that beach for a couple of days before the alarm was even raised.'

'And Alice?' she asked. 'You said she was downstairs.'

'Alice is here, my love.' The rounded figure of the cook bustled through the doorway. 'I heard voices and reckoned it was time to put the kettle on. Here, drink this.'

Flora took the offered cup and sipped. 'Thank you, Alice.' She sipped again. 'I never thought tea could taste so lovely!' She looked anxiously at her friend, perched on the end of the bed. 'Was it you who undressed me?'

Jack gave a loud laugh. 'I didn't, if that's what's worrying you. Once I had you out of that hellhole, I had one of the waiters at the Priory call a taxi, while Charlie ran ahead. He ran all the way to Alice's cottage to tell her what had happened and she was here, Kate alongside, within half an hour of my carrying you through the door.'

'You looked some awful, my love.' Alice shook her head as though wanting to dislodge the memory. 'How are you feeling now?'

'Better with every minute.' Flora took another sip of tea, trying not to succumb to the lethargy overwhelming her.

'That man—' Alice began.

'We decided it must be Elliot who imprisoned you,' Jack went on. 'You didn't land in the priest hole by accident.'

'It was Elliot all right,' Flora said bitterly. 'After I found Anselm's directions. They were just where I said they'd be, Jack. In the *Malleus Maleficarum*.'

Alice was looking bewildered, and Flora hastened to explain. 'It's an old book, Alice, the oldest volume the Priory possesses.'

'Did Elliot find you in the library?' Jack asked, his face grave.

'Not there – in his office. I'd tucked both documents away in my handbag and gone looking for the typewriter, but there didn't seem to be one.'

'Just an empty rubber mat,' he concurred.

'That's right. I reckoned Elliot must have tried to hide it and that if I looked at the room from a different angle, I might be lucky. It didn't work, but as I was starting to leave, I tripped on the rug and stumbled against the old bookcase. I heard a click and the whole thing started moving.'

'And there was the typewriter, ready and waiting.'

'A typewriter that had a wonky "s", the one used to order those flowers. I'd just tested the keys when that dreadful man appeared. He murdered Kevin with water hemlock, just as we thought, killing Cyril in the process. He admitted it. He was quite brazen – in fact, proud of what he'd done.'

'He killed Cyril! I knew there was somethin' wrong. I never said anythin' to Kate – she had enough to contend with – but Cyril goin' like that didn't seem right.' Alice had turned bright red, her hands twisting her rings compulsively.

'He'll pay for it,' Jack said softly. 'And Mitchell, Flora? Did Elliot say anything about him?'

Flora lowered her voice as though Kate might still be in the house. 'Bernie Mitchell was his accomplice. He planted the hemlock, kept it alive, and then burnt what was left of it immediately after Cyril died. No wonder Kate said her husband was Elliot's right-hand man.'

'Why did the wretch disappear then?' Alice asked, still twisting her rings in agitation. 'Not that I can't be grateful that he has, even with Kate breakin' her heart over him.'

'Elliot threatened that he would be next in line for a swift death if he dared to spill the beans, and that prompted Mitchell to take off in a panic. Kate mentioned how much pressure her husband had been under, and now we know why.'

'His disappearance can't be suicide then,' Jack remarked. 'If he was trying to save his skin, he'd hardly go swimming – and naked.'

'You wouldn't go swimming in any case if you were trying to escape, unless you were hoping to fake a suicide.'

'That's it,' Alice said decidedly. 'It's the kind of low thing Mitchell would do. Sacrifice his wife's peace of mind to keep himself safe.'

'I hope for Kate's sake that the mystery of Bernie's whereabouts is soon cleared up,' Flora said. 'At least, then, she can begin to come to terms with what's happened.'

'Something is bothering me.' The creases in Jack's forehead deepened.

'Only something?' Pallid and exhausted as she was, it was Flora's weak attempt at a joke.

'Presumably Vernon Elliot found out what Kevin had been researching and knew he had to look for a manuscript that was in the Priory library. He must have searched every book on the library shelves, either with Kevin or alone.'

'With Kevin,' Flora confirmed.

'They couldn't have found the letter because we found it in your books, but why didn't they find the clue that Anselm left? You went straight to it.'

'I thought about that when I was in the black hole. I had a lot of time to think. I reckoned that either Elliot's search was slapdash, which doesn't fit with the man we know, or he did find the strip of parchment that I discovered and didn't realise its significance. You haven't seen it, Jack, but it's just one long, narrow strip. It could easily be taken for a bookmark. Elliot wasn't looking for a bookmark. He was looking for a manuscript and could have dismissed what he found as unimportant.'

'But if he read what was written on it – I don't imagine Anselm wrote in invisible ink.'

'There *was* nothing written on it. Just three drawings, which would make very little sense to anyone who hadn't read the letter that we found.'

Jack shifted in his seat. 'I'm intrigued. We seem to be dealing with one devious monk here. Tell me, what exactly did he draw?'

'The top image was of a statue, which I worked out had to be Minerva. Remember that cryptic line in the letter?'

'Minerva? Wisdom!'

'You're right. And the drawing at the bottom was of a tree, the tree of sorrow. In between the two, there was a large cross.'

'Sounds like a tall tale,' Alice said, looking from one to the other. 'That tree of sorrow…'

Flora smiled. Jack liked to get to the bottom of things. 'The dule tree. It was used for centuries to make gallows.'

'Would Elliot have worked that out?' he asked doubtfully. 'The man didn't strike me as someone close to nature.'

'He would recognise the statue of Minerva, I'm sure. Everyone who's ever walked in the Priory grounds knows it. I guess he'd start digging between that and the nearest tree.'

'Like I said, a tall tale.' Alice bounced up from the bed, smoothing down her pinafore.

'One that has led Elliot to whatever Anselm buried all those centuries ago.' Flora's voice was tinged with bitterness. She looked across at Jack, still sprawled uncomfortably in the too small chair. 'We might have uncovered the murderer but, in the end, we failed.'

'Why do you say that?'

'Elliot will have found the treasure by now, whatever it is, even if he had to dig for hours. He'll have used it to escape and he'll never face justice.'

Jack levered himself from his seat, walking over to the bedside again, and shaking his head. 'Not so, Miss Steele.'

'That's right,' Alice confirmed. 'The police have got him.'

'Really?' Flora sat bolt upright.

'He's at Brighton police station. Locked safely in a cell,' Jack added.

The news turned Flora's world upside down. 'How did the police know what he was up to?' Her head was spinning.

'I called in one more favour. Inspector Ridley sent two of his men to search the Priory grounds – for you, incidentally – but lo and behold, they found Elliot instead, with a shovel, a pile of earth and a chipped wooden casket in his hands.'

'They couldn't arrest him for that,' she protested. 'He was digging on his own land. They couldn't arrest him for murder either. With the flowers gone, there's no proof that he killed Anderson, only his confession to me, and that won't stand up in a court of law. It will be one voice pitted against another.'

Jack pulled a face. 'You're right – up to a point. It's infuriating that the Anderson murder will go by the board. Ridley has no proof beyond the statement that you'll make, but he does have evidence of what happened to you. After I called him, he ordered his men to be on the lookout for Elliot and, if his officers were at all suspicious, they were to bring the man in for questioning. Since then, Elliot has admitted to imprisoning you in that dreadful place, and Ridley knows it was with every intention of letting you die there. That's attempted murder. Then there's the little matter of growing poisonous flowers and the accidental killing of a pensioner. It would mean exhuming Cyril to prove it, I'm afraid – Kevin is beyond reach – but I think we'll find that Elliot will spend quite a number of years behind bars.'

'Good riddance to him, I say.' Alice hovered in the doorway. 'The man's a monster and now the village knows just what he's done. I'm telling everyone I meet that it was him, not ghosts or poisonous fumes that killed that young man in your bookshop. You'll have plenty of customers coming back, you'll see.'

'The right kind of notorious?' Jack queried, his eyes laughing.

Flora grinned, recalling the boast she'd made what seemed a lifetime ago. 'Let's hope so. But what will happen to your work at the Priory, Alice?'

'I dunno if I'll have a job at the end of all this, but right now I don't much care, and whoever takes over the hotel has to be better. Now, my love, what can I get you for breakfast? While Jack was sitting with you, I went back home and collected a couple of new-laid eggs. My hens must have known what was needed.'

'I don't think—'

'Yes, you could. You're too skinny already and you've not eaten for days. Any case, eggs are good for shock.'

Flora looked surprised.

'You didn't know that, did you?' Jack said, straight-faced.

'Have them soft boiled, with some soldiers for dipping,' Alice put in. 'I've just baked a fresh loaf and the milkman's delivered a slab of his best butter.'

Flora gave in graciously. 'You're so kind.'

When Alice had clattered down the stairs, she gestured to Jack to come closer, reaching out for his hand. 'I haven't said thank you, and I need to. You saved my life.'

He took her hand and held it for a while. 'Strictly speaking, it was Charlie Teague who saved your life. He was the one who told me about the priest hole.'

Flora nodded reminiscently. 'Charlie would know – the children used to play in the library. Edward Templeton loved having them there.' She levered herself up to sit a little straighter. 'I must think of an especially good treat for Charlie as a way of saying thank you.'

'I've been working on it. What do you say to a day in Brighton? Candy floss, the Palace Pier, a fish and chip supper and to round it off, a show at the Hippodrome?'

She grinned. 'I'd say that Master Teague will be in heaven.'

'Me, too. I've never been on a pier.'

'Jack, you have had such a strange life!' Her expression grew serious. 'Thanks to your calling the police at just the right time, that wretched man will go to prison. I hope it's for a very long time, but I'm sad that when he comes out he'll still own the Priory and still be able to claim the treasure. *Was* it a casket of jewellery?'

He nodded.

'Just as I thought. Tudor gold and silver will be worth a fortune. It's so unjust. I know any treasure over three hundred years old has to be offered for sale to a museum, but there's bound to be plenty who'll want it. Elliot will become a rich man. He'll be able to pay off his debts and escape his past.'

'I'm not sure any museum will want it.' Jack, she noticed, had a sly smile on his face.

'The jewellery will still be there when he gets out of prison,' she said a trifle tartly. 'And still be his to sell. He can't lose.'

Jack was now smiling broadly.

'I don't see there's anything to smile about.' Flora was cross and plumped her pillows with unnecessary force.

'Oh, there is. That priceless Tudor jewellery, it seems, is nothing but a fake. Mere paste…'

She gaped at him. 'What!'

'That's right. While you were lying prone, I went up to London. Ridley allowed me to take the box of goodies and have its contents valued. They were well-preserved – we're lucky the casket was lead-lined. There were several bracelets, a necklace and three rings. Lovely-looking items, but Lady Ianthe was a naughty girl. She must have sold the real jewels and substituted them for paste replicas. They were troubled times – she probably needed the money.'

'But then why did the priest go to all the trouble of burying the box and leaving instructions where to find it? It makes no sense.'

'Lady Templeton would hardly have broadcast the fact that she'd sold her jewels, would she? She would have been keen to keep up the fiction, even when she was carted off to prison. Anselm must have thought he was burying the real thing, saving the Templeton jewels from destruction.'

Flora swung her legs out of bed, shrugging herself into her dressing gown. She walked to the window and looked out on the curling drifts of copper and gold leaves, trying to absorb this amazing turn of events.

Eventually, she turned to face Jack. 'So Elliot will get nothing for them?'

'They are beautiful pieces, so perhaps two and sixpence for the lot.'

At this, she laughed aloud.

'It's good to hear you laugh again. I was beginning to wonder if I ever would. There's something else that will make you laugh, or smile at least. When I was at the London auction house, I asked their books and manuscript valuer to have a look at Anselm's letter. Unfortunately, the strip of parchment – the bookmark, you called it – was ruined in Elliot's digging, but the letter excited the valuer greatly. It has considerable historical significance, apparently, and, along with the Book of Hours that your aunt bought, turns out to be worth a good deal of money. My expert reckoned that together they would fetch well over two hundred pounds in a sale.'

Flora was stunned. 'It will save the bookshop,' she stuttered. 'Even if the village doesn't come back as quickly as Alice thinks.'

'It will do a great deal more than that. There'll be enough for you to hire an assistant, make her your manager and allow you to travel to your heart's content. On those proceeds, you could manage a good year away.'

She was dumbfounded. Was an impossible dream becoming reality? Would she get to all those places she'd had in her heart for so long: Paris, Rome and way beyond? Her spirits quickened at this stunning development. Then, just as swiftly, they plummeted. She would be leaving a village she loved, leaving her beloved bookshop in unknown hands, and travelling alone. Seeing those long-desired sights with no one by her side. Somehow it no longer carried the appeal it once had.

'I don't know,' she said uncertainly. 'After all this time, I'm not sure that I'd make a good solo traveller.'

Jack walked over to the window and stood silently by her side. Meeting his gaze, Flora was aware of grey eyes that changed from light to dark and back again. It was as though he was struggling to find the right words.

'I'm off to Cornwall early in the summer,' he said at last. 'I've had no time to tell you, but it's part of the project my agent has lined up for me. It's a few months distant and not exactly France or Italy, but Cornwall is a beautiful county, especially in May. You could always travel with me.'

Flora felt a tingle of pleasure. A sensation of warmth. Cornwall and Jack? She definitely liked the sound of it. And May was months away, so time enough to rebuild trade after such a disastrous period. Time to make the All's Well buzz again. Travel was exciting but Abbeymead was where her heart lay.

'Thank you for the invitation. I'll certainly think about it,' she said, not wanting to sound too enthusiastic. 'We make a good team, don't we?'

A LETTER FROM MERRYN

I'd like to say a huge thank you for choosing to read *The Bookshop Murder*. If you enjoyed it and want to keep up to date with all my latest releases, just sign up at the following link. Your email address will never be shared and you can unsubscribe at any time.

www.bookouture.com/merryn-allingham

The 1950s is a fascinating period, outwardly conformist but beneath the surface there's rebellion brewing, even in Sussex! I've lived in the county for many years now and love it – the small villages, the South Downs, and the sea – and I hope you enjoyed Flora and Jack's adventures there as much as I loved imagining them. If you did, you can follow their fortunes in the next Abbeymead mystery.

In the meantime, I love hearing from you all – I promise, it will make my day! – so do get in touch on my Facebook page, through Twitter, Goodreads or my website, and if you enjoyed *The Bookshop Murder*, I would love a short review. Getting feedback is amazing and it helps new readers to discover one of my books for the first time.

Thank you for reading,
Merryn

MerrynWrites

merrynwrites

www.merrynallingham.com

Made in the USA
Columbia, SC
18 September 2023